MERMOUSE MYSTERY

MILLIE

JUNIPER

PEDRO

There is a lot of tiny text on this page and the
Adventuremice were wondering if you would read it.
If you have read it: congratulations!
You have keen eyes and would make an
excellent member of our Adventuremice team.

First American Edition 2024
Kane Miller, A Division of EDC Publishing

First published in Great Britain in 2023 by David Fickling Books
Text © Philip Reeve & Sarah McIntyre, 2023
Illustrations © Sarah McIntyre, 2023
The right of Philip Reeve and Sarah McIntyre to be identified as
the authors and illustrator of this work has been asserted.

For information contact:
Kane Miller, A Division of EDC Publishing
5402 S 122nd E Ave
Tulsa, OK 74146
www.kanemiller.com
www.paperpie.com

Library of Congress Control Number: 2023939604

Manufactured by Regent Publishing Services, Hong Kong, China
Printed September 2023 in Shenzhen, Guangdong, China
1 2 3 4 5 6 7 8 9 10

ISBN: 978-1-68464-854-2

FSC
www.fsc.org
MIX
Paper | Supporting
responsible forestry
FSC® C013314

ADVENTUREMICE

MERMOUSE MYSTERY

BY

PHILIP REEVE

AND

SARAH McINTYRE

Kane Miller
A DIVISION OF EDC PUBLISHING

CHAPTER
1

THE GREAT STORM

A wild west wind was howling over the
Mouse Islands. Big white waves burst
against the shores. Rain rattled on the
windows of the Mousebase, where the
brave Adventuremice were waiting, ready
to go out and rescue anyone who was in
danger from the storm.

Pedro, the youngest and newest Adventuremouse, looked out at the booming waves in wonder. The storm was scary, but it was beautiful too.

"A storm at sea is one of the things I was hoping to see when I came looking for adventures," he said. "It's wonderful!"

"It won't look so wonderful when we're out in it, saving shipwrecked mice," said

Skipper, the leader of the Adventuremice.
"This will be a busy night."

Suddenly there was a flapping of wet
feathers outside the window and a gray
beak tapped loudly on the glass. Skipper
and Juniper ran to heave the window
open, and a storm petrel stuck its head
into the room.

"Message from Big Island!"
it chirped. "The sea wall at
Mousehaven is about to collapse!"

"Action stations!" shouted Skipper. "Ivy, Bosun, you come with me on the *Daring Dormouse*. Make sure there are plenty of sandbags aboard to repair that sea wall!"

Ivy and Bosun scurried off downstairs to start loading the ship. A moment later, a far-off flare burst like a beautiful pink flower in the dark sky. It startled the messenger bird, who gave a squawk and flapped off into the storm.

"That was a distress signal!" said

Juniper, running to

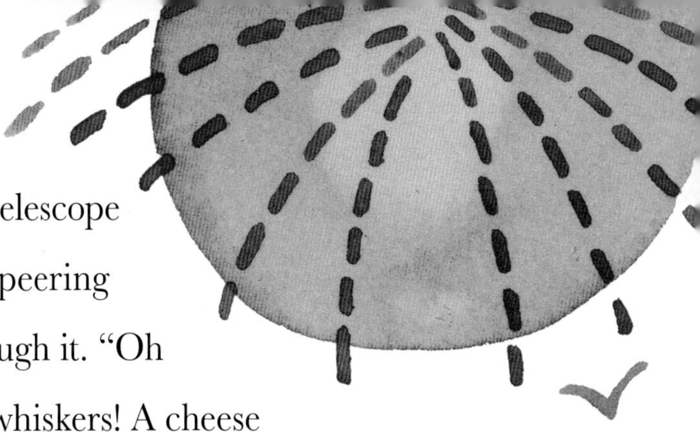

the telescope
and peering
through it. "Oh
my whiskers! A cheese
ship has run aground on the rocks at West
Wainscotting!"

"That sounds like a job for you, Millie,
and Fledermaus," said Skipper, fastening
the toggles of his sailor coat. "Take the
helicopter over there and rescue the crew—
and the cheese, if you can!"

Millie and Fledermaus grabbed their
wet-weather gear and hurried off to the
helipad.

"What shall I do?" asked Pedro, who wanted to help.

Skipper patted him on the shoulder before he followed Ivy and Bosun downstairs. "You stay here with Juniper, in case any more distress calls come in while we're gone," he said.

The helicopter took off, with Millie at the controls and Fledermaus waving from the open door. Soon afterward, the *Daring Dormouse* set off into the storm too, plowing her way through the steep waves

6

in the direction of Big Island. Juniper and Pedro were left all alone in the Mousebase, waiting for another flare, or another bird bearing bad news.

But no more birds arrived, and no more flares lit up the sky. The storm

roared on for a while, but it seemed to be getting tired. The wind grew quieter, and the rain stopped hammering quite so loudly against the windows.

Juniper was getting tired too. She yawned a big yawn.

"You should go to bed," said Pedro. "I can keep watch."

"Well, if you're sure," said Juniper. "I think the worst of the storm is over. But be sure to wake me if anything happens."

Pedro promised he would, and Juniper went off to her nest. Pedro was left alone. He felt very important, but also a bit nervous. What if some new emergency struck the Mouse Islands and he didn't notice? It was a big responsibility. He stood in Skipper's place by the big window and struck important-looking poses. He peeked through the telescope, looking out into the blackness of the night for any sign of more flares or signals. But he didn't see any, and slowly the night turned from black to gray and a new morning broke over the islands, with the sky full of hurrying, torn-up clouds.

Pedro realized he had been awake all night, which made him feel even more important. He didn't feel tired yet, just hungry, so he went quickly to the kitchen and poured some mouse-sized cornflakes into a bowl. (They were made from human-sized cornflakes, which had been smashed into little bits by mice with mallets at the East Wainscotting Cornflake Factory.) Then he stepped

outside onto the balcony to eat them.

And that was when he saw something.

"Oh!" he said.

The sea, which had been so high and
fierce last night, was very quiet and calm
this morning, and the first light of the new
day shone on rocks and patches of sand
which the tide had bared. There were

gleaming tide
pools among the
rocks, and in one of them,
just for a moment, Pedro
thought he saw a little mouse struggling.

"A shipwrecked sailor!" said Pedro to
himself. But he could not be quite sure
because the mouse had ducked down out
of sight behind a rock. It had looked too
small to be a sailor, though. Perhaps it
was just a mouselet, washed out of its nest

by the storm! Or perhaps he had only imagined it?

Pedro didn't want to wake Juniper without a good reason, so he went running downstairs to make sure it really was a mouse that he'd seen.

"Hello!" he shouted, as he scrambled across the seaweed-slithery rocks outside the base. "Get off!" he added, as his tail trailed through a tide pool and a sea anemone grabbed him with its sticky little tentacles.

He tugged himself free, clambered over a washed-up shampoo bottle, and there was the stranded mouse, sitting in a tide pool just in front of him.

Only it wasn't a mouse. It was very small, and instead of back legs it had a tail, just like a little fish.

It was a mermouse.

CHAPTER 2
MEEPIE

"Meep!" said the mermouse.

Pedro tugged on his whiskers three times to make sure he wasn't dreaming. Mermice were another of the things he had been hoping to see when he came to the Mouse Islands, but Skipper and the other Adventuremice had laughed when

15

he asked about them.

"Mermice?" they had said. "There's no such thing!"

"They're just tall tales mouse sailors tell," Skipper had explained.

"I thought I saw a mermouse once," Bosun had said, "but it was just a trick of the light, and when I looked again it had vanished."

But here was a real, live, little mermouse boy, and he showed no sign of vanishing. His tail was covered in shiny yellow scales, just like a goldfish, and he was clutching a soggy red woolen thing in his tiny pink paws.

"Where have you come from?" Pedro asked.

"Meep!" said the mermouse sadly.

Pedro wondered what to do. He looked all around, but there was no sign of any other mermice on the shore, and the sea was making grumbly noises as if it was thinking about coming back and covering the rocks again. Pedro made a decision.

"Come with me, little mermouse," he said, scooping him out of the tide pool. "Juniper will know what to do with you."

"Meep!" said the mermouse.

A big white wave came rushing over the rocks. Pedro turned and ran, with the mermouse in his arms, all the way back to the Mousebase.

"Juniper!" he shouted, running up the stairs. "Juniper, help! I've found a mermouse, and it isn't a dream or a tall tale or a trick of the light, and it goes *meep!*"

"Meep!" said the mermouse.

There were
a lot of
stairs in the
Mousebase.
Pedro stopped
to catch his
breath halfway
up, and Juniper
ran down to meet
him, still in her
pajamas.

"It really *is* a mermouse!" she gasped. "But where on earth can he have come from? I wonder what his name is?"

"Meep!" said the mermouse.

"I think he's too small to talk," said Pedro.

"We'll call him Meepie," decided Juniper, taking the mermouse from Pedro and carrying him through to the bathroom. They half filled the bathtub with cool water, and the mermouse settled into it happily and splashed about while Pedro ran to the kitchen to fetch some food for him. Juniper watched the mermouse with shining eyes. She had loved the stories of mermice when she was a mouselet. She was so happy to find out they were real!

Pedro brought cornflakes, bread crumbs, and a sliver of cheese, but the little mermouse would not eat any of them. "Meep!" he said, in a disgusted tone, when they were offered.

"What do mermice eat?" asked Pedro.

"I don't know," said Juniper. "I don't think anybody does. Poor Meepie can't stay here. We need to get him home to his own people. He's only a baby. His family must be so worried about him."

"But we don't know where he comes from!" said Pedro.

Juniper frowned. "In the stories, the mermice live in an underwater city called Mousehole, but nobody knows where it is. If only Meepie could tell us where he came from . . ."

Meepie was happily swimming lengths of the bathtub. The red knitted thing he

had been carrying when
Pedro found him floated
beside him in the water.
Juniper fished it out and
looked at it. It was a
hat, and it had four letters written on it:
"BIMC."

"This is a clue!" she said.

"Is it?" said Pedro. "I thought it was a
hat. And what does 'BIMC' mean?"

"That stands for Box Island Mining
Company," said Juniper. "That's what
makes it a clue: this hat must belong to
one of the miners on Box Island."

"I think it belongs to Meepie now," said Pedro because the little mermouse was reaching out for it and saying, "Meep! Meep!" Juniper gave it back to him, and he snuggled down with it in the bottom of the bathtub.

"So maybe he comes from Box Island," said Pedro. "Or maybe he lives near Box Island, and that's where he found the hat. Either way, that's where we should look for mermice!"

"We can get there in my submarine," said Juniper. "I'm just sorry the others won't get a chance to meet little Meepie."

"Meep!" said Meepie.

CHAPTER 3
BOX ISLAND

Pedro had not yet been aboard Juniper's submarine. He was a little nervous about it because it went underwater and Pedro had always thought the whole point of boats was that they *didn't* go underwater. But he trusted Juniper, so he helped her put Meepie in a mixing bowl full of water and together they carried the little mermouse into the elevator and rode down the long, long shaft which led to the submarine pen, in a cave deep beneath the Mousebase.

The submarine was called the *Water Vole*. It was as sleek and streamlined as a deep-sea fish and as bright yellow as a deep-sea banana. Juniper and Pedro carried Meepie aboard. The inside of the submarine was snug and cozy. It looked just like a neat little living room, except for all the control panels and wheels and levers and the periscope sticking down

from the ceiling. Juniper started the

engines, and the *Water Vole* sank into its

pool. Peering over Juniper's shoulder, Pedro watched big underwater doors slide open ahead, and the submarine swam out through them into open sea.

They sailed west, passing lots of little islands where mice were busy repairing the damage that the great storm had done. Pedro soon dozed off to sleep.

When he woke up, the *Water Vole*
was almost at Box Island.

Box Island wasn't really an island at all.

It was an actual box: one of those enormous, metal boxes which human beings like to put on ships and send all over the world for some reason. This one had fallen off its ship and come to rest among some rocks, with just its top half sticking out of the waves. When mouse explorers

landed on it and found a way inside, they found it was full of thousands of smaller boxes, and inside the smaller boxes were toy boats and planes, dollhouse furniture, batteries, and all sorts of other things mice could use. The brave miners of the Box Island Mining Company spent their time venturing deeper and deeper into the layers of boxes, and winching their treasures out.

"Even my *Water Vole* was just a human bath toy until Ivy fitted some engines and made her properly waterproof," said Juniper, as she steered the submarine in

to dock at the big wooden jetty which had
been built around the edge of Box Island.
Mouse miners in their orange helmets
came scurrying out of the warehouses
there and scampering down the rickety
wooden stairways which zigzagged up the
island's sides. They crowded around the
landing stage as the *Water Vole* moored.

They were as surprised as

Pedro and Juniper had

been when they saw Meepie.

"So you've never seen mermice here before?" asked Juniper.

"No, never!" the miners all said, shaking their heads.

"But this is a Box Island hat?" said Pedro, taking the soggy red hat from Meepie and holding it up to show them.

"Meep!" said Meepie, reaching out for it with his little pink paws opening and closing like starfish.

"It's my hat!" said one of the miners, taking it from Pedro and trying it on. "I lost it down in Number Seven Shaft . . .

But how did a baby mermouse end up
with it?"

"Meep!" wailed Meepie, and the miner
hurriedly gave him back the hat. "I've got
a new one anyway," he explained.

"That hat isn't the first thing to go
missing down Number Seven Shaft," said
a big gray mouse. She was Marge, the

chief miner, and she was looking very thoughtful. "Number Seven is our deepest shaft. It goes right down almost to the bottom of Box Island. Mice who work down there often hear strange noises, and things go missing . . ."

"My lunch box disappeared!" agreed one of the miners. "It still had half a cheese puff in it, too!"

"I found a whole box of plates and cups," said another, "and when I went back down the next day, it had been nibbled open and emptied out!"

"It's ghosts!" said a little gray miner nervously. "I've heard their voices whispering, down there in the dark water at the bottom of the shaft!"

"Is there water inside Box Island?" asked Juniper.

"The bottom of Shaft Seven is flooded," said Marge.

"So there must be a hole down there," said Pedro. "And if sea can get in, so can mermice!"

"Meep!" said Meepie.

"Come on!" said Juniper. "Let's take a look!"

Pedro and Juniper carried Meepie back aboard the *Water Vole*, and Marge came with them. Juniper closed the hatch tightly behind them. When they were all seated in the cockpit, with Meepie in his mixing bowl between them, Juniper pulled a lever and the submarine sank down past the

huge rusty cliff face that was the side of
Box Island.

The bottom of the huge box was
wedged tightly between underwater rocks.
It was dark down there. Juniper switched
on the submarine's headlights as she
steered it around the corner
of the island.

The circle of pale light went sliding across the rusty metal, startling shrimp and making barnacles blink and hide inside their shells. At last it lit up a small, dark, jagged hole where Box Island had been bashed against the rocks as it sank.

"So that's why the lower levels are flooded," grumbled Marge. "We never could find that hole from inside."

"I'll come back with underwater welding gear and fix it," promised Juniper.

"But first we need to get Meepie home."

Pedro looked hard at the hole. Inside it, in the darkness, something was moving. He just had time to say, "Look!" before two mermice popped out. These were full-grown mermice, and they were carrying a net full of things they must have taken from inside Box Island.

"Blithering baboons!" shouted Marge. "Box Island's being burgled!"

Pedro tapped on the inside of the *Water Vole*'s window and held up Meepie in his bowl so the mermice could see him. But the mermice were too startled at finding the submarine there to notice, and too dazzled by the submarine's lights to see. They dropped their net and swam quickly away.

"After them!" yelled Marge.

Juniper spun the *Water Vole* around and turned the engines to full power. The submarine shot off so fast that Pedro sat down unexpectedly and the water from Meepie's mixing bowl splashed all over him. Far ahead, in the beam of light from the submarine's headlights, the two mermice went squiggling through the water.

"When we catch up with them I'll give them a piece of my mind all right," said Marge.

"Oh, no you won't!" said Juniper. "We'll just ask them very nicely to take Meepie home to his family."

But the mermice were moving almost as fast as the *Water Vole*. Where the submarine had to go around the big rocks and tangled clumps of seaweed which dotted the seafloor, the mermice could find their way through the narrowest of gaps. Deeper and deeper they went, through whole forests of seaweed and past the wrecks of ancient mouse ships, until Pedro began to feel quite scared. But he didn't mind too much because he was an Adventuremouse, and all Adventuremice know that if you aren't a *little* bit scared, you aren't really having an adventure, just an outing.

So he peered through the front window,

watching the deep, dark sea . . .

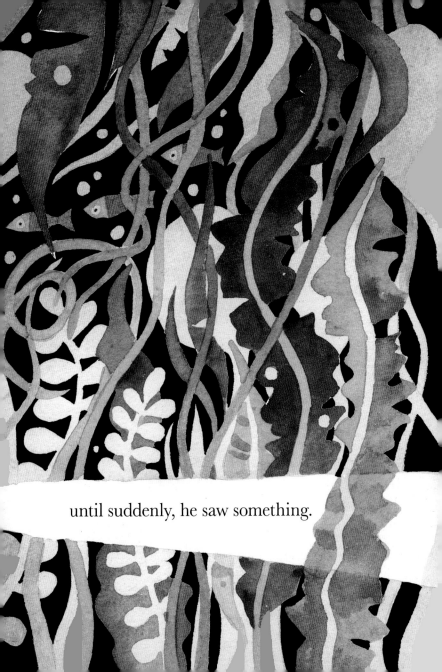

until suddenly, he saw something.

It was a light, shining in the gloom on the seafloor. Soon there was another and then another and another. The dark stony sides of a big rock stack towered up ahead, and on the seabed at its base lay a city.

"That must be Lonesome Rock," said Juniper.

"And that must be Mousehole!" gasped Pedro. "The mermouse city, just like in the stories!"

The houses of
Mousehole had big
seashells for roofs,
and their walls were
decorated with
smaller ones. Coral
and barnacles had
grown over them, so
that the whole place
seemed bejeweled.

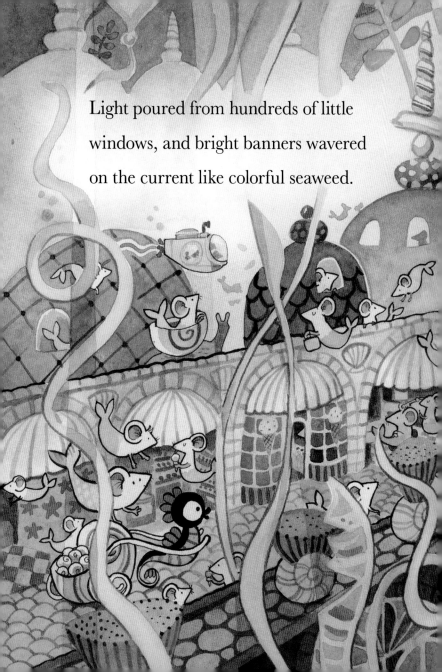

Light poured from hundreds of little windows, and bright banners wavered on the current like colorful seaweed.

The two mermice from Box Island were still far ahead of the *Water Vole* when the city came into sight. They swam down into the shelter of its rooftops, and they must have raised the alarm, for by the time the submarine arrived, the underwater streets were full of mermice. Some were swimming, some were riding on the backs of crabs or seahorses, and they were all rushing to meet the *Water Vole*.

"I hope they're friendly," said Pedro nervously. He had noticed that some of the mermice were carrying swords made from the spines of sea urchins, and spears tipped with sharp bits of seashell.

"They will be when they see we've brought Meepie home," said Juniper.

"Meep!" said Meepie.

It was hard for Juniper to know where to moor her submarine because there were so many mermouse buildings, and so many delicate coral trees growing in the parks and squares between them. But important-looking mermice in shell armor swam ahead of her, pointing the way with their spiny swords, and at last the *Water*

Vole arrived at a kind of shallow cave in the base of Lonesome Rock.

Juniper let down an anchor, and some of the mermice helped to hook it on a handy boulder. Then Juniper and Pedro climbed into their diving suits. There were diving suits for all the Adventuremice in the *Water Vole*'s lockers, and Marge was

able to squeeze herself into the biggest, which was Bosun's. Meepie had been snoozing underwater in his mixing bowl most of the way from Box Island, so they knew he didn't need a diving suit. Pedro picked him up and the three mice climbed out through the submarine's air lock hatch.

The mermice waiting outside looked

confused. They hadn't seen diving suits before, and they weren't sure what these strange creatures were, with their heads encased in glass bubbles. But as soon as Meepie woke up and said, "Meep!"

a mermouse who had been swimming right at the back of the crowd gave a squeak of happiness and quickly pushed her way to the front.

"Meepie!" she squeaked, as the tiny mermouse swam toward her. She took the mouselet and hugged him tight. "Oh Meepie, my own little mouselet!"

"Is his name really Meepie?" asked Pedro.

"That's what I call him because 'meep' is all he's learned to say yet," said the mermouse.

"Meep! Meep! Meep!" said Meepie happily.

"My name is Tessa," said Meepie's

mother. "Meepie was washed away in the storm tide last night. Oh, thank you, thank you, for bringing him home!"

Pedro felt very proud. "We are Adventuremice," he said, "and that is what we do."

A stern-looking mermouse with bushy whiskers arrived, riding on a crab who looked particularly pleased with itself.

"You must come and meet our mermouse queen," he said. "Outsiders are not allowed in Mousehole. She will decide what is to be done with you."

CHAPTER 5

THE MERMOUSE QUEEN

The queen of the mermice was called
Queen Frangipani Camembert-de-Mer
the 44th. She lived in a grand palace
with seashell walls and a domed glass
roof made from a large glass bowl.
Inside, the palace was decorated with
tapestries woven from seaweed, and

clever portraits of
Queen Frangipani's
ancestors done in
colored sand. Small glowing starfish clung
to the ceiling, casting a warm yellow light.
But not everything was made of sand
and seashells. Here and there Pedro and
Juniper saw other things which must have
come from Box Island.

"These subaquatic
sneak thieves must
have been robbing us

for years," muttered Marge.

The queen herself sat on her throne under the glass dome of the large bowl, looking very beautiful and wise and grand.

"How did these strangers come here, General Angmering?" she asked.

"They chased Horace and Hilary all the way from Box Island in an underwater

boat, Your Majesty," said the stern, bushy-whiskered mermouse who had brought them to the palace.

"How extraordinary!" said the queen. "I always thought the whole point of boats was that they *don't* go underwater."

"If you please, Your Majesty," said Pedro, "I always thought so too, but the *Water Vole* is *designed* to go underwater."

"Hmmm," said the queen, looking at him in a very queenly way. "And why were you chasing Horace and Hilary? They are two of Mousehole's bravest adventurers, who have brought us all sorts of treasures."

"Brave adventurers, my foot!" said
Marge angrily. "Beastly burglars is
what they are!" She was so cross she
had steamed up the inside of her diving
helmet, but luckily when Ivy designed
the Adventuremouse diving suits she had

thought of that, so two tiny windshield wipers cleared a gap for Marge to glare through at the queen.

"The treasures in Box Island belong to the mice of the Mouse Islands! You deep-sea delinquents can't just go helping yourselves to them!"

"But that's not why we followed Hilary and Horace here, Your Majesty," said Juniper hurriedly. "We needed to find our way to your city because the storm

washed little Meepie ashore on our island,
and we wanted to bring him home."

"And they did, Your Majesty!" said Tessa.

"Meep!" agreed Meepie.

"That was very brave," said the queen.
"You shall be rewarded. You shall have
a house to live in, and I will have the
royal builders make it airtight, and fetch
air down for you from the world above.
But you must never leave. The city of
Mousehole is a secret, and no one who has
found their way here can ever be allowed
to leave again, in case they tell others how
to find us."

"Oh, we won't tell anyone," said Juniper.

"We promise," said Pedro.

The queen shook her head sadly. "It is the law," she said. "You must stay in Mousehole forever."

"But that's not fair!" said Pedro.

"You can't keep us here!" shouted Marge. "I have work to do at Box Island, sealing up that hole so your scaly-tailed scallywags can't steal our stuff!"

"General Angmering!" ordered the
queen. "Seize these mice!"

"No!" said Tessa.

"Meep!" said Meepie.

"Er . . ." said General Angmering.

"Look!" said Pedro.

While the others were all talking, a
movement had caught Pedro's eye. He
was pointing up through the clear glass
ceiling. Something was falling through
the water. It was a big, black stone, and
it was heading straight toward Queen
Frangipani's palace.

"Look out!" shouted Pedro.

Adventuremice and mermice scattered in all directions as the stone smashed down on the glass roof. General Angmering hurried the queen off her throne. Marge stood dithering in the middle of the floor, but Tessa swam over to her and pulled her out of the way, just as the ceiling gave way and the stone came crashing in. It landed on the queen's throne and squashed it flat. Everyone watched, crouched under tables or in handy alcoves,

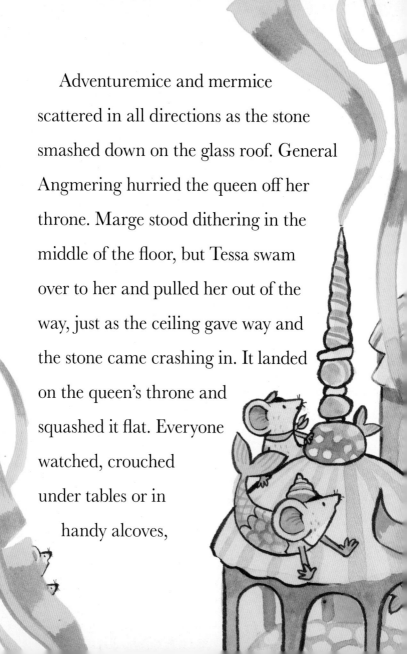

while a few smaller stones came down.
They fell quite slowly underwater, but they
were still big and heavy enough to hurt a
mouse.

"That's the third stone that's fallen on Mousehole today!" said Tessa. "And it's the biggest yet!"

"Lonesome Rock must have been damaged by the storm," said Juniper. "Bits are dropping off it."

A frightened-looking mermouse messenger came swimming in. "Your Majesty! Your Majesty!" he squeaked. "I've been to the surface. Terrible news! An even bigger piece of rock is about to fall! It will crush the whole city!"

The mermouse queen put her head in her paws. "Oh," she sniffled, "this is

awful! Our poor city! This is the end of
Mousehole!"

"Not if we can stop it!" said Juniper.

The queen and all the mermice stared
at her. So did Pedro. "How?" he gasped.

"I don't know," admitted Juniper. "But,

Your Majesty, if you will let us go and call our friends, I'm sure the Adventuremice can find a way to save your city!"

The queen shook her head. "If your friends come here, Mousehole will be a secret no more."

"Humph," said General Angmering. "If their friends *don't* come here, Mousehole will be squashed as flat as a pancake. I'm not entirely sure what a pancake is, since I'm an underwater sort of mouse, but I've heard about them, and I gather they're jolly flat."

"Please, let them help!" said Tessa.

"Yes, yes!" chorused the other

mermice. "Save our city!"

"Meep!" said Meepie.

"Very well," said the queen. "Juniper,

Pedro, you may call your friends and see if

there is some way they can help us."

Pedro, Juniper, and Marge scrambled quickly back into the *Water Vole*. A crowd of mermice swam with the submarine as it soared back to the surface. It popped up in a drift of floating seaweed, startling a seagull, who flapped away with an angry squawk.

Pedro looked up through the wet windows at the dark pinnacles of Lonesome Rock. He could see a crack in the rock face where the storm had battered and battered at it. A big, jagged shard was wobbling like a loose tooth as the wind blew around it, ready to break free and fall off into the sea.

"That chunk of rock looks as big as the *Daring Dormouse*!" he gasped. "And it's probably twice as heavy! How can we possibly stop it from falling?"

Juniper pushed the hatch open and leaned out with a flare gun in her hand.

WHOOOOOOSH, went the flare, shooting high into the sky. **BOOM,** it added, bursting like a little sun.

"The Adventuremice will find a way,"
she promised.

LONESOME ROCK

The other Adventuremice had arrived
home at the Mousebase to find a note
propped against the teapot. It read:

We have found a mermouse,
and we are taking him
home to Mousehole.
Juniper and Pedro
x

"Is it a joke?" asked Fledermaus.

"It must be," said Ivy. "There are no such things as mermice."

"Then where have Juniper and Pedro gone?" wondered Bosun.

"We must look for them," said Skipper.

"Found them!" said Fledermaus, pointing out of the window.

An orange flare hung in the sky, far to the west of the Mouse Islands. As they watched, it slowly sank toward the sea.

"A signal from Juniper!" cried Skipper. "It looks as if she's beyond Box Island, out near Lonesome Rock . . . "

Tired though they were after their long night, Skipper and Bosun piled back aboard the *Daring Dormouse*. Millie ran to her helicopter, and Fledermaus scampered downstairs and jumped into his yellow seaplane. Soon they were all zooming toward Lonesome Rock. It wasn't long before Fledermaus spotted the submarine wallowing in the swell at the rock's foot.

"Hello, Juniper!" he shouted, landing
on the sea nearby. "Hello, Pedro! What's
the trouble? Have your batteries run out?"

"No," Juniper called back. "We have to
stop that rock from falling on the mermice!"

"On the what?" said Fledermaus. "This is no time for jokes, Juniper! There are no such things as mermice!"

"Yes, there are!" said Tessa, poking her head out of the waves beside his seaplane. "Yes, there are!" added dozens of other mermice, popping up all around him.

"Meep!" said Meepie.

"Goodness gracious!
Great balls of cheese!" gasped
Fledermaus. He waved up at Millie,
whose helicopter came whirring
overhead just then. "Millie!
We've got to stop that rock
from falling!"

Millie set down her helicopter
on the top of Lonesome Rock. She got
out and peered at the wobbling shard.

"It's no use," she shouted. "It's too big!
Even if we can get ropes around it, there's
no way we can lift it."

A seagull flapped overhead, screeching
with annoyance when it saw that Millie
had stolen its favorite perch. But seagulls
had learned not to get into fights with
the mice of the Mouse Islands, so it flew
off again. A single feather came drifting
down to land on the mats of seaweed
that floated near the rock. Pedro watched
it thoughtfully as it settled there. He
said, "What if we could put something

underneath the rock to break its fall?"

"Good thinking, Pedro!" said Millie. "We could anchor a raft underneath it, and it would land on that instead of sinking down on top of the mermice."

"But it would have to be a HUGE raft!" said Fledermaus. "Where would we find something like that?"

They all thought hard. Then Marge said, "I have just the thing!"

Juniper and Millie stayed with the
mermice, keeping watch on the teetering
rock while Pedro and Marge squeezed
into Fledermaus's plane, and Fledermaus
flew back toward Box Island. The *Daring
Dormouse* was just passing on its way to

Lonesome Rock, but Fledermaus waggled the seaplane's wings to signal to it, and Bosun turned the ship to meet them on the Box Island jetty.

While Pedro told Skipper, Ivy, and Bosun about the danger hanging over Mousehole, Marge rounded up some of her miners and scurried over to one of the huge warehouses where the things they had found inside Box Island were kept. They were soon back, dragging an enormous cardboard box. A picture on the box showed a pillowy sort of raft floating on the sea.

"These things are called 'pool floats,'"
said Marge. "Humans float about on them."

"Why?" asked Pedro.

"No one knows. But if a pool float can
carry the weight of a human being I'm sure
it can hold a rock or two. Come on, miners!"

The miners heaved the box lid open,
and pulled the pool float out. It looked
nothing like the picture on the box at all.

It was just a bundle of rubbery yellow plastic.

"But that's not a raft!" said Pedro.

"Not yet," said Marge. "We have to pump it full of air first. It'll be ten times bigger and as light as a feather, you'll see."

While the Adventuremice spread the pool float out flat on the jetty, Marge and her miners delved into the box and fetched out a foot pump with a long tube which Ivy and Bosun connected to a nozzle on the pool float. The foot pump was made for human feet, but when twenty or thirty miner mice jumped on it, it squeezed down and pumped a puff of air into the pool float.

All through that long afternoon, groups of mice took turns to work the pump. It was fun at first, but it soon grew tiring. For a long time nothing seemed

to be happening, and some of the miners grumbled and wanted to give up. But then the bundled-up pool float slowly started to change shape, unfurling at the edges, and plumping up in the middle, and the mice all cheered and carried on pumping.

But the mice were small, and the pool float was big, and the sun was going down in the west by the time their work was done. Pedro glanced uneasily toward Lonesome Rock. He could see the lights of the *Water Vole* out there. The wind was rising. That shard of rock might fall at any moment.

Bosun and Ivy pulled the tube off the pool float nozzle. There was a horrible moment when it seemed as if all the air the mice had pumped in was going to rush straight back out again, but Bosun, Ivy, and Marge all working together managed to cram the lid onto the nozzle. Soon the pool float floated on the swell beside Box

Island docks. It was bigger than any vessel that had ever sailed the Mouse Island seas before.

"But lighter, too!" said Skipper. "Quick, tie a line from it to the *Daring Dormouse*. We'll tow it out to Lonesome Rock before night falls."

The miners lit the lamps on

their helmets and stood in the twilight waving as the *Daring Dormouse* motored away, towing the enormous inflatable behind it. Pedro ran to the prow of the ship and watched Lonesome Rock draw slowly closer. He knew Queen Frangipani would be leading her people out to shelter in the seabed fields around their city, just in case the Adventuremice's mission failed.

"But we can't fail!" said Pedro, clenching his paws tightly. "We can't! Not after all that work!"

Just then, wide
white wings
swept over
the *Daring
Dormouse* like a ghost.

It was that annoying seagull from earlier.
It was heading home to Lonesome Rock
to roost for the night, and this time it
wasn't to be put off by any pesky mice.

Pedro and the others watched in horror as it came in to land right on top of the loose bit of rock.

The extra weight of the gull was all it took to overbalance the rock. It toppled forward, leaning far, far out over the sea, ready to fall. But luckily, Millie and Juniper had tied ropes to it. Millie took off in her helicopter, and its engines strained as it tried to take the weight of the huge rock. Teams of mermice who had scrambled up the sides of Lonesome Rock held other ropes. But the rock was heavy, and as it leaned out farther and farther over the sea it dragged them after it.

"They can't hold it for long!" shouted Skipper. "Quick!"

A rope snapped, and the mermice who had been holding it fell over backward in a heap. Another broke with a *ping!* catapulting mermice into the sea. The rock lurched forward. Millie cut her rope just in time to stop the helicopter from being dragged down with it as it began to fall.

The *Daring Dormouse* surged through the sea. Little pebbles clattered on the decks and the cabin roof as she raced under the falling rock. Pedro squeaked with fright. He shut his eyes and braced himself for the great splash which the rock would make when it hit the sea.

But the splash never came.

Pedro opened one eye, then the other.

Behind the *Daring Dormouse* the huge rock lay on the pool float like a giant

sunbather. It was so heavy that the pool float was tilting to one side, and so jagged that air was hissing out through lots of little holes where the rock had punctured it.

"Let's get it safely away from Mousehole before the pool float collapses!" called Juniper. She swung her submarine around behind the pool float and started pushing, while the *Daring Dormouse* pulled, and Millie hovered overhead, shining a

light down on them. The waves all around
were filled with cheering mermice.

The Adventuremice towed the deflating pool float farther and farther away from Mousehole, until the rock rolled gently into the water. It sank down on a stretch of empty seafloor where it did no harm at all, and made a useful home for small fish.

CHAPTER 7

MOONLIGHT & CAKE

The poor old pool float was too floppy to take the weight of a rock anymore, but it could easily support some mice. The Adventuremice jumped aboard it, and Marge and her miners arrived on tugboats from Box Island. The mermice came shyly out of the deep to meet them there.

Queen Frangipani herself swam up to thank them for their help, and Skipper and the others went down with her to see the underwater city for themselves.

A fat, full moon was rising by the time they returned.

"Well," said Skipper, as he pulled off his helmet, "it just goes to show–you can sail these seas for years, and still find there are things in them you didn't know about."

"What will happen to this huge great pool float?" asked Queen Frangipani.

"Oh, don't worry about that, Your Queenship," said Marge. "We'll tow it to Big Island. It can be cut up to make waterproof coats and hats for mouse sailors."

The queen thanked her. "I am sorry
we took things from Box Island without
asking," she said.

"That's all right," said Marge. "We
never thought there might be mermice

down below who
needed them.
There's plenty
in that big old
box for everyone,
land mice and mermice alike. Let's say
everything that's underwater belongs
to mermice, and everything that's not
belongs to land mice. Is that fair?"

"Very!" said Queen Frangipani, and they shook paws to make it official.

Pedro and Juniper sat on the pool float's edge with Tessa, nibbling snacks while Meepie played beside them. The lights of the Mouse Islands twinkled in the night. The moonlit sea shone like silvery fish scales, and far-off unknown islands lay dark against the glitter of it.

"I wonder what else we'll find out there?" said Pedro.

"Adventures!" shouted the other Adventuremice. Then Ivy fetched her accordion, and Bosun came out of the *Daring Dormouse* carrying a big cake he'd

just baked, and the Adventuremice and their new friends ate, and talked, and danced, and laughed, and sang until long after the moon had gone to bed.

EAST WAINSCOTTING

CORNFLAKE FACTORY

LONESOME ROCK

MOUSEHOLE

WEST WAINSCOTTING

BOX ISLAND

SANDPIPER STRAITS

RUMMAGE

THE TWITCHLETS

WHISKERY

SNIFF

THISTLE ROCK

THE MOUSE ISLANDS

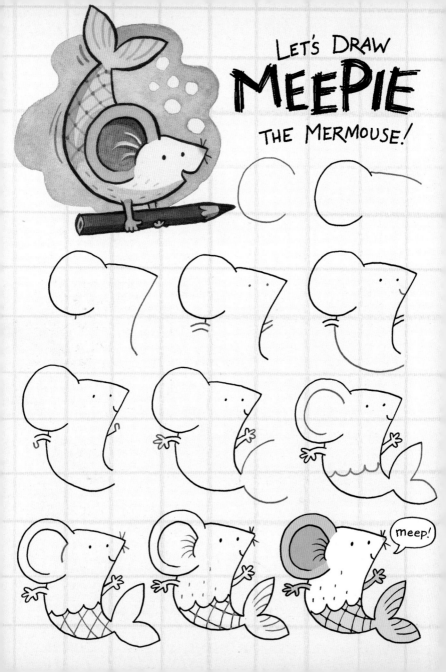

LET'S DRAW
MEEPIE
THE MERMOUSE!

meep!

ABOUT THE AUTHORS

SARAH McINTYRE

LOVES DRAWING MORE THAN WRITING. BUT SHE OFTEN HELPS HER COAUTHOR PHILIP WITH THE WORDS WHEN HE WANTS SOME NEW IDEAS.

PHILIP REEVE

LOVES WRITING MORE THAN DRAWING. BUT HE HELPS SARAH WITH THE PICTURES SO THEY WON'T TAKE QUITE SO LONG TO MAKE.

THEY BOTH LOVE BEACHES, DRIFTWOOD, AND THE SEA, AND MAKING UP STORIES ABOUT MYSTERIOUS ISLANDS.

READ THE FIRST ADVENTURE!

ADVENTURE MICE

OTTER CHAOS!

REEVE & McINTYRE

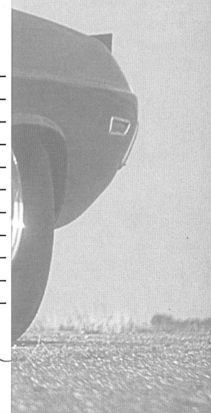

THE ULTIMATE GUIDE TO
AMERICAN CARS

THE ULTIMATE GUIDE TO
AMERICAN CARS

Peter Henshaw

LORENZ BOOKS

This edition published in 2011 by
Lorenz Books, an imprint of
Anness Publishing Ltd
Blaby Road, Wigston
Leicestershire LE18 4SE, UK

Email: info@anness.com

Web: www.lorenzbooks.com;
www.annesspublishing.com

ETHICAL TRADING POLICY
Because of Anness Publishing's ongoing
ecological investment programme, you,
as our customer, can have the pleasure
and reassurance of knowing that a tree
is being cultivated on your behalf to
naturally replace the materials used to
make the book you are holding. For
further information about this scheme,
go to www.annesspublishing.com/trees

PUBLISHER'S NOTE
Although the information in this book is
believed to be accurate and true at the
time of going to press, neither the authors
nor the publisher can accept any legal
responsibility or liability for any errors
or omissions that may have been made.

Contents

Introduction

Every nation has its car enthusiasts, and most have a motor industry to go with them, but nowhere is the car more strongly a part of society and a means of personal expression than in America. Whether it's for the daily commute to work, a weekend trip to a national park or simply a visit to the supermarket, the car is an essential part of daily life.

Los Angeles was famously the first city in history to be built around the car, where no one walks more than a block if they can drive. The rest of the world appears to be going that way, which isn't necessarily a good thing, but it's happening nonetheless.

But for Americans, this love affair with the automobile goes deeper even still, America, after all, being a nation founded on free movement of populations. Before the first European settlers arrived, Native Americans changed locations with the seasons, following their animals to new hunting grounds, while the coming of the founding fathers saw wagons moving west as new townships were established. These were many miles apart, the nearest many days away.

Which is why the private car, when it arrived, had such an explosive effect on early 20th-century America. Henry Ford did not invent the automobile or even perfect it, but he was a pioneer of mass-production. Consequently the cars he produced, notably the Model T, were made increasingly affordable to the ordinary man in the street. Americans lived in a big country and had vast distances to travel, so the private car opened up new horizons to thousands of people. In Europe, by contrast, where few people lived more than a few miles from towns, simpler types of transport were able to do the job almost as well.

It follows, therefore, that there was a huge home market for cars as well as the potential for huge profits, which gave the American car industry a massive kickstart with little need to look beyond its borders. Within a few years it was out-producing the rest of the world put together, which continued until it was overtaken by Japan in the late 20th century.

This world dominance, and mastery of the techniques of mass-production, meant that Detroit, America's car capital, had all the confidence of a world leader, which was not confined to Henry's pile 'em high, sell 'em cheap philosophy. William Durant's General Motors Company, Chevrolet in particular, demonstrated that it was possible to produce affordable cars in bright colours with chrome trims, which accordingly set the trend.

Detroit built cars with the consumer very much in mind, which is why automatic transmission, power steering and power brakes were pioneered in the States. Even the Depression of 1929 failed to destroy the buoyant confidence of these early manufacturers. A period of austerity may have decimated production for a time, but it was swiftly forgotten as it recovered later in the 1930s.

The industry was diverted to military vehicles in the early 1940s and when civilian production resumed after the Second World War it was much revitalized, unlike Europe, whose motor industry was now in decline, many of its factories razed to the ground. In America, however, because people had been starved of cars for so long, Detroit found it could sell everything that rolled off the lines.

It was a golden era for Motor City, when hot new V8s offered more power and more features than ever before, and tailfins sprouted in homage to the space age. But Ford, Chrysler and General Motors also kept their ears close to the ground, producing a new generation of compacts to counter the flood of cars coming in from abroad. In the early 1960s, Ford's Mustang created a whole new genre – the pony car – with Pontiac's GTO doing the same for muscle cars, the two burning rubber right through that hedonistic decade. It seemed that Detroit could do no wrong.

But a fuel crisis, tightening emissions and safety legislation and ever-increasing imports from Japan and Europe were seen as something of a

wake-up call in the early 1970s. Once again, Detroit rose to the challenge, though gas-guzzling dinosaurs persisted for a few years more. The second fuel crisis of 1978 saw queues at gas stations, spiralling prices and talk of rationing – a warning that the world was changing fast. But as gas came back on stream and memories began to fade, Americans began to demand bigger cars. Front-wheel-drive four-cylinder compacts conceived in the 1970s were given V6 options, and their replacements were bigger and heavier, while V8 engines, now with fuel injection and four-valve heads reappeared. Performance was back in fashion and while car sales made no great strides in the 1990s, those of SUVs began to rocket

By the early 21st century, the American car had become more efficient than of old. Detroit now had a wealth of heritage on which to draw, and several cars, such as the Dodge Viper and 2005 Mustang, now owed much to the past, which was perceived to have been a happier, simpler time. But one thing hadn't changed: America was still in love with the automobile.

AMERICAN AUSTIN/AMERICAN BANTAM (1930–41)

Unlikely as it may seem, the little American Austin can claim to be a distant cousin of the Jeep. It began life in 1930 when, in an attempt to offer a tiny four-cylinder four-seater along European lines to the American public, a licence-built version of the Austin Seven chassis and running gear was married to all-American coupé or roadster bodies styled by Alex de Sakhnoffsky. Unfortunately, its price of $445, actually slightly more than a full-sized Model A Ford, meant that it saw only limited production.

The American Austin nevertheless had a unique appeal of its own, being sufficiently novel and eye-catching to establish a niche market of its own, even though sales fell short of the maker's ambitious target of 180,000. Less than 9,000 were sold in 1930, and only a few more before the factory closed in 1932.

The operation was rescued by a car dealer named Roy S. Evans, who disposed of the unsold stock at giveaway prices, raising sufficient cash to resume production in 1934. Once again, the American Austin sold in limited numbers for a couple of years, though none was built in 1935–36. But it was relaunched, in restyled and updated form, as the American Bantam in 1937. Yet again, production dwindled to a mere 800 cars in 1940, when the plug was finally pulled for good. But the company itself was far from finished and went on to design the first Jeep, destined to become a world-class icon in its own right.

AMERICAN MOTORS (1968–87)

American Motors Corporation (AMC), one of Detroit's 'Big Three', gained a stranglehold on the post-war U.S. motor industry. Here was a company that

AMC's Javelin had some success in the Trans Am series. Here Mark Donohue in his Sunoco Javelin chases the Mustang of Parnelli Jones.

general. But the company was only intermittently profitable, and in 1987 it succumbed to a takeover by Chrysler, whose main purpose was to acquire Jeep rather than AMC's cars.

The company had its beginnings in the 1954 merger between Hudson and Nash. Four years later, the entire line-up was renamed Rambler, but it wasn't until 1968 that the AMC name finally appeared on a car – the Javelin – part of chairman Roy D. Chapin's bold plan to revitalize the company with a new range of modern cars. The Javelin was certainly of its time, being a sleek, four-seater fastback capable

LEFT
AMC made a good job of selling Jeeps, such as this Wagoneer, though the cars were less popular.

BELOW and BELOW LEFT
1971 Javelin AMX. This is the short-wheelbased two-seater version of the standard car.

pioneered compact cars, hatchbacks and four-wheel-drive sedans. It offered small cars at a time when the American public was waking up to their benefits in the late 1950s, and did much to popularize four-wheel-drive SUVs with the public in

RIGHT
The Javelin was created to rival
contemporary pony cars, such as the
Mustang and Camaro, but sold in smaller
numbers.

OPPOSITE
The Pacer looked like a European compact
but with U.S. dimensions.

of challenging the almighty pony car and the Mustang and Camaro in particular. It came with the choice of a 233-ci (3818-cc) six and V8s of 288ci (4719cc) and 344ci (5637cc), over 55,000 of which were sold in the first year. An interesting spin-off was the AMX, a two-seater short-wheelbased version with the same engine options. Unfortunately, the American public didn't find it all that interesting, and fewer than 20,000 where sold before it was dropped in 1970.

There was better news that year when the takeover of Jeep was announced. Roy Chapin had forseen the huge potential of four-wheel-drive family transport, and Jeep sales expanded as a result, supporting AMC's ailing car line-up for the next decade or more. This was helped by the subcompact Gremlin in 1970 (beating the Ford Pinto and Chevy Vega to market), powered by 233-ci or 258-ci (4228-cc) sixes and later by a 123-ci (2016-cc) VW four.

Billed as the 'first wide small car', the Pacer offered the width of a full-sized car in a compact package.

were sold before it was dropped in 1980.

By then, AMC had its range of Eagle four-wheel-drives on sale, based on the compact Concord, with 153-ci (2507-cc) fours and 233-ci sixes. Once again it seemed that AMC was a pioneer ahead of its time. Four-wheel-drive cars are popular now but were regarded as oddities in the early 1980s, and the Eagle failed to sell well. More successful, at least at first, were the AMC-Renaults. The company sold the

The rest of the line-up consisted of the compact Hornet and medium-sized Rebel, later renamed the Matador, as well as the full-sized Ambassador, the latter being an old-fashioned remnant of the Rambler era. The Sportabout, a fastback station-wagon version of the Hornet, was a notable variation that sold well. With the first fuel crisis of the 1970s in full swing, AMC dropped the big Ambassador and sporty

Javelin, launching the innovatively conceived Pacer. Billed as the 'first wide small car', this combined near full-sized width with a compact wheelbase and acres of glass. Designed originally to take a General Motors rotary engine, it used AMC's own six and a V8 when this failed to materialize. But it was too radical for its time: the Pacer was not the roaring success that had been envisaged, though 280,000

Renault 5 and Fuego coupé in the U.S.A., and from 1982 built the 9 and 11 in its own Kenosha factory, selling them as the Alliance and Encore respectively. Over 200,000 left the showrooms in 1984, but a reputation for poor quality saw a rapid slump in sales. AMC sold out to the newly revitalized Chrysler in 1987, having lost money and market share with equal rapidity.

APPERSON (1902–26)
In the 1890s the Apperson brothers, Elmer and Edgar, were running the Riverside Machine Works in Kokomo, Indiana, when they were approached by Elwood Haynes. It was the beginning of a partnership that would last for several years, the Appersons building cars to designs by Haynes to which they added their own contributions.

This arrangement came to an acrimonious end in 1901, when Elmer and Edgar formed the Apperson Brothers Automobile Company. The Haynes-Apperson cars had been one- or two-cylinder machines, and while the first pure Apperson was a twin, using a Stintz engine, a four-cylinder car appeared in 1903 and the twin was dropped the following year.

Apperson cars were far from cheap, ranging from $2,500 to $5,000, the brothers clearly having no ambitions to beat Henry Ford at his own game. In 1907, when Ford unveiled the Model T, Elmer and Edgar announced their Jack Rabbit sports car, a spartan two-seater which

lasted for six years. The year 1908 saw a six-cylinder Apperson unveiled, though it took another six years or so to reach production as the 6-45 and 6-55. By that time, the company was offering six different models.

The brothers were certainly not behind in engine layouts, replacing the fours with a V8 in 1918 and dropping the short-lived sixes the following year. A new low-priced six, the $1,535 6-23 appeared in 1923, using a Falls engine, but by now the company was on a slippery slope. Production had peaked in 1916, but Elmer's death early in 1920 severed a lifelong partnership.

Despite an outside injection of capital, and a reorganization in 1924, Apperson's days were numbered. The V8 lingered awhile, now offered alongside a 276-ci (4523-cc) Lycoming straight-eight, though by 1926 even that had gone. Apperson finally closed in July 1926.

AUBURN (1902–36)
The history of Auburn, one of the most stylish American cars of the 1920s and '30s, divides into two parts. Established and run by the Eckhardt brothers, it produced a line of competent but unremarkable cars until 1924, when it was taken over by Errett Lobban Cord, who

Errett Lobban Cord transformed the dowdy Auburn into one of America's most stylish cars.

transformed the marque into an icon of style and glamour. In the end, however, nothing could ensure Auburn's survival and it closed in 1936.

Frank and Morris Eckhardt began to build a conventional small runabout in 1902. It followed the conventions of the time, with a single-cylinder engine, open two-seater body and tiller steering. They named the car Auburn after the company's Auburn, Indiana, location. The Auburn's development was conventional enough and the early single was soon supplanted by a twin, while a four-cylinder car, using a Rutenber engine, arrived in 1910 and a six two years later. Although Cord is generally acknowledged as the man who beautified Auburn, the Eckhardts launched their own 'Beauty Six' in 1921, with bevelled-edge

OPPOSITE and THIS PAGE
A glamorous, well-restored two-seater Auburn, complete with dicky seat. When this car was built, in 1931, the company was enjoying its best year ever.

bodywork on open versions. Despite this, only 2,443 cars were sold in 1923, down from 6,000 in 1919, and by 1924 production was a mere six cars a day.

It was at this point that Cord comes into the picture. A super-salesman who had made his name selling Moon cars, he could see the potential beyond Auburn's dowdy image. By then, he had already realized that looks rather than technical features were more likely to sell cars, so he struck a deal. He would join Auburn at a low salary and in the event of turning the company round would eventually take control.

Which is exactly what happened. Cord's first task was to find a way of shifting the 500 unsold Auburns that were sitting outside the factory gathering dust. He had them repainted in two-tone colours, exposed the bright nickel plating on the radiator and door handles, and sold the lot. The car was completely restyled the following year, again with a two-tone finish and a distinctive belt of moulding across the hood, while a Lycoming straight-eight power unit added to the appeal.

The ever-restless Cord was now on the lookout for fresh projects, which led to the acquisition of Duesenberg, but in the meantime Auburn thrived. Its new-found glamour was abundant in the 1931 cars, styled by a young Alan H. Leamy, and its lean sports-car look was suggestive of power and grace. They weren't even that expensive, starting at $945, with the result that Auburn sold over 34,000 cars in 1931, nearly three times the 1930 total. It was an extraordinary figure, not only because it

represented a step-change in Auburn production, but also because it was in the aftermath of the Wall Street crash. To actually increase sales of an upmarket car as the Depression began to bite was a very real achievement.

But Auburn couldn't escape the Depression, and its effects were felt the year after as sales sank to a little over 11,000. Never again would they reach the heights of 1931. Not that the company didn't fight back. It slashed its prices to a base price of $725 in 1932, and added a sub-$700 six two years later. There was also a big twelve-cylinder, though even this was modestly priced, listed at $1,175 or $1,275 in 1932 in its two body styles, the top-priced straight-eight costing more.

All of this was to no avail. Sales dropped to just over 5,000 in 1932, and though they did rally to 7,770 when the new six was launched, they were back to 6,316 in 1935, and this despite the launch of supercharged versions of both six- and eight-cylinder cars, plus a two-seat boat-tailed speedster. When in 1936 only 1,263 Auburns were sold, it was clear the end was nigh. There were plans for a 1937 range, which never came to fruition, and that was the end of Auburn. Cord abandoned the car industry altogether, selling his companies for over $2.6 million and going on to make more money in uranium, real estate and all-music radio.

AVANTI (1965–91)
Some cars just aren't prepared to lie down and die, at least not until well after their

allotted span, the Avanti being one such an example. Originally built by Studebaker from 1960, the Avanti had striking Italian-type styling by Raymond Loewy, based on a shortened Studebaker Lark chassis, with the company's own 289-ci (4736-cc) V8 providing the power. It looked good, handled well and promised to be an all-American coupé with a degree of European sophistication into the bargain. Individual and distinctive though it was, the Avanti was not destined to be Studebaker's saviour, which was now a small and struggling concern.

When Studebaker decided to close its South Bend, Indiana, plant, in order to concentrate production in Canada, it seemed like the end for Avanti, except that two ex-Studebaker dealers – Leo Newman and Nathan Altman – couldn't bear to see the car die. Instead of wringing their hands, they tried to interest other manufacturers in making it, and when that didn't work bought all the tooling, plus a small section of the South Bend factory, and resumed production themselves.

The reborn Avanti II could not use a Studebaker engine, so now came with a 300-hp Chevrolet Corvette V8 of 327ci (5358cc), while the fibreglass body was supplied by Molded Fiber-Glass of Ashtabula, Ohio. Otherwise, it was little different from the original, though it is clear that Newman and Altman were not aiming at mass-production, for the car could be personalized with a choice of 700 interior colours and styles. Only 45 Avanti IIs were delivered in 1965, which was its first year.

The project was a success, in a limited way, and around 100–125 cars a year were built through the late 1960s and '70s, while in 1984, 287 were made. The Corvette V8 was used throughout, though it was soon upsized to 350ci (5735cc) and 400ci (6555cc). It hardly mattered that the styling stayed the same, as the Avanti was on its way to becoming a modern classic. The company changed hands several times in the 1980s, when there were variations such as a long-wheel-based coupé and a four-door sedan. Production finally ended in 1991.

BOCAR (1958–62)

The Bocar was a serious sports racer designed and built by Bob Games, from whom the name derives. It used a shapely fibreglass body, which owed something to contemporary Jaguars and Lotuses, based around a tubular steel spaceframe, with VW or Porsche front suspension and Chevrolet brakes and rear axle.

Carnes originally built the Bocar for hill climbs and road racing, so it was powerful as well as light, the first power unit being the 283-ci (4637-cc) Corvette V8, with the option of a 370-ci (6063-cc) Pontiac V8; either could be had in the 1958 Bocar XP-4. The Corvette's power was boosted to 315hp for the XP-5 in 1959, with a claimed top speed of 120mph (193km/h).

Bocars could be bought either in kit form or complete, and though designed for competition could theoretically be used on the street as well. Only the brave would have used the 400-bhp supercharged XP-6 on the road, likewise the similarly powered Stiletto, which was to be the last Bocar model before the factory burned down in 1962.

BRADLEY (1971–)

Of the many car kits based on the ubiquitous VW Beetle, the Bradley GT was one of the most successful; in fact, the company claimed that over 5,000 were sold. One of the reasons for the Bradley's popularity was its simplicity and relatively low price. It had no doors, for example, access to the interior being through the fold-up plexiglas windows.

Reflecting the simple-is-best philosophy, the more complex Bradley GT-II, with its gullwing doors and higher price, was not quite as successful, though there was an electric version, the GTE.

Aware of the danger of keeping all its eggs in the GT basket, Bradley bought kits from other manufacturers to broaden its range, such as the MGT MG and Veebird Thunderbird replicas, all of which were still Beetle-based. But the original GT proved more enduring than any of them. When Bradley itself closed in 1981, Sun Ray Products bought the design and resumed production in 1993.

BREWSTER (1916–25)

Brewster was most famous for its carriage-built bodywork, used by Rolls-Royce among others, but the company also made its own car. Available, naturally enough, in a variety of body styles, the Brewster was aimed at wealthy people who had no wish to flaunt the fact. It was smaller than the big Duesenbergs and Cadillacs, and powered by a quiet sleeve-valved four-cylinder engine that Brewster built itself.

As befitted the marque and its customers, most aspects of the car could be altered as required, even the left- or right-hand position of the steering wheel.

Production ended in a takeover of Brewster by the U.S. branch of Rolls-Royce in 1925, though the name was later used on a number of rebodied Fords, Buicks and others.

BRIGGS & STRATTON (1918–24)

Cars don't come much simpler than this, provided that this basic buckboard can be regarded as a car at all. There was no suspension (the flexible slats were deemed to cushion the bumps adequately) and power came from a 2.5-hp single-cylinder engine, mounted on a fifth wheel which hinged down onto the road. Engine-maker Briggs & Stratton did not actually design this buckboard, but bought the rights to it from A.O. Smith & Co.

The price was only $200, ready to roll, and it must have been fun to drive despite its modest performance. The company produced several hundreds of them before selling the rights to the Automotive Electric Service Co. in 1924, which continued to build both petrol and electric versions.

In the 1950s, the Banner Boy was sold as a Briggs & Stratton-powered replica of the original.

BRUBAKER (1972)

Unlike other VW Beetle-based cars, the Brubaker Box made no attempt to emulate a sports car, either classic or futuristic. It was a mini-van – rather more spacious and practical than a two-seater built from a kit.

However, its maker, Curtis Brubaker, was soon in trouble when VW refused to sell only the chassis, forcing him to buy complete Beetle cars and sell the bodyshells to accident repair centres. Only three fully-assembled Boxes were built before the project collapsed, though it was resumed by Automecca of California,

which is thought to have made 1,500 as the Roamer Sport Van throughout the 1970s.

BUFFALO (1901–15)

There is nothing new about electric vehicles, and for a few years battery power was a strong contender to the early gasoline engine, at least for use in town. The Buffalo Electric Carriage Co. of Buffalo, New York, built a whole series of battery-powered cars, everything from golf buggies to a full four-seater tourer, though lighter-weight runabouts were more typical. Taken over by F.A. Babcock in 1906, the Buffalo name re-emerged in 1912 and a range of electric roadsters, broughams and coupés was offered until 1915, when the company closed.

BUICK (1903–)

The Buick was America's archetypal upper-middle-class car. Safe, conservative and well-made, it was the one to which people outgrowing their Chevrolet or Ford could aspire, perhaps on promotion to a lower rung of management. Buick advertising emphasized the dependability and solidity of the cars: 'So nice to come home to' (1943) and 'Buick ownership is the knowledge that you have entered the House of Quality'. If a Chevy was too commonplace and a Cadillac too expensive, then a Buick was the obvious choice.

David Dunbar Buick was born in Arbroath, Scotland, but emigrated to the U.S.A. with his parents in 1856, aged two.

He became a talented engineer, even inventing an enamelling process that was used in baths. Two attempts at engine manufacture ended in failure, however, and it was only after outside finance had been obtained, first from the Briscoe brothers and subsequently from James H. Whiting, that the Buick Motor Co. was able to develop its overhead-valve stationary engines.

Early in 1904, Whiting agreed that Buick and his fellow engineers should build a complete car, and by July that year it was up and running. The first Buick was a four-seater tourer with a horizontally-opposed twin-cylinder engine of 160ci

BELOW LEFT
William C. Durant.

BELOW
Buick Model C.

RIGHT
Buick barrel-chested racing cars of 1910.

BELOW RIGHT
Buick Model 10 racer

BELOW FAR RIGHT
The first Buick, built at Flint, Michigan.

OPPOSITE
LEFT
A Buick in Egypt. The car was taking part in a 1925 round-the-world race.

OPPOSITE
RIGHT
Independent front suspension and styling by Harley Earl helped Buick 90s to fly out of the showrooms. This is a model from 1936.

(2622cc) and 16hp. By the end of the year, 37 had been sold and engine power had been tweaked to 22hp.

By now, however, the unfortunate Whiting, manager of one of the largest wagon manufacturers in Flint, Michigan, had nearly exhausted his capital, and it looked as though the Buick venture would follow its predecessors into oblivion. Fortunately, William C. Durant, later of

General Motors fame, was sufficiently impressed by the car to buy a controlling interest in the company and production of the Buick Model C could begin in earnest.

In 1905, 750 Model Cs were built, and nearly twice that amount the year after. Production cleared 4,600 in 1907, a momentous year in which Buick production came second to Ford, and when a new four-cylinder car was launched. This 256-ci (4195-cc) side-valve unit came with a three-speed gearbox in roadster or tourer bodies. By now, however, David Buick was on shakier ground. More concerned with engineering finesse than production, he began to question Durant's methods. He left the company in 1908, with a golden handshake of $100,000, and had no more to do with the concern that bore his name.

Meanwhile, Durant was engaged in the serious business of making cars, and a new Model 10 in 1908 underlined Buick's success. It was no great technical advance, but it was reliable, good-looking, well-made (three Buick keynotes) and sold well.

Power came from a new ohv 166-ci (2720-cc) four of square bore and stroke dimensions, with a two-speed epicyclical transmission. The range was expanded for 1909, when over 14,000 Buicks left the factory, the Model 10 being the best-seller.

That same year, assembly of Bedford-Buicks began in London, with U.S.-

OPPOSITE, ABOVE LEFT and ABOVE
The 1937 Special Tour. Buick recovered rapidly from the Depression, going on to break new production records.

LEFT
The Buick Century of 1936, the year the company built its three-millionth car.

Roadmaster is a name usually associated with post-war Buicks, but it also appeared on this 1939 example.

made running gear and locally-built bodies, a similar arrangement having already been made with McLaughlin of Ontario, Canada.

A Small Diversion

Until then, all Buicks had been aimed at the middle classes, but in 1910 the company decided to challenge Ford with

the Model 14, equipped with a 128-ci (2097-cc) twin-cylinder engine. The Buggyabout was around half the price of Buick's standard Model F twin, but failed to attract buyers and only 3,300 were sold. Buick dropped the car after a little over a year and decided to concentrate on the market it knew best.

Meanwhile, the range of four-cylinder cars was still selling well, bolstered in 1914 by a 333-ci (5457-cc) straight-six. It proved to be another success, so Buick followed the roadster six with a tourer, and in 1916 with a 225-ci (3687-cc) version, also available in a sedan. The company was now

experimenting with alternative power units, such as a V6 in 1912 and even a V12 in 1915, but its message from the marketplace was that it was the tried and tested designs that sold best. In fact, over 120,000 of these solid fours and sixes found homes in the year that Buick engineers were contemplating their exotic V12.

Not that the company was wedded to four cylinders. The old four was dropped in 1918, and its replacement, the Model 22

launched in 1921, only lasted three years. (Buick refused to put its badge on another four until the front-wheel-drive X-cars came along in the 1980s.) In its place came a new 192-ci (3146-cc) Standard Six alongside the existing 256-ci (4195-cc) Master Six.

Otherwise, the 1920s was a quiet decade for Buick, when useful advances were made, such as front-wheel brakes and a wider choice of colours, but with no

Ten years later and the 1949 Roadmaster looked quite different, even though it was mechanically similar.

Skylark was another long-running Buick name. This is a convertible from 1953.

major steps forward. There was another attempt to offer a cheaper car, the Marquette, in 1930, though it was no more successful than before.

There were big changes the following year, however, when the entire range of sixes was replaced by straight-eights – the Series 50 (222ci/3638cc), 60 (274ci/4490cc), 80 and 90 (both 347ci/5686cc). A synchromesh gearbox was part of the deal, but no sooner had Buick renewed its range

than the Depression struck and sales slumped to a little over 40,000 in 1933.

Fortunately, over a decade of profits enabled Buick to survive, helped by the management skills of Harlow H. Curtis, ex-AC Spark Plug Co., and the 1930s saw a steady stream of improvements. After that sales low, a peppy 80-mph (129-km/h) Series 40 was launched and all the cars received independent front suspension. The entire range was restyled by Harley

Earl in 1936, with coil-sprung suspension arriving two years later, along with Dynaflow transmission. The latter brought more power from higher compression pistons, now up to 141bhp on the biggest eight, and 1939 saw the fashionable steering-column gearchange made standard.

If there had been any doubts that Buick would survive the Depression, they were unfounded. The company had made its three-millionth car back in 1936, and by the early '40s was breaking sales records once again, with over 300,000 cars delivered in both 1940 and '41. Civilian production ceased in February 1942, due to the war effort, and the majority of cars was virtually unchanged when it was resumed less than four years later. This applied throughout the U.S. motor industry, but Buick was better placed than most. Its 1942 models had been up-to-the-minute, so the 1946 Special, Super and Roadmaster, still powered by straight-eight engines, did not look like pre-war cars with an extra dash of chrome.

After four years of negligible production, the American market was starved for new cars, so there were few major changes in the mid-1940s, but for 1948 Buick announced the option of Dynaflow automatic transmission on the Roadmaster. So popular was the two-pedal system that the option quickly spread across the range, and by 1950 only 15 per cent of buyers were opting for manual transmission.

image for 1950 with a garish buck-toothed front end, with incisor-like vertical fender guards covering the grille. It was a chrome grin too far, and the buck-toothed Buick was toned down for 1951.

But more substantial developments were in the pipeline, and 1953 saw the first ever V8 Buick, powered by an all-new 324-ci (5309-cc) V8, offering 164bhp in the

The New Look

If there is one model associated above all with Buick, it's the Riviera. It first appeared in 1949, a sleek two-door coupé with no B-post. This pillarless look was an immediate hit, and Buick followed it with a pillarless four-door sedan and, later still, a station wagon. Initially available only with the top Roadmaster engine, the Riviera was soon offered as a 263-ci (4310-cc) Super as well. So popular was the new style that other manufacturers followed

suit, and it would feature for over 20 years until fashion and predicted safety legislation killed it off. The Riviera name also endured for many years, and it was thanks in part to the Riviera and the profile of its faux convertible that Buick was able to sell just short of 400,000 cars in 1949.

Good though the Riviera was, it was no faster than the more staid Buicks, which were now seen as solid, reliable – even a little dull. Buick tried jazzing up its

Super and 188bhp in the range-topping Roadmaster, either as sedan, convertible, station wagon or Riviera coupé. As with every other new-generation overhead-valve V8, it set a new standard of performance and marked the beginning of Detroit's ongoing love affair with the layout. For 1953, only the base-model Special persevered with the ageing straight-eight, but by the following year that too had the V8.

The V8 may have been a big step forward, but the Skylark convertible was something of a flop. It was a special edition of the standard Roadmaster open-top, with a lower screen, wire wheels and other cosmetic touches. At a time when Buick was selling nearly half a million cars a year, the provision of a Skylark owner's signature on the steering-wheel must have

OPPOSITE
This line-up of late-1950s Buicks demonstrates the trend towards the lower, wider look.

LEFT and BELOW LEFT
Fins were at their most popular in 1958 and four-door Buicks were beginning to look like coupés.

seemed a nice personal touch. Unfortunately, few buyers were prepared to pay an extra $1,000-odd for the privilege, and the first Skylark was dropped after two years. However, the name would return.

After the excitement of the V8 had worn off, Buick seemed to lose its way, depending too much on fins, chrome and generally over-fussy styling, with the result that buyers stayed away in droves. Between 1956 and '59, Buick sales more than halved, while the company slid from its regular fourth to nineth place in the U.S. sales league.

From there, things could only get better, and they did. The early 1960s marked Detroit's first wave of compact cars with the advent of the Ford Falcon,

Chrysler Valiant and Chevy Corvair. Buick's contribution was the Special, with a 112-in (2.8-m) wheelbase and a new small aluminium V8 of 216ci (3540cc). Its 155hp gave the compact Buick sprightly performance and the sedan and station wagon were soon joined by a Skylark coupé and convertible. A 199-ci (3261-cc) V6 was soon added, though Buick later sold the aluminium V8 to Rover, which used it to great effect, while the Americans reverted to cast iron. As for the Special/Skylark, that would grow into an intermediate through the 1960s, leaving its origins as a compact far behind. Nevertheless, it still heralded a new generation of cleaner, sharper-looking Buicks.

The same was true of the new Riviera for 1963, a sporting four-seater coupé aimed fair and square at the Ford

OPPOSITE and LEFT
The styling appears confident, but Buick sales were heading for the floor when this 1958 Riviera left the production line.

BELOW
The 1958 Roadmaster, latest in a long line of roomy, comfortable Buick sedans for the middle-class buyer.

Thunderbird. This latest model was a step up from the new pony cars, pioneered by the Mustang, and had no great pretentions to performance: the standard power unit was the same 325-bhp 403-ci (6604-cc)V8 used in the Electra and Le Sabre sedans, though one could pay extra for 427ci (6997cc) and another 15bhp. It was the Riviera's styling that was its distinguishing feature. Ned Nickles of General Motors' Special Production Studio headed the team responsible, having been told by Bill Mitchell that the new car must resemble something between a Rolls-Royce and a Ferrari. Consequently, a design classic was born: the full-sized Riviera would run until 1976, then survive by downsizing and be revived in the early 1990s.

OPPOSITE and BELOW
By 1958, Buick was offering a range of powerful overhead-valve V8s, as in this Roadmaster, but so was just about everyone else.

PAGES 38 and 39
Just six short years on, and the American car had been transformed into something far simpler. This is a 1964 Le Sabre.

Was this a 'gentleman's muscle car'? Buick certainly thought so, aiming the luxury Gran Sport a little above the Mustangs and GTOs.

Meanwhile, Buick was playing a modest part in the muscle-car decade with the Gran Sport, or GS, a package of sporty extras optional on the Skylark and Riviera. So popular was this that the GS became a model in its own right, earning the description 'gentleman's muscle car'. But in the early 1970s, the GS threw aside its restrained appearance and became the garish GSX option, complete with big spoilers and bright colours, and with the biggest 455-ci (7456-cc) V8 under the hood really was a serious performance car.

Farewell to Muscle

But by 1972/3, what with soaring insurance rates, the first oil crisis and increasing gas prices, the days of gas-guzzling V8s were numbered, though they were to return. Buick's response was the Apollo in 1973, which, with an 111-in

(2.8-m) wheelbase, stole the position occupied by the Special a decade earlier. Being a General Motors compact, it used many of its components, including a Chevrolet Nova bodyshell and a 251-ci (4113-cc) Chevrolet straight-six as base engine alongside Buick's own 352-ci (5768-cc) V8. The subcompact Skyhawk hatchback, which joined it a couple of years later, would have been similarly familiar, being a Chevrolet Monza with rejigged trim, badging and equipment, plus the addition of a new 232-ci (3802-cc) V6. The Skylark badge also returned on the only V6-engined compact, while the Skyhawk had the option of a five-speed manual gearbox.

The public seemed to approve the new generation of compact Buicks and sales soared by over 50 per cent in 1975, when a Buick was chosen to pace the Indianapolis 500. The car in question was a turbocharged Century, and the inevitable pace-car replica followed in its wake.

Meanwhile, the reality of more expensive oil was forcing Buick, along with the rest of Detroit, to downsize its bigger cars. For 1977, the Le Sabre, Electra and Riviera all shrank, with smaller V8s to suit, the biggest engine now measuring

OPPOSITE and LEFT
By 1970, the Gran Sport could be had in far
flashier GSX guise. This has been modified
for drag racing.

403ci (6604cc) and Chevy 330 V8s joined the range. They sold well, enabling Buick to achieve record-breaking sales in 1977. The following year, the mid-sized Regal and Century were given the same treatment with a smaller 196-ci (3212-cc) version of the V6, though a turbo V6 was also an option on the Regal and Le Sabre sport coupés.

Some thought the 1979 Riviera had returned to its 1960s roots. Although it now had front-wheel-drive it was also more compact and sporty than the long, heavy boat-tailed Riviera of the 1970s. It was less of a Buick than before, sharing its chassis with the Oldsmobile Toronado and Cadillac Eldorado, but it did have all-round independent suspension, and four-wheel disc brakes were an option, with a 232-ci turbo V6 or 352-ci (5768-cc) V8 the choice of power. With the turbo, it

became the Riviera S Type, with suitably sporty extras.

In fact, Buick underwent a front-wheel-drive revolution during the 1980s. First to follow the Riviera was the Skylark in 1980, then the subcompact Skyhawk

and intermediate Century in 1982; even the full-sized Electra followed the front-wheel-drive route in 1984, as did the Regal coupé in '87. Only the big station wagons retained the 'conventional' layout, though even these had been given a lockup

converter clutch to improve fuel economy.

The Skylark was now Buick's version of General Motors' compact X-car, a range of hatchbacks and sedans designed to take on both imports and Detroit's fellow compacts. The Chevrolet Citation,

OPPOSITE
The 1971 Riviera, still filling the role as Buick's coupé.

ABOVE
The 1971 GS with 455-ci V8.

BELOW
*The Riviera was still a full-sized Buick of
the old school.*

OPPOSITE
*By 1973, even the Gran Sport had been
downsized, though Buick tried to preserve
the coupé look.*

Pontiac Phoenix, Olds Omega and Cadillac
Cimarron were all X-cars under the skin.
Similarly, the Skyhawk was now just
another variation of General Motors'
worldwide J-car, powered by a four or V6,
the 113-ci (1852-cc) available with
turbocharging from 1984. Turbo fours were
to become a feature of Detroit in the 1980s,

in which V6 (or ever V8) performance with
four-cylinder economy could be achieved. It
was a sign of the times that, for the first
time in 30 years, Buick was offering no V8
of its own, though customers could opt for
the diesel V8 built by Oldsmobile. Born in
the aftermath of the oil crisis, this was
undeniably economical, but doubts as to its

reliability proved something of a deterrent.
Thereafter, drivers seeking a modest
improvement in economy were likely to opt
for the more familiar gasoline V6, now in
252-ci form as well as the 231-ci original.

Meanwhile, the bigger Buicks were
restyled in such a way as to reflect the
growing preoccupation with aerodynamics,

RIGHT
1976 Gran Torino.

the Century, Regal, Le Sabre and Electra all following this route. The Regal was Buick's best-seller in the early 1980s, its image enhanced by the all-black Regal Grand National coupé, which became a collector's item. Buick sold its last diesel in 1985, while the Skylark X-car, which had sold quite well, was replaced by the new Somerset Regal.

Buick hadn't quite finished with special editions, and in 1988 the Reatta joined the line, being a two-seater coupé based on a shortened Riviera platform. The Reatta was not intended to compete with Pontiac's Fiero, but was a low-production car, built at the Reatta Craft Center in Lansing, Michigan. There were plans to build 25,000 a year, but buyers balked at the list price of $25,000, which

made it the most expensive Buick yet, and only a little over 20,000 were sold in a three-and-a-half-year run, despite the addition of a convertible in 1990.

Of more relevance to more buyers that same year was a new Park Avenue sedan with the 231-ci V6, later in supercharged form. The traditional rear-drive V8 Roadmaster made a return the following year, in sedan and station wagon forms. Big, roomy and good value (it was cheaper than the Park Avenue), the 1990s Roadmaster seemed like a return to the days of gas-guzzling dinosaurs. But the revival lasted only a few years and the reborn Roadmaster was dropped in 1996.

In 1994 the Riviera was relaunched with all-round independent suspension and the same supercharged 231-ci V6 as the

Park Avenue, which by 1998 was producing 243bhp. Styled by Bill Porter, the Riviera remained a stylish, distinctive coupé and production ended in 1999. By then, Buick's line-up was very different from that of 20 years before, being all V6 and all front-wheel-drive. But as for the names – Century, Regal, Le Sabre, Riviera – well, some things never change.

Recent years

Overall sales of the Buick brand peaked in the 1984 model year with the popular styling of the Buick Regal and Oldsmobile Cutlass Supreme, in combination with the popularity of newer, smaller offerings and performance-oriented turbocharged models. Buick Regal Grand National was Buick's muscle car, the fastest production

OPPOSITE
1976 Gran Torino.

ABOVE LEFT
1996 Regal Limited Edition sedan.

ABOVE RIGHT
A Century Special Wagon from the same year, though it looks more dated.

RIGHT

The Le Sabre Celebration, another 21st-century interpretation of the traditional American sedan.

BELOW

Maserati? Acura? No, this is a 2005 Buick LaCrosse sedan.

car at one time. Equipped with a 3.8L V-6 engine with a turbo charger, the FBI had a GN with twin turbo chargers.

The number of Buick models in the line-up fell over time, with the compact and performance segments being abandoned altogether. By the 2000s, Buick had become a traditional luxury brand in the GM group, emphasizing comfort and safety, whereas Cadillac has focused more on cutting-edge products that are performance-oriented and of avante-garde style.

Buick introduced its first SUV in 2001, the Buick Rendezvous crossover, which provided the much-needed success

for the marque and single-handedly brought a large number of younger, wealthier 'conquest' buyers into Buick showrooms who otherwise would not have considered purchasing a Buick. The Buick LaCrosse and Rendezvous are slotted against the Lexus ES and Lexus RX, respectively, while the Cadillac CTS is intended to compete against luxury performance imports from German and Japanese manufacturers.

Certainly a major contributor to the Rendezvous's success was an aggressive value-pricing strategy that made the Rendezvous $6,500 cheaper than a comparably equipped Acura MDX and $8,000 less than the Lexus RX300. The Rendezvous handily exceeded GM's predictions of 30,000 to 40,000 units a year by a large margin, which helped offset the poor sales of the Pontiac

The 2008 Buick Enclave crossover has been a much needed sales success for Buick.

Aztek with which it shared its Ramos Arizpe, Mexico, assembly line. The truck-based Buick Rainier was added to the line-up in 2004.

Buick began consolidating its line-up in 2005, replacing the Century and Regal with the LaCrosse and the LeSabre and the Park Avenue with the Lucerne in 2006. Both of its SUVs, the unibody Rendezvous and truck-based Rainier, were discontinued in 2007 to make way for the new and highly successful 2008 Enclave.

In January 2009, Buick unveiled the new 2010 LaCrosse sedan, an all-new styling direction. After its first year in production, the car has drawn praise from enthusiasts and critics, auto journalists and satisfied owners, significantly lowering the age demographic and broadening Buick's customer base. Another bright spot for Buick, especially when the car was compared with the similarly placed Lexus ES, is that the LaCrosse emerged the winner on nearly all counts. Meanwhile,

sales of the luxury crossover Enclave have increased each year and the reintroduction of the Regal has reinforced Buick's emerging image as an upscale, capable and elegantly appointed automobile.

At its extended product review in August 2009, GM announced Buick's future line-up. LaCrosse and Lucerne models will continue in production to cater to Buick's traditional upper medium price/entry-level luxury markets. The Regal has returned to strong demand and its GS

ABOVE
The 2010 LaCrosse is the second generation of the model.

OPPOSITE
The 2012 Buick Regal GS.

version will be the first Buick in almost 20 years to be offered with a manual transmission and a turbocharger. Buick also offered a new compact sedan to be assembled in China, which with LaCrosse-based styling will be targeted against the Acura TSX and Volvo S60.

In worldwide sales, Buick showed a huge resurgence during the months following the release of the new LaCrosse, although Buick has hinted that the Lucerne will soon be discontinued. There are also two other concepts: the Buick Verano, a compact sedan, and the unnamed small crossover expected in 2013–14.

Currently, Buick's North American line-up consists of the Regal entry-level luxury/sports sedan, the LaCrosse mid-size luxury sedan, the Lucerne full-sized luxury sedan, and the Enclave full-sized luxury crossover.

CADILLAC (1903–)
Cadillac – the Rolls-Royce of America – or is it? Despite being the ultimate car, as far as countless Americans are concerned,

RIGHT
The first production Cadillac, a 1903 Model A runabout.

BELOW
The first-ever Cadillac, dating from 1902.

Cadillac's image was, and is, very different from that of Rolls-Royce. It personified glitz and glamour, especially after the Second World War, when it was more likely to be seen cruising the boulevards of Hollywood than transporting men in suits around Washington, D.C. Politicians may have preferred the gravitas of a Lincoln or Imperial, but nothing could beat a Caddy in announcing that one had arrived. In terms of European marques, however, the Cadillac was more Jaguar/BMW than Rolls or Mercedes-Benz.

Yet behind the glitz lies a tradition of technical innovation, the history of

Cadillac dividing into three parts. There were its beginnings in humble economy cars before the company went rapidly upmarket, via innovations such as electric lighting/starting, V8, V12 and V16 engines, with production remaining relatively low. After the Second World War, with an order book of 100,000 cars and stronger centralized control from General Motors management, the strategy changed again. Cadillac became the mass-production prestige car, with sales reaching unprecedented heights, while fins, chrome and equipment became more important than technical advance.

Cadillac's origins lay in a series of chance encounters, and it would probably never have existed had Henry Ford not quarrelled with one of his first groups of investors. Henry Leland was the key figure in all of this. Older than many of the U.S. motor pioneers, he was already a well-established engineer at the turn of the 19th century, and was approaching 60 when his engineering concern built its first automobile. Previously, there had been transmissions and single-cylinder engines, supplied to Ransom Olds for his famous Curved Dash. They were reliable and well-engineered, superior to their contemporaries, which didn't prevent Olds from rejecting Leland's latest engine on grounds of cost. It was while Leland was searching for an alternative market that the directors of the Henry Ford Company asked him in to value the company, Henry having left and his investors being about to shut up shop.

So, with one empty, tooled-up factory, one new engine and a group of investors, it was obvious to Leland what should be done: he suggested building a new car. The new company couldn't use the Ford name (Henry had been there before them), so they named it Cadillac, after Antoine de la Mothe Cadillac, the French colonial founder and governor of Detroit in the early 18th century.

The first Cadillac car, completed in October 1902, gave little indication of the exotic creations that would follow. Like the contemporary Ford and Olds, it was a small, simple machine. Leland's single-cylinder motor lay horizontally under the seat, driving through a two-speed epicyclical transmission and chain final drive. Displayed at the New York Automobile Show in January 1903, the Cadillac Model A attracted over 2,000 orders in a week: exact production figures for that first year are uncertain, though it is clear that the new company got off to a good start.

In 1905, the new Model D marked the first move upmarket. Unlike the simple single-cylinder A, this was a 303-ci (4965-cc) four and cost $2,800, nearly quadruple the price of the little single. However, the Model D made up only a tiny proportion of Cadillac's production that year (156 cars out of a total of 3,712) but it clearly showed where the company's direction lay. Later that year, Leland's engine production works was taken over and Leland himself became general manager.

Just as significant was the way in which the cars had been made. Henry

ABOVE
The Model 30, the first Cadillac to sell in large numbers.

LEFT
Henry Leland (seen here with a 1905 Osca) was the founder of Cadillac.

ABOVE
An elegant Model 57 coupé from 1918.

ABOVE RIGHT
The 1927 La Salle convertible. The first
models were lighter and smaller than other
Cadillacs but used many of the same parts.

Leland had long valued precision engineering, and a spell working at the Colt Revolver Works as a young man had taught him the importance of maintaining consistent production standards. He transferred this to car production in 1907, after importing the 'Jo Block' gauges from Sweden. Invented by Carl Edward Johanssen, these ensured that every component was identical. So instead of filing and fashioning individual parts until they fitted, they could simply be bolted on, which speeded production and made for more reliable cars, which was a considerable breakthrough as far as the motor industry was concerned.

This was graphically demonstrated by Leyland's British importer, Frederick S. Bennett, in 1908. Three single-cylinder Cadillacs were taken to the Brooklands track and completely dismantled. All the parts were mixed up, then reassembled into three cars, which started and ran without a hitch. This interchangeability of parts was something of a step-change in the early motor industry, taking it from craft-based high-volume to consistent-standard production.

Not that Cadillac had ambitions to tackle Ford. This was underlined in 1909 when the single-cylinder cars were dropped, finally leaving the company's

origins in economy cars far behind. The singles were replaced by the four-cylinder Thirty (the name deriving from its horsepower), cheaper than the existing four but a big advance on the single. The Thirty's engine measured 227ci (3720cc), enough to give a reasonable performance. There was a range of three body styles, yet prices started at $1,400. Affordable and well-engineered, the Thirty was a good-seller, and nearly 6,000 found buyers in the first year.

Enter Mr. Durant
This success didn't go unnoticed, and Cadillac was acquired by William C.

Durant for $5.6 million in 1909. Henry Leland remained at the helm, assisted by his son, Wilfred, though this was not to last. When war broke out in Europe in 1914, Leland was keen to produce aero engines to support the effort, but was overruled by Durant. A furious Leland and son resigned, setting up shop to make engines themselves. They succeeded, and the Lincoln company went on to build luxury cars after the war. Within a few years, however, they were facing bankruptcy and succumbed to a takeover by Ford. That didn't work out either, and both Henry and Wilfred Leland left within months, Henry going into active retirement.

Back at Cadillac, 1912 saw another major advance in the use of Delco electric starting/lighting. This neat, all-in-one system was designed around a dynamo

A La Salle, photographed with Charles Lindbergh's Spirit of St. Louis *in 1927.*

RIGHT
Just as Cadillac pioneered the V8, so it did the V16. This is a 1931 Sport Phaeton.

RIGHT
Just as Cadillac pioneered the V8, so it did the V16. This is a 1931 Sport Phaeton.

OPPOSITE
The V12 in this 1931 sedan was really a smaller version of the same thing, with four fewer cylinders and 8 inches lopped from the wheelbase.

that could double as a starter motor, charging the battery and supplying both lights and ignition. In a world of hand-cranking and kerosene lamps, it was a huge step forward, and allowed Cadillac to leapfrog the opposition. It was therefore no surprise that production also leapt ahead to over 12,000 in 1912 and over 17,000 the following year.

But Cadillac had another bold innovation up its sleeve: for 1915 it announced the first series production V8. The French company of De Dion Bouton had been offering a V8 for several years, but Cadillac's Model 51 was rather different, in that it utilized its famous standardization of parts to build an exotic power unit in large numbers. It was a 90° V8 of 316ci (5178cc), with a single camshaft operating side valves. Producing 70bhp at 2400rpm made it powerful enough to push the Model 51 along at up to 65mph (105km/h), speeds more appropriate to racing cars. The refined, electric-start Cadillac was offered in a range of nine body styles, starting at less than $2,000. Once again, the opposition was left floundering, though it wouldn't be long before rival V8s were on the market. Cadillac sold over 13,000 V8s that first year.

Large technical advances were few throughout the 1920s, perhaps because of the departure of Henry Leland, with items like detachable cylinder heads and front-wheel brakes merely following industrial trends. However, the V8 did get a power boost, the 77-bhp maintaining its position

RIGHT and FAR RIGHT
With a hood emblem like this, maybe
Cadillac was emulating Rolls-Royce
after all.

OPPOSITE
Simple elegance describes the dashboard of
this 1931 V12.

as one of the most powerful cars on the
market. Instead, the company
concentrated on taking the V8 upmarket
by offering specialist bodywork from
coach-builders such as Fleetwood, later
absorbed by General Motors, and Judkins.
When the new Series 341 Cadillacs were
announced, they came with either mass-
produced Fisher bodies, starting at $3,295,
or coach-built Fleetwoods ($4,095 to
$6,200), the reason for the Fleetwood's
higher price being the choice in a range of
37 styles against a mere seven Fisher
bodies. The 341 Cadillacs got their name
from an enlarged version of the 341-ci
(5588-cc) V8 and sold alongside the new

A Cadillac at the 1933 World's Fair.

range of La Salles (see La Salle), smaller cadillacs designed to fill a gap in General Motors' range.

This strategy of choice worked, despite higher prices, and Cadillac sales and production boomed throughout the 1920s. From fewer than 20,000 in 1920, they peaked at just over 56,000 in 1928 before the Depression took its toll. But Cadillac was still far from being a mass-producer, like Ford, or indeed any of its General Motors stablemates; by now, the company was well-established as the relatively low-production, prestige American marque, even though it was still a rung below the Duesenbergs and Cords.

But Cadillac's (and General Motors') ambition was to pose a direct challenge to the aristocracy of American motoring, and in January 1930 the car was launched to

do just that: the V16. To unveil such a car so soon after the Wall Street crash was unfortunate, but Cadillac didn't know it would happen when Owen M. Nacker began work on this impressive new power unit three years earlier. It was really two straight-eights bolted together at an angle of 45°, each with their own fuel and exhaust systems but sharing a common crankshaft. The total capacity was a massive 455ci (7456cc) and power a sky-high 165bhp, enough for a top speed of up to 90mph (145km/h).

All in all, the V16 Cadillac was an extraordinary car for its time, whether the basic Fleetwood roadster ($5,350) or a fully coach-built car by Murphy or Waterhouse was chosen. Thanks to hydraulic tappets, it was said to be so quiet that the only thing audible at idle was the

sparking of the contact-breakers. Ownership was an exclusive club, with special service standards where the dealer had to provide regular reports to the factory, which didn't prevent nearly 3,000 customers from ordering a V16 in its first year. But in 1931, partly as a result of the Depression, sales slumped to 364, trickling along until production ended in 1940.

The Multi-Cylinder Endures
The V16 was followed in late-1930 by a V12 based on the same principles and with 8in (20cm) lopped from the wheelbase. It was more successful, with prices starting at $3,795; over 5,700 were sold in the period 1930–31. As with its big brother, there was a range of body styles on offer, both mass-produced Fishers and semi-coach-built Fleetwoods, but they remained an affordable route to multi-cylinder motoring. The V16 was renewed in 1938 with a new engine, now of monoblock construction (that is, a true V16 rather than two straight-eights), side valves and a 135° angle between the cylinders. It was unusual in that it had square bore and stroke dimensions, and at 185bhp was slightly more powerful than the original V16, capacity being 433ci (7096cc). Cadillac's final V16, also the world's final V16, struggled on for three years with a little over 500 sold.

Meanwhile, Cadillac's bread-and-butter V8s weren't making the headlines as often as the 12s and 16s, but they were making profits. A new lightweight monoblock V8 appeared in 1936, available

Multi-cylinder V12s and V16s were grabbing the headlines, but Cadillac profits came from big-selling V8s, like this 1933 CV-8 saloon.

as 330ci (5408cc) or 348ci (5703cc) in the Series 50 and 60/70 respectively. These cars, in a choice of three mass-produced body styles, sedan, coupé and convertible, were a world away from the coach-built V16, but even the most expensive was only $1,725, doubling Cadillac sales to over 25,000 in 1936.

Throughout the 1930s Cadillac managed to keep its cars fresh with regular updates, with hydraulic brakes, no-draft ventilation, independent front suspension and all-steel bodies all coming on stream within a few years of one another.

The late 1930s was a time of styling advances, and Harley Earl's protégé, Bill Mitchell, made his mark with the 60 Special Cadillac in 1938. Based on the Series 60, it led the industry with a longer, lower look. It was 3in (8cm) lower than the standard 60, yet had a 32 per cent greater area of glass, plus an integral trunk and no running boards. It set the style for most American cars in the late 1930s and was Cadillac's best-selling model.

General Motors was quick to notice, and the following year the new 61 used many of the Special's styling features, sharing its bodyshell with Pontiac, Oldsmobile, La Salle and Buick, the first

time that General Motors rationalization had been imposed on Cadillac. By 1940, Cadillac's La Salle operation had been dropped, as had the V16, the V12 having died three years earlier, but there were no adverse effects on the core range of 60 Special, 61, 62, 63 and long-wheelbased 75, all of them V8-powered.

Cadillac ceased civilian production in 1942, along with most of Detroit, but would face a backlog of demand when it resumed four years later. It had been its best year yet with over 66,000 cars sold. The company order book actually stretched to over 100,000 cars, so it would clearly have to concentrate on production rather than innovation in the first post-war

standard 61 convertible with wraparound windshield, cutaway door-tops and a flush-fitting cover for the folded and stowed top. Cadillac added wire wheels and priced the first Eldorado at $7,750, to which 532 customers responded. However, the Eldorado lost some of its exclusiveness the following year, when all Cadillacs were given the wraparound shield; but the company slashed $2,000 from the price,

LEFT
A 1953 Cadillac Le Mans.

BELOW
President Eisenhower, using a Caddy as a platform in 1953.

years. In fact, the pattern was set for the next three decades. Not until 1948 were there any major changes, with lower, wider styling across the range. However, this was a mere prelude to the big news for 1949, which was an all-new overhead-valve short-stroke V8 that was smaller than its predecessor at 333ci (5457cc) yet slightly more powerful at 160bhp. Given that Cadillac was a pioneer of V8s back in 1915, it was fitting that it should come early to the new generation of post-war ohv power units. The motor would prove remarkably durable and adaptable and would be in production for nearly 20 years, at one point producing more than twice the power of the 1949 original.

Automatic transmission was rapidly gaining popularity, and by 1951 the 75 limousine was the only Cadillac that offered manual: the Hydra-Matic had proved so successful that between 1955 and 1980 there were no manual Cadillacs at all.

Eldorado!
A famous name was born in 1953 with the Eldorado convertible. Like the Chevrolet Corvette, it had featured as a showcar in Motorama, General Motors' corporate travelling show, and like the Corvette created such a stir that it went into production straightaway. The difference was that the Chevy sports car was a new design, whereas the Eldorado was a

early '60s, from the original 333 to 367ci (6014cc) and 265bhp in 1956 and ultimately to a 340-bhp 431-ci (7063-cc) unit. Sales climbed in parallel with engine size and fin height as Cadillac led the way through a chrome-encrusted decade and beyond. The company broke the six-figure barrier in 1950, at a little over 103,000 cars, with over 140,000 five years later and just short of 166,000 in 1964. In fact, apart from a blip in 1969, Cadillac sales could trace an upward curve right through the 1960s and early '70s, approaching one-third

OPPOSITE and THIS PAGE
A 1953 Eldorado.

selling more cars in the process and the Eldorado was here to stay.

General Motors may have thought it was Cadillac's duty to offer dream cars as flagships for the entire corporation, and the Eldorado Brougham of 1957 was certainly that. A pillarless hardtop was nothing new, but the Brougham came loaded with equipment and the innovation of air suspension. The latter was fed by a central compressor, with an air chamber, rubber diaphragm and piston at each

corner, constantly adjusting the ride to suit conditions on the road. In practice, however, the system leaked and proved impractical, and most of the owners who had paid over $13,000 for the privilege abandoned it. Only 700 air-suspended Broughams were made in two years.

But as in the 1930s, while the exotic Cadillacs were stealing the show, the common V8s were selling in ever-increasing numbers. The standard V8 grew in size and power during the 1950s and

of a million in 1973. Only the oil crisis called a halt to this post-war boom, and even then Cadillac emerged from the 1974 model year with increased market share. It is significant that the company took 47 years to make its first million cars, only another nine to make the second million and just six more to make the third.

The 1967 model year saw the first-ever front-wheel-drive Cadillac in the form of the Fleetwood Eldorado. Sharing its body and layout with the Olds Toronado and Buick Invicta, the latest Eldorado was radical by Cadillac standards. Front-wheel-drive packaging allowed it to seat

OPPOSITE and THIS PAGE
A 1953 G2-series coupé in all its chrome-plated glory, not to mention an effective overhead-valve V8.

six in comfort, in spite of it being smaller than any other Cadillac, and it also offered variable-ratio power steering and automatic level control. Cadillac's own 431-ci V8 provided the power, with Hydra-Matic transmission mounted alongside. It was a huge success, with nearly 90,000 built up to 1970, while a 1971 facelift added a convertible to the line-up, which lasted until 1976.

Meanwhile, the full-sized Calais and De Ville lines had been given Cadillac's biggest ever V8 of up to 475ci (7784cc) in 1968 and a massive 503ci (8243cc) in 1970,

the latter offering more cubic inches than any other car on the market. However, this was the high tide of size, weight and guzzling gas, for Cadillac was no more immune to the effects of the oil crisis than any other manufacturer. For 1977 the mighty 500-ci was squeezed down to 425ci (6964cc), while the full-sized cars each lost nearly half a ton in weight.

The Euro-Sized Cadillac
More serious downsizing arrived with the new Seville in 1975, which was the first attempt to build a slightly more compact

Cadillac since the pre-war La Salle. And compact it certainly was, being almost three feet shorter than the full-sized Sedan de Ville. It was still V8-powered, albeit by a relatively modest 350-ci (5735-cc) unit offering 180bhp. The Seville was well-equipped and hid its corporate platform well (shared with the Chevrolet Nova among other General Motors cousins), thanks to its own razor-edged bodywork.

Aimed directly at Mercedes, the Seville actually cost considerably more (over $12,400) than the traditional full-sized Cadillacs, which started at less than

OPPOSITE
The 1959 Eldorado convertible. Never again
would the world see fins like these.

LEFT and PAGE 76
Period sun visor, split windshield and simple
chrome grille identify this V8 coupé. Note
also the split rear window.

PAGE 77
A 1959 convertible in England, though few
Cadillacs were exported to Europe at the
time. Here was a car that reflected
American tastes.

$8,200. Neither would its ride and handling have worried Jaguar or Mercedes; however, as a modern, compact Cadillac, it was the right car at the right time for American buyers, and thousands of them were sold.

The Seville was renewed in 1980 with front-wheel-drive and a standard diesel engine (the 350-ci unit that would be relinquished after a few years). It also received an odd hump-backed trunk that was supposedly reminiscent of a 1950s

Rolls-Royce. The full-sized Cadillacs were also being downsized, notably with a smaller 368-ci (6030-cc) V8 and the option of a Buick V6, the latter being a shock to traditionalists. It was the first time a non-Cadillac engine had been used, if the first-ever Cadillac of 1903 is excluded, which also used a bought-in power unit. Even more radical was the V8-6-4 engine of 1981, which automatically cut four, six or all eight cylinders in and out, depending on power demand: four cylinders for

trundling downtown, six for the freeway, eight for passing. The idea was to cut emissions and improve economy, but the variable-capacity Vee proved troublesome in practice and was soon dropped in favour of a conventional 250-ci (4097-cc) V8.

After an oil crisis, perhaps of more relevance to a brave new world was the Cadillac Cimarron, launched the same year – or to be more accurate, the 'Cimarron by Cadillac', as it was officially known – though it wore not a single Cadillac badge.

OPPOSITE and THIS PAGE
In contrast to its flamboyant exterior, the engine bay and interior of this 1959 coupé was positively spartan. There was ample space, however, and the simple overhead-valve V8 was powerful if thirsty.

Front-wheel-drive came to the bigger Cadillacs in 1985, the new-generation De Ville and Fleetwood being 2ft (61cm) shorter than their predecessors, with transverse-mounted V6 or V8 engines. Surprisingly, the traditional rear-wheel-drive Fleetwood Brougham still sold well (sales actually increased by 30 per cent in 1986) but buyers appeared to like the newly downsized Cadillacs and sales held up well.

Nineteen-eighty-seven saw yet another departure from the Cadillac mainstream with the launch of the European-influenced Allante. Billed as a luxury sports car, the Allante was styled by Pininfarina and was aimed directly at the Mercedes SL convertible. It was, of course, front-driven, but performance fell well short of its sports-car aspirations, even after the V8 was boosted to 274ci (4490cc). Sales were also disappointing, due in part to the sky-high price tag of $54,000, for which one could buy two Eldorados.

ABOVE and RIGHT
It was now 1960, and even Cadillacs were given quieter, more conservative styling to greet the new decade.

The Cimarron was no more nor less than the front-wheel-drive J-car (Chevrolet Citation, Buick Skyhawk, etc.) with extra equipment, a 113-ci (1852-cc) four-cylinder engine and four-speed manual gearbox. From some angles, it made sense, offering Cadillac equipment and prestige in a smaller, more fuel-efficient car. But unlike the restyled X-car Seville, the Cimarron looked exactly like the cheaper J-cars, and for $12,000 something more was expected. Later on, the subcompact Cadillac did better with a 174-c (2851-cc) V6 and five-speed transmission, though it was dropped in 1988.

The 1961 coupé took this process further, though the world wouldn't see a downsized Cadillac for another 20 years.

CASE (1910–27)

Better known for its agricultural machinery, the JI Case Threshing Machine Company also built cars for a while, which happened more by accident than design when Case bought the Pierce-Racine company's factory. It decided to continue the production of the 40-hp Pierce-Racine, but with Case badges, though later added 25- and 30-hp models, all of them with four cylinders.

The Case motor cars were never mass-produced, and their most prolific year was 1915, when 2,630 left the factory. Many components were bought-in, though Case produced the four-cylinder engines itself until 1918, when it switched to six-cylinder units from Continental. The first was of around 239ci (3916cc) and gradually grew in size to around 325ci (5326cc).

One thing the company didn't have to worry about was distribution, as it already had a nationwide network of dealers capable of selling a car as easily as a tractor. In spite of this, however, sales had dwindled to just over 600 by 1926, forcing Case to cease production the following year.

CHADWICK (1904–16)

Lee Sherman Chadwick was the man behind the Chadwick car, though its origins lay in his work for the Searchmont company. He designed a twin-cylinder car for them and was working on a fourth when the firm went bankrupt in 1903. Undaunted, Chadwick bought a wagon-load of parts from the defunct company,

and assembled them into a complete vehicle – the first Chadwick car – and was installed in his own factory by 1904.

At $4,000 for the 7-seater tourer with 32-hp four-cylinder engine, Chadwicks were not cheap. A bigger 40/45-hp version was added in 1906, at $5,000, but the ultimate Chadwick was the Great Six. This was quite a machine, powered by a 711-ci (11650-cc) low-revving six that produced 75bhp, enough for 80mph (129km/h). Some Chadwicks were even supercharged; racing driver Willy Haupt developed the system, which was later offered on production cars at $375 extra.

But cracks began to appear in 1910 when Chadwick's main supplier refused to do business because of late payment. Lee Chadwick left the company a year later, and though the cars that bore his name continued for a few more years, production fell to a trickle before finally ceasing in 1916.

CHALMERS (1908–23)

Hugh Chalmers was vice-president of the National Cash Register Co. before taking over the Thomas-Detroit car in 1908. This was rapidly renamed the Chalmers-Detroit, becoming plain Chalmers in 1911.

There was nothing radical about the four-cylinder Chalmers, though it did feature a self-starter as early as 1911, and a six-cylinder car was added two years later. At $l,500–$3,000, the cars held the middle ground between Ford and more exotic makes, and sold in respectable numbers; 21,000 cars were delivered in the peak year

of 1916, though production did fall off thereafter, averaging 10,000 a year through to 1920.

It may have been this that persuaded Hugh Chalmers to lease part of his factory to his greatest rival, the Maxwell concern. The plan was to use Maxwell production expertise and Chalmers would market both marques. But in the financial climate of post-war America, this was not enough to ensure success and by 1922 both companies had been swallowed up by Chrysler. Production of Chalmers cars was stopped in 1923 in favour of the Chrysler six.

CHECKER (1923–82)

Checker, the ubiquitous American taxi, also offered a private car during its final 23 years of production, though it was no more than the basic vehicle with a few minor changes. As such, it was surely the dream car of anyone who hated Detroit's obsession with planned obsolescence, the Checker being a solid, straightforward, utilitarian device for transporting people from A to B, with no concessions to fad or fashion.

The Checker Cab Manufacturing Co. was founded in 1923 out of a series of earlier companies. First using Buda four-cylinder engines, then Continental sixes, the Checker soon became the standard taxi, though only a few were sold for private use as special orders or one-offs. It wasn't until 1959 that Checker made a concerted attempt to target private buyers, first with the Superba sedan with a 226-ci (3703-cc) Continental six, and from 1964

BELOW and RIGHT
Louis Chevrolet was the Swiss-born racing driver and engineer who gave his name to the company.

with the similar-looking but updated Marathon, which came with a Chevrolet six or V8. There was also a roomy station wagon, plus an eight-passenger Custom Limousine, the Marathon being also available right through to 1982 when Checker closed.

CHEVROLET (1912–)

Chevrolet was the one manufacturer that managed to out-Ford Ford in terms of value-for-money, mass appeal and sheer sales. Unlike Ford, Chevrolet was never a family dynasty, and there was no one strong personality keeping control over the decades. Louis Chevrolet, the engineer who lent his name to the enterprise, left after just a couple of years, and it was William C. Durant who set the company up in the first place, before losing control in 1920. The Du Pont family was a leading investor

in the 1920s, but they were not car people. Instead, high-ranking men from General Motors were instrumental in shaping Chevrolet's fortunes: William S. Knudsen, Alfred P. Sloan and Ed Cole, while Zora Arkus-Duntov helped to make the Corvette the world-class sports car that it eventually became.

Far from hindering the company, this wealth of talent allowed Chevrolet to thrive as General Motors' mass-market division. In 1917, Ford was outselling its products by more than ten to one, but by 1926 it was down to three to one, with Chevrolet taking the blue oval the following year. For most of the 1930s, more people bought Chevys than Fords. In

fact, right through the remainder of the 20th century, the two marques vied for the top-selling slot, with Chevrolet coming first more often than not, which it achieved by combining economies of scale with customer choice and keeping technically up to date. Yet by the standards of America's long-standing marques, Chevrolet was a late starter. By the time the first Chevrolet-badged car had rolled off the production line, Henry Ford had been in business for over a decade.

William Crapo Durant was the man responsible. He was a constant presence in the early days of the American motor industry, the salesman-entrepreneur with a hand in Buick, Cadillac, Oldsmobile and many other. He called this first group of companies the General Motors Co., but within two years had run out of money and was forced by the bankers to resign. Determined to fight back, he decided to establish a rival, setting up the Little Motor Car Co. to build a small car (though the company was actually named after the ex-Buick man, William H. Little). For a big car he turned to Louis Chevrolet.

Chevrolet was a Swiss-born racing driver who had emigrated to the U.S.A. in 1900, working as a chauffeur before racing Buicks. Louis had no formal training in engineering, and described himself as 'a rough-hewn and tough racing-car driver

and engineer'. His personality would soon bring him into conflict with Durant, who nevertheless recognized Chevrolet's engineering talent and asked him to help develop the new big car which would bear his name. Chevrolet, in turn, invited fellow countryman, Etienne Planche, an experienced designer, to participate.

The Chevrolet Classic Six was the result, not a cheap car at $2,150, but large and powerful and an equal to the contemporary Cadillac and Haynes. At its heart was a 301-ci (4932-cc) T-head six-cylinder engine, driving through a conventional three-speed gearbox mounted in a five-seater tourer body. Production did

not actually start until late in 1912, a year after the new Chevrolet Motor Car Co. had been incorporated, but once it did, the Classic Six sold reasonably well, with nearly 3,000 delivered in the first two months. It was updated with an electric starter the following year when around 6,000 cars were sold.

This was all very well but it wasn't fulfilling Durant's ambition of making a mass-selling car to rival his erstwhile colleagues at General Motors, not to mention Henry Ford. He renamed the Little Six the Chevrolet Light Six, but at

ABOVE
Russian-born Zora Arkus-Duntov was instrumental in the development of the Corvette.

LEFT
William C. Durant is not sitting in a Chevrolet but a 1910 Buick.

$1,475 it was not going to worry Mr. Ford. More significant was the new Series H of 1914, priced at $875 for the five-seat tourer Baby Grand or $750 as the oddly-named two-seater roadster, the Royal Mail. Both were powered by a bought-in Mason ohv four of 171ci (2802cc). Louis Chevrolet was aghast: he had never expected his name to appear on a cheap car, and left the company in disgust. In fact, the Series H was something of a last straw for the rough-hewn engineer; there had already been friction between himself and Durant when Durant strongly objected to the cigarettes Chevrolet smoked, Durant maintaining that an executive should only smoke cigars. Chevrolet left, going on to build his own Frontenac racers, and Planche also left to join Dort.

OPPOSITE and THIS PAGE
A 1950 Chevrolet sedan, with period bench seat and column gearchange, plus a straight-six in the engine bay. It would be another five years before Chevrolet fitted a V8.

RIGHT
A former racing driver, Zora Arkus-Duntov did much of his own test driving. Here he is behind the wheel of a Corvette racer.

OPPOSITE
The 1952 Chevrolet Starline. It was solid, good value and just a little dull.

It may have been too cheap for Louis Chevrolet, but the Series H wasn't cheap enough for the booming U.S. car market. Durant, however, had the situation in hand and for 1916 dropped the expensive six-cylinder Chevys, announcing the ultra-low-priced 490 in their place. The name came from the price ($490 brand new), which was reflected in the pared-to-the-bone specification with no electric lighting or starting, though it retained the H's Mason engine. Typically, Henry Ford responded within months by cutting the price of the Model T to only $440, though it didn't prevent Chevrolet from selling 18,000 490s in 1916 and over 57,000 the following year.

Union with General Motors
By this time Chevrolet was part of the General Motors empire. William Durant had been quietly buying shares in GM and assumed control in 1916, which technically Chevrolet had taken over. Whatever the case the upshot was the same, though within five years Durant would once again have run out of money and be forced to leave General Motors for good. As for the cars, the Series H was enlarged for 1916, with a longer wheelbase and bigger 225-ci (3687-cc) engine. More ambitious was the D-series launched the following year, powered by a 55-bhp 288-ci (4719-cc) V8. It was good value at less than $1,300, but Chevrolet was a latecomer to the V8 market, which Cadillac had pioneered three years earlier.

Once Durant had left, General Motors' new president, Pierre S. Du Pont,

98

BELOW and OPPOSITE
It looked glamorous, but this 1954
convertible had the same basic Stovebolt six
that had been used in countless Chevys over
the previous 20 years.

decided to drop Chevrolet completely, but was persuaded otherwise by vice-president Alfred P. Sloan. This turned out to be a good decision as far as General Motors was concerned, for Chevrolet eventually became its top-selling division.

But there must have been times when even Sloan questioned the wisdom of persevering with the division. Durant's financial problems had been well-publicized, which led to a hiccup in 490 sales in 1920–21, and the disappointing adventure with the V8 was followed by the technical failure of the copper-cooled engine.

Unveiled in 1923, this was really air-cooled, the cooling fins consisting of U-shaped copper plates mounted on the cylinders. Being air-cooled, the new 136-ci (2229-cc) unit would not freeze or boil its coolant, and at 22bhp was only slightly less powerful than the 490's 172-ci (2818-cc) water-cooled engine. In practice, power plunged when the copper-cooler overheated, which it did frequently, and Chevrolet rapidly revised its ambitious plan to build 50,000 such motors a month. In the event, only100 were sold and Chevrolet wisely abandoned the whole idea.

Meanwhile, Alfred Sloan had decided, probably correctly, that even Chevrolet could not compete with Ford on price, and in 1922 replaced the 490 with the Superior, which aimed to offer a little more comfort and convenience than the Model T. It was a good move, as Henry Ford was refusing to contemplate any major updates on his best-seller, insisting, above all else, on keeping its rock-bottom price. But as the 1920s progressed, customers were more willing to pay for extra features, and Chevrolet was there to meet the demand. This was reflected in sales as Chevy played a rapid catch-up game in the early 1920s: it was outsold by Ford six to one in 1924, which was cut to three to one just two years later, when Chevrolet sold over 580,000 cars. When Ford shut his line down in 1927, to swap from Model T to Model A production, Chevrolet was quick to take advantage, selling over 1.7 million and for the first time toppling Ford from its premier position.

The division had William S. Knudsen, a Danish-born production expert who had joined General Motors in 1922, to thank for much of this. An ex-Ford man, he had grown tired of Henry constantly undermining his authority, with the result that General Motors in general and Chevrolet in particular were the beneficiaries, and Knudsen remained with General Motors for the rest of his career.

So 1920s Chevrolets gained the features that Fords didn't yet have, such as a range of cellulose colours and more modern styling. The Superior became the

National in 1928, with a larger engine and front-wheel brakes. Annual renaming was a Chevrolet trademark at this time, the car becoming the International in 1929, then Universal, then Independence and Confederate in the following three years.

But more significant than this was the new engine that came with the International. It was Chevrolet's first six-cylinder motor since 1915, and appeared to be a simple, conventional ohv engine with nothing in particular to distinguish it. It was 'not a high-quality power unit', according to motoring historian Richard Langworth, 'Every part of it had been designed to be just good enough and no more.' The new engine even used cast-iron pistons when everyone else was turning to aluminium. Yet the 'Stovebolt Six', as it was nicknamed (from the slotted cylinder-head bolts), proved to be immensely enduring. It powered every Chevrolet car between 1929 and 1954 and would be developed from its original 46-bhp/195-ci (3195-cc) form into the 150-bhp Blue Flame that powered the Corvette.

From 1933, it powered the Master Six, now sold alongside a cheaper version named the Standard Six, with a 183-ci (2999-cc) engine. Now locked in a struggle with Ford, Chevrolets were updated each year to keep them looking fresh. The big six gained a synchromesh gearbox and free wheel and the Stovebolt was boosted to 60bhp. In 1934, independent front suspension gave it another advantage over Ford, likewise the stylish Fisher all-steel

body, and hydraulic brakes for 1935 and '36. All this paid off and, with a couple of exceptions, Chevrolet led Ford in production right through the 1930s, '40s and '50s.

There were fewer changes in the late 1930s, though the Stovebolt six was upsized to 218ci (3572cc) for 85bhp in 1937, with the internals uprated to cope. There were body advances, too, with a station wagon in 1939 and the disappearance of running boards in 1941. The following year, the last

before the Second World War, called a halt to civilian production and also saw a new fastback coupé and a convertible with a power-operated top.

A Slow Start

Chevrolet was in the same boat as every other U.S. car manufacturer after the Second World War. It was faced with a huge demand for cars and no time for extensive redesigns, so the 1942 cars were simply returned to production with only a

OPPOSITE and BELOW
Beneath this subtle custom job lay the new shape Chevy for 1955, in this case a Bel Air, with the small-block V8 that would transform the image of the marque.

few changes. The main line-up now included the Stylemaster and Fleetmaster, which replaced the pre-war Master Deluxe and Special Deluxe respectively, the latter with a higher standard of trim. The Fleetline Aerosedan was most popular, selling nearly 160,000 in 1947. It was a two- or four-door version of the short-lived fastback of 1942, and was surely the most attractive of the early post-war Chevys. All three basic models were powered by the same 217-ci (3556-cc) version of the Stovebolt six, now offering 90bhp at 3300rpm. This was not sufficient for exciting performance, however, and Chevrolet's V8-driven image shift of the 1950's was still several years away.

In fact, the Stovebolt was unchanged for 1949, when Chevy unveiled all-new styling across the range that left the late 1930s behind, still in notchback and Aerosedan fastback form. The 'woody' station wagon gained an all-steel body and the Bel Air hardtop was introduced as a new model in 1950, which, though based on the same running gear as every other Chevy, had automatic Powerglide transmission as a major new option at $159. The Stovebolt was coaxed up to 115bhp in 1953, due to a capacity boost to 236ci (3867cc), but the 24-year-old design was by now reaching the end of the road.

In the history of Chevrolet, the year 1953 is not remembered for the 115-bhp Stovebolt, but for something far more significant: the Corvette. America's only mass-produced sports car began life as a show car at General Motors' annual Motorama, but the public reaction was so overwhelming that it was rushed straight into production. It looked good, at first glance being a low-slung short-wheelbased roadster which promised to beat the European imports at their own game. The force behind the Corvette was General Motors' head of design, Harley Earl, who envisaged an image-building design to rival Jaguar.

Constraints of cost and time, however, dictated that mostly off-the-shelf Chevrolet parts (apart from the Corvette's glassfibre body) be used. The chassis consisted of the standard frame shortened by 13in (33cm),

The 1955 Bel Air four-door sedan, the most significant picture being that of the engine bay. The overhead-valve engine, concocted by Ed Cole's engineers, lifted the Chevrolet way out of the ordinary to something approaching a hot rod.

and featured the Stovebolt six, now producing 150bhp due, among other factors, to triple carburettors and higher compression. But it was never designed as a performance engine, and was hampered still further by the Powerglide automatic. The car could top 105mph (169km/h) and reach 0–60mph in 11.0 seconds, which was respectable but trailed behind an XK120.

On sale in mid-1953, the first Corvette was an odd machine. It didn't quite have true sports-car performance, yet the interior had been stripped bare in basic sports-car style, with flimsy plexiglas side windows rather than glass. Nor was it cheap at $3,550, making it twice the price of any other Chevrolet. The plan had been to sell the car in limited numbers to VIPs before full production was offered to an eager public. But in reality, very few of the thousands who had shown interest in the Corvette at the Motorama actually bought one. Over 3,600 were built in 1954, but many ended up in dealer lots, gathering dust, and only 700 cars were sold in 1955. Chevrolet's new flagship was turning into an embarrassing mistake.

Or it would have been, had Chevrolet not made a milestone announcement in 1955 that was even more significant than the Corvette itself – something that would transform the company's image and appeal to younger people as never before. It was a V8.

Chevrolet was late adopting the new generation of post-war V8s. By 1955, its

OPPOSITE and LEFT
Prior to the Nomad, most station wagons
had been slow-selling, wood-trimmed
specialities. But Chevy's new wagon for
1955 had a distinctly rakish look.

PAGE 108
The Nomad station wagon adapted well to
customizing.

PAGE 109
The 1956 Chevrolet Tri. The public loved its
original 265 V8, so Chevy responded with
bigger, powered-up versions.

General Motors cousins – Cadillac and Buick – already had one, while Ford had replaced its old flathead V8 with an overhead-valve unit the year before. But when it came, Chevy's first small-block made a huge impact. Originally designed as a mild-mannered 231-ci (3785-cc) unit, Ed Cole's team punched it out to 265ci (4342cc). The combination of short stroke, good breathing and lightweight valvegear meant the new V8 could happily reach 6,000rpm and had plenty of tuning potential into the bargain. It offered 162bhp or 180bhp in standard form with the option of 'Power Pack'. Predictably, it transformed the performance of the previously stodgy Chevy sedans, the '55 becoming something of a hot-rod classic as a result. Zora Arkus-Duntov demonstrated the fact by power-sliding a 1955 V8 up Pikes Peak, breaking the current record by two minutes. Within months of the small-block's arrival, Chevrolet had been transformed from a bank clerk's car, and a middle-aged one at that, to 'the Hot One'.

completed by manual transmission, new styling and a more luxurious interior with wind-up windows. From then on, the Corvette's progression to American sports-car legend was assured. While Ford's big-selling Thunderbird proceeded further along the route to becoming a luxury personal car, so the Corvette became more of a sports car each year. This was largely due to the hard work of Zora Arkus-Duntov, the General Motors development engineer who had been passionate about the Corvette from the start. Under his guidance, and with the option of the fuel-injected small-block, the Corvette became a 130-mph (209-km/h) sports car with sales exceeding 6,000 in 1957 and 10,000 in 1960.

By now, the Corvette's future seemed secure and the car was even making a

OPPOSITE and LEFT
Later Impalas became early muscle cars in 409 V8 SS form. This is a 1956 example.

BELOW
A plainer 1956 Sport Coupé.

There was now no stopping it. The V8's potential was exploited the following year with standard power up to 205 or 225bhp with a four-barrel carburetor, while the Stovebolt was still available if required, now with 140bhp. For 1957 the V8 was taken up to 283ci (4637cc) with Ramjet fuel injection taking power to 283bhp, thus reaching the magic one horsepower per cubic inch. Few customers actually paid the extra for Ramjet, but it helped to boost Chevrolet's image all the same.

Naturally, none of this passed the Corvette by. After the first two disastrous years, some within General Motors were arguing that the car should be dropped. But by fitting Ed Cole's V8 it had been transformed. The transformation had been

RIGHT
A 1957 Chevrolet 150. It was still possible
to buy a cut-price sedan with the Stovebolt
six, if one really wanted to.

OPPOSITE
There was a facelift for the 1958 Corvette,
the twin headlights, more chrome and garish
grille generating more sales.

profit. Arkus-Duntov's ambition had been to make a world-class sports car and he succeeded, by and large, in the 1963 Stingray, a striking coupé with all-round independent suspension and fine handling, though it still used as many standard General Motors components as possible.

With up to 360bhp available, the Stingray could top 145mph (233km/h) and over 21,000 were sold in its first year. Constant development kept it popular, with all-round disc brakes and a 396-ci (6489-cc) big-block V8 in 1965, and with a 427-ci (6997-cc) and 425bhp the following year.

This was the height of the muscle-car boom and the big-block Corvette was only a part of Chevrolet's response.

Meanwhile, the Chevrolet sedans had been given more chrome and bigger fins throughout the late 1950s, particularly the 1958-only body and the '59 that followed it,

OPPOSITE and LEFT
It is hard to believe that Chevrolet nearly axed the Corvette early in its life, but by 1959, when this car left the line, it was wildly popular and a permanent part of the line-up.

ABOVE
Chevrolet's rear-engined Corvair could have been the thinking driver's compact, but found its niche as an enthusiast's car.

OPPOSITE
Stingray! Was there ever such a striking American car in mainstream series production?

which was a standard General Motors shell. But 1960/61 saw more subtle styling throughout the industry, in fact the 1961 Chevys had practically no tailfins at all. On the other hand, the Biscayne, Bel Air and Impala were being offered with a whole range of V8s, from the standard 283-ci through to the new 348-ci (5703-cc), which came in four levels of tune, from 250bhp to 335bhp. Nor was that the end. They were joined by a Turbo Fire 409-ci (6702-cc) option in 1961, which the following year

came in high-compression 409-bhp form. A Bel Air coupé with a 409 under its hood was an early muscle car of its day, its engine held in such reverence that the Beach Boys even wrote a song about it.

Corvair & Chevy II
But alongside these ever more powerful V8s, the American public was flocking to buy the new generation of compact cars, the popularity of AMC's Rambler sparking conventional responses from Ford

(the Falcon) and Chrysler (the Valiant) and a highly unconventional one from Chevrolet (the Corvair). Launched in the fall of 1959, the Corvair turned almost every Detroit convention on its head: it was rear-engined and powered by an air-cooled flat-six; the body/chassis was of unit construction and there was all-round independent suspension. There was much to admire in the Corvair, and 250,000 were sold in the first year, with a total of 1.25 million in the first three years of production. But its tail-heavy handling was undeniably tricky, and led to safety campaigner Ralph Nader condemning it as 'unsafe at any speed'. As Nader acknowledged, the problem only affected early Corvairs, but by then the damage had been done. Sales slumped and though the sporty Monza coupé acquired a keen following of enthusiasts, as a mass-selling compact the Corvair was effectively dead. It was finally dropped in 1969.

But the Corvair episode didn't even cause Chevrolet to draw breath, because only three years after it unveiled the Chevy II as a thoroughly conventional front-engined answer to the Falcon. Available with a 154-ci (2524-cc) four-cylinder engine or a 195-ci (3195-cc) six, the Chevy II came as a sedan, station wagon or (as the upscale Nova) a convertible or hardtop. It was followed in 1964 by the intermediate Chevelle, with the same six-cylinder engine or the 283-ci (4637-cc) V8. Both Chevy II and Chevelle sold well, the latter making over 369,000 in 1967, and both later come with larger V8s to make them genuine

OPPOSITE
Chevrolet followed Corvair with the more conventional and better-selling Nova.

LEFT
The 1966 Malibu, an upmarket coupé descendent of the Nova.

BELOW LEFT and BELOW
Corvette convertibles from 1958 and 1968. They may have been ten years apart, but the basic mechanical package was little changed.

OPPOSITE
A late-1950s Bel Air in the pillarless coupé
style popular at the time.

LEFT
A Camaro Z28 of 1971, inspired by Trans
Am racing and built to take part.

muscle cars. The Chevelle chassis was later used as a base for the upmarket Monte Carlo coupé, available with Chevy's biggest-ever big-block, the 454-ci (7440-cc) unit, though at 390bhp it was slightly less powerful than the earlier 427-cc (6997-cc).

Chevrolet had nothing in direct response to Ford's Mustang until 1967, but when it arrived, the Camaro was another hit. In the same pony-car mould as the Mustang, it was a sporty four-seater with a wide range of options and engines from a mild six to a high-compression big-block V8. The Z28 was a famous model, derived from the Trans Am racing experience, and over 19,000 of these were sold in 1969 alone. The Camaro was restyled in 1970 and was in production right through to 1981 in this form, managing to survive oil crises and new safety and emissions legislation along the way.

The Corvette had received another makeover in 1968 as the curvaceous Stingray though the first examples suffered

had the same engine options, plus a 265-ci (4342-cc) diesel. Both were crosses of General Motors cars, but the Corsica sedan and Beretta coupé, unveiled in 1987, were both exclusive to Chevrolet. With Chevy's own four-cylinder and V6 engines,

they were effective competition for the Japanese imports, and were built through to 1997.

In fact, the lines between U.S.- and Japanese-built cars were becoming blurred, with some Japanese designs built

in the States and others sold with Detroit badging. Thus the three-cylinder Suzuki Swift was rebadged and sold as the Chevrolet Sprint from 1984; the Toyota Corolla became the New Chevy Nova and the Isuzu Gemini was otherwise known as

OPPOSITE
A 2010 Aveo RS.

ABOVE
The 2008 Volt concept electric.

ABOVE
The 2011 Cruze, Chevrolet's medium-sized family car.

OPPOSITE
The formidable ZR-1 returned for 2010 and is shown here with the new, next-generation C6-R racecars that were derived from it.

the Chevrolet Spectrum. From 1989, these various imports were sold by a Chevrolet sub-division, named Geo, but the arrangement lasted for only seven years before there was a reversion to Chevrolet badges.

While all this was happening, the classic rear-drive Chevrolets were still in production, albeit in downsized and aerodynamic forms. The Caprice sedan and Monte Carlo coupé endured through the 1990s, with the 307-ci (5031-cc) V8 squeezed to 265ci (4342cc). Keen drivers

could still opt for the hotter Impala SS, powered by the Corvette's 350-ci (5735-cc) V8, but this was really the last gasp. In 1996, the big rear-wheel-drive Chevys were finally dropped. This would have given Chevrolet a range that was all front-wheel-drive, were it not for the Corvette and Camaro, both of which had been regularly updated and renewed right through the 1980s and '90s. A high point was the 1990 Corvette ZR-1, with a Lotus-developed dohc 350-ci V8 of 385bhp, with new-generation Corvettes launched in 1993,

1997 and 2004. Fifty years after Chevrolet's first 'Hot One', it was still possible to buy a rear-drive V8 Chevrolet.

Chevrolet carried on successfully producing cars until 2007. Today, however, the Chevrolet division is currently recovering from the economic downturn of 2007–10 after sales of GM vehicles plummeted and the company were forced to create more fuel-efficient vehicles in order to compete with foreign auto manufacturers like Toyota, Honda and others.

General Motors showed the Volt MPV5 concept at Auto China in 2010, this being an MPV based on the electric Volt sedan, with a range of 32 miles (51km). In late 2010 General Motors began a small production of this plug-in electric car, and production numbers are set to reach 60,000 in 2012. Chevrolet is starting a second-generation Aveo which will be released in the summer of 2011. A sport version of the car, the Aveo RS, already features.

CHRYSLER (1924–)
Chrysler was the last of the Detroit Big Three to enter production. Henry Ford had been a pioneer, building his first production car in 1903 after years of experimentation, and General Motors' origins also lay pre-1910. But Walter Chrysler didn't begin building the cars that bore his name until 1924 – not that he was inexperienced in the field. He was then approaching 50 and had been involved with both General Motors and Willys-

BELOW RIGHT
Walter Chrysler was determined to take on Ford and General Motors.

FAR RIGHT
An imposing Chrysler from 1926.

BOTTOM RIGHT
Chrysler in 1924, with one of the first cars to bear his name.

BOTTOM FAR RIGHT
Early Chrysler car bodies being taken for final assembly.

OPPOSITE PAGE
A 1926 Chrysler two-seater in all its boat-tailed glory.

Overland, having been given a million-dollar salary to join the latter.

Walter Chrysler had a reputation in the car industry as an effective troubleshooter, and succeeded in cutting Willys' debt significantly. Even before the Willys contract had terminated, he was invited do the same for Maxwell-Chalmers. He was soon convinced that what Maxwell

needed was a new, up-to-date car, and brought in three young designers from Willys to come up with the goods.

When it was unveiled in 1924, the Chrysler 70 (not a Maxwell, note, but a Chrysler) proved to be just what the company needed. It offered sprightly performance (up to 75mph/12lkm/h) from its advanced 203-ci (3326-cc) side-valve six, which featured a relatively high compression ratio, full-pressure lubrication and aluminium pistons, not to mention 68bhp. The Chrysler 70 also had hydraulic four-wheel brakes and offered nine different body styles starting at $1,335.

The public was impressed by this new name, and 32,000 Chrysler 70s were sold in the first year. As if to underline its arrival, Maxwell-Chalmers became Chrysler, and its smaller four-cylinder car was renamed the Chrysler 58. Both cars were uprated for 1926: the four-cylinder Model F-58 was given a 187-ci (3064-cc) engine and the 70's six was punched out to 220ci (3605cc). There was also a new Series E-80, powered by a 290-ci (4752-cc) six and given the Imperial badge that would be used for upmarket Chryslers until 1954.

Chrysler's rapid rise was helped by the large network of Maxwell-Chalmers

dealers. There were around 4,000 of them, and they sold over 180,000 cars in 1927, making Chrysler the seventh best-selling marque in the U.S. that year. In fact, Chrysler would rapidly become one of the Big Three, alongside General Motors and Ford, though it was always in third place with no prospect of overtaking either of its rivals. As for the Chrysler marque itself, as opposed to the Dodge and Plymouth divisions, it rarely repeated that early success. It took nearly 20 years to exceed the sales total of 1927 and was usually placed outside the top ten U.S. marques. Chrysler's post-war performance saw alternating periods of good and poor sales which would see the company close to bankruptcy by the late 1970s.

But the 1920s were optimistic times. Only four years after its original launch,

OPPOSITE and LEFT
By 1931, when this car left the factory, Chrysler was offering a full range of cars, from value-for-money Plymouths to eight-cylinder Imperials.

BELOW LEFT
The radical Airflow was ahead of its time though sales were disappointing.

BELOW
Upmarket Chryslers, such as this, wore the Imperial badge.

Chrysler took over Dodge, giving it a place in the intermediate market, and launched Plymouth, competing with Chevrolet and Ford. Straight-eight engines of 242ci (3966cc), 262ci (4293cc), 284ci (4654cc) and 387ci (6342cc) were added to the range in 1931, the latter used by the new Series CG Imperial. The biggest eight offered 125bhp, enough to propel the large Imperial to 95mph (153km/h) as long as the buyer chose one of the lighter body options. And there was plenty of choice, with both factory and Le Baron semi-custom styles available. The straight-eight Imperial seemed like good value next to Lincoln or Cadillac, but the early 1930s was not a good time to be selling luxury sedans and sales were low.

The Radical Airflow

Chrysler had not produced any milestone cars up to this point, but that was about to change. The story goes that Chrysler designer Carl Breer, one of the original 'Three Musketeers' brought in by Walter Chrysler from Willys, saw a group of fighter planes in the sky which were so streamlined that he mistook them for geese. He reasoned that a streamlined car would look as good and slip through the air as efficiently, with the result that six years of experimentation would follow before the Chrysler Airflow was finally launched in early 1934.

With its faired-in radiator, headlights and fenders, plus a steeply-raked windshield, the Airflow was as radical as it seemed. It retained Chrysler's familiar

straight-eights, now in 301-ci (4932-cc) and 325-ci (5326-cc) forms, as well as the big 387-ci, but the packaging was all-new, with the engine mounted well forward and tilted 5° to the rear. The occupants all sat within the wheelbase and the Airflow's streamlined shape was of all-steel construction, which

was unusual at the time. The car was a bold step forward but in practice proved just a little too radical for the buying public. Only a little over 11,000 were sold in the first year as opposed to more than 25,000 of the conventional CA/CB six. A milder version, the Airstream, was launched in 1935 and

OPPOSITE
After the failure of the Airflow, Chrysler reverted to more conventional cars.

ABOVE and PAGE 140
A 1941 Chrysler, production of which resumed after the Second World War.

the Airflow was toned down a little, though sales actually dropped. Production ceased after only three years, even though the Airflow's influence on car design had been so important.

Other rechnical advances in the late 1930s followed industrial trends, with independent front suspension, steering column gearchange and a semi-automatic transmission in 1939. Many American manufacturers were beginning to make station wagons at the time, and Chrysler's appeared in 1941, being partly of wooden construction – the familiar 'woody' treatment so popular in the late 1940s. This was the Chrysler 'Town & Country' look which was extended post-war to the sedans and convertibles as well.

ABOVE LEFT
A 1946 Town & Country with the fashionable 'woody' look.

ABOVE
A New Yorker convertible of 1951. Chrysler launched its V8 the same year.

LEFT
A fast, luxurious Chrysler 300 of 1955.

OPPOSITE and THIS PAGE
Chrysler's two-door 300 became a legend in
its own right, its high performance coming
a decade before the heyday of the muscle
cars. This 1958 300D has a Fire Power hemi
V8 beneath the hood, with twin four-
barrelled carburetors. The 1962 300H
packed over 400bhp and was capable of
135mph (217km/h).

Chrysler's late-1930s/early-'40s models, such as the six-cylinder Windsor and eight-cylinder New Yorker, were continued after the Second World War, though they were completely restyled in 1949.

For a quarter of a century, Chrysler had relied on straight-six and straight-eight engines, but 1951 saw its response to the new generation of ohv V8s. The 'hemi' was so named because of its hemispherical combustion chambers, which allowed big valves and good breathing. The hemi produced 300bhp by 1955, and the 1960s hemi which succeeded it gave up to 500bhp. The 333-ci (5457-cc) unit produced a healthy 180bhp, more than its

But even Chrysler wasn't immune to the 1970s trend of downsizing, an example being the Cordoba two-door hardtop, which combined a 318-ci (5211-cc) V8 with a modest 115-in (2.9-m) wheelbase. It was the company's best-seller in 1975, though the late 1970s saw the V8s downsized, while six cylinders made a return, offered in the Le Baron station wagon and Newport sedan. A new Le Baron in 1982 was smaller still, being the first four-cylinder Chrysler since 1929. It was Chrysler's corporate K-car, also sold as a Plymouth or Dodge. Available as a sedan, convertible or coupé, it used Chrysler's own 136-ci (2229-cc) four or a bought-in unit of 157ci (2573cc) from Mitsubishi. The Laser was a more potent coupé version produced in 1984, having the option of turbocharging, while the same year saw the slightly bigger H-cars with the same engine options.

By this time, Chrysler was finally emerging from the near-insolvency of the

ABOVE and RIGHT
If the 300 was for covering long distances very quickly, then the New Yorker was a luxurious cruiser of the boulevards, here in 1959 convertible form.

OPPOSITE
The most luxurious Chryslers, this imposing four-door sedan, for example, were still badged Imperials in 1959.

rivals, and started the horsepower race of the 1950s, which Chrysler usually led.

The new Chrysler 300 of 1955 reflected this numbers game, being a two-door hardtop based on the New Yorker with the 300-bhp hemi. It was a precursor of the muscle cars of the 1960s, the 1962 300H offering up to 405bhp and a top speed of 135mph (217km/h). The 300s never sold in droves, but did a lot for Chrysler's image, and the name lasted through the 1960s. Other Chrysler sedans of the '60s were less exciting, being large, heavy and conventional.

ABOVE
The four-cylinder, front-wheel-drive Neon was Chrysler's modern compact for the 1990s.

ABOVE RIGHT
2000 Cirrus LXi

RIGHT
The Crossfire is a distinctive sports coupé. This is a 2005 example.

OPPOSITE
The retro-styled PT Cruiser adds a touch of individuality to family transport.

the 1935–37 810/812, with its streamlined profile and pop-up headlamps.

Errett Lobban Cord was no stranger to the motor industry and when he finally built the car that bore his name he was already owner of Auburn and Duesenberg. Front-wheel-drive wasn't completely unknown in America in the late 1920s, when Cord began to consider the design of a new car. Miller racing cars had used the format successfully, and it was their performance that inspired Cord to build one himself. Harry Miller was a consultant, and designer Cornelius van Ranst modified the Miller layout to make it suitable for the road.

At first glance, the new Cord L-29 (announced in September 1929, hence the name) looked like a conventional big car, albeit with particularly low, clean lines and a handsome V-shaped radiator grille. But under the hood the Lycoming straight-eight had been turned around to drive a three-speed gearbox to the front wheels. The Cord wasn't cheap in any of its forms, its four body styles starting at just over $3,000, but it was hailed as a great innovation by the motoring press.

But Cord's plans to sell 5,000 cars a year were scuppered by the Wall Street crash, which hit the financial sector just two months after the car was launched. In the event, a little over 1,800 L-29s were sold in its first year, and the planned L-30 and L-31 updates never saw production. Cord responded by drastically slashing prices, with the cheapest body (there was a sedan, convertible sedan, coupé and

The 810, the Cord that everyone knows, with its distinctive coffin-nosed styling and wind-up headlights. Under the skin, it retained the front-drive layout, but now with a Lycoming V8. There was plenty of interest from the public but very few sales.

155

brougham) coming in at just under $2,400. But even with a bigger version of the Lycoming (now measuring 303ci/4965cc) it was not enough to tempt buyers, and production ceased in December 1931. Of course it was very bad luck to have launched a luxury car only months before a worldwide slump, but it's unlikely that the conservative buying public would have warmed to something as radical as front-wheel-drive in large numbers.

Typically, Cord the entrepreneur was undaunted by any of this. In fact, he seemed to see the Depression as a new market opportunity, laying plans to make a less expensive, more compact luxury car to combat falling sales of the big Duesenberg. Designer Gordon Buehrig came up with what would become the classic Cord, which was rounded and streamlined, with the distinctive horizontal grille wrapping itself around the length of the hood.

The year before its launch it was decided that the new car should be badged as a Cord rather than a Duesenberg, and that it would have front-wheel-drive like the L-29. The first prototype had twin radiators, but the production car was simpler, with a single radiator in the conventional position. Lycoming again provided the power, this time a V8 designed especially for the car. Its 290ci (4752cc) produced 125bhp, enough to push the Cord 810 to over 90mph, though acceleration was hampered by the slow-acting pre-selector four-speed gearbox.

The car caused a sensation when it was unveiled at the Chicago and New York

motor shows in November 1935. Despite the high price (the 810 was $500 more than the equivalent Cadillac), Cord came away with 3,600 firm orders for it in his pocket, plus 7,000 enquiries. Many of these buyers were smitten by the 810's striking looks, and the car gained huge attention worldwide, especially when racing drivers and Hollywood celebrities clamoured to buy one.

Alas, the 810 had been shown before it was really ready, and it was three months before cars began to trickle off the assembly line. By then, many buyers on the waiting list had cancelled their orders in frustration, and sales for 1936 came to only 1,176. There were also rumours of problems with the front-wheel-drive layout. But Cord persevered, announcing the improved 812 for 1937. This had more room for passengers and luggage, while the Lycoming V8 was supercharged up to 190bhp, giving a substantial boost in performance. It cost more to buy (up to $3,000 for the long-wheel-based Custom) but the Depression was fading into memory as America's affluent classes began to re-emerge and conspicuous consumption was once again in fashion. None of this seemed to do the Cord much good, however: when production was halted in August 1937, sales for the year stood at 1,147, though some cars had been exported. It was the end for the big front-drive Cord, though Cord himself turned his hand to real estate and uranium, finding them more profitable than building cars.

CROSLEY (1939–52)

Contrary to popular belief, America built a whole range of small cars during the 20th century. All were offered by tiny companies and had a relatively short lifespan, and most were very simple in an attempt to undercut the already low prices offered by the Detroit Big Three. The Crosley was different, being more advanced than any other American small car, certainly after the Second World War, and for a short time was most successful, selling over 28,000 in 1948.

Powel Crosley Jr. made his fortune in radio and refrigeration before spending some of it building cars. The first Crosley was unveiled at the 1939 New York World's Fair, powered by an air-cooled 15-hp Waukesha twin-cylinder engine. There was a convertible, sedan and station wagon, all produced until 1942 when production was halted to allow concentration on the war effort.

The first few post-war years turned out to be a golden opportunity for Crosley. The Detroit Big Three were unable to keep up with the demand, and rather than wait for a full-sized car, many were willing to downsize, provided they could have their longed-for engine and wheels. But instead of a rehash of his pre-war twin, Crosley announced a miniature four-cylinder car. During the war, he had bought the rights to a 44-ci (721-cc) overhead-cam stationary engine named the Cobra. This lightweight, high-revving unit performed surprisingly well, and for a short time the latest Crosley sold well.

Once full-sized sedans were back in regular supply, however, and for the same price as the Crosley, demand soon vanished. The company persevered for another couple of year, adopting four-wheel disc brakes in 1949 (a world first) and offering the tiny Hotshot sports car that same year.

CROW-ELKHART (1911–23)

The name Crow-Elkhart grew out of the company's origins (the Black Crow Car of Chicago) and its production base in Elkhart, Indiana. Early production concentrated on four-cylinder cars, with bought-in engines from a whole range of suppliers, though Crow did offer its own overhead-valve four in 1918, with sizes ranging from 20 to 40hp. A six-cylinder car was added in 1913, again with proprietory engine.

Crow-Elkharts were neither particularly cheap nor luxurious, and even in the best year of 1917, only 3,800 were built, the Elkhart factory running well below capacity. A useful sideline was the supply of cars to Bush of Detroit, which sold them with its own badge attached. But that wasn't enough to keep the enterprise viable and despite new ownership in 1919 the company went into receivership three years later. It was taken over by a subsidiary named Century Motors, but production remained on a downward spiral, with only 236 cars built in 1923, many of them powered by four-cylinder Lycomings or Herschell-Spillman sixes. That was the final year of official production for Crow-Elkhart.

CUNNINGHAM (1907–36, 1951–56)

Two Cunninghams built cars in the U.S.A., the first being James Cunningham, a long-established carriage and buggy-maker, who diversified into gasoline cars in 1910 after experimenting with electric power. The company concentrated on coach-built hearses and ambulances, and only offered private cars as a sideline.

Based on the same substantial four-, six-cylinder or V8 chassis as the core vehicles, Cunningham cars were highly-priced and exclusive, with a chassis alone costing around $4,800 in 1920, and coach-built body work could result in a total bill of up to $12,000. They were not even sold through dealers, but via hospital officials and funeral directors already familiar with the make. Not surprisingly, the Cunningham was far from being a massive seller, with fewer than 200 cars sold in the peak year. Car production ended in 1931, though the company went on to build town-car bodies for the Ford V8.

Most enthusiasts will be more familiar with the products of Briggs Cunningham. Best known for his racing sports cars of the 1950s, this Cunningham also sold a limited number for the road, though only because he was required to make 25 cars to qualify for entry to Le Mans. The Cunningham C-3 was the result, with Ferrari-like coupé or convertible bodywork by Vignale of Italy. Power came from the 225-hp Chrysler hemi

Replica of the Briggs Cunningham C-3 Le Mans entry, seen here at the famous circuit in 2000.

Quite a threesome: 'Jo' Eerdmans, Sir Williams Lyons and Briggs Cunningham himself.

V8, mated to either automatic or three-speed manual transmission.

The C-3 was a heavyweight at 3,500lb (1588kg) and with its live rear axle not particularly sophisticated. In spite of this, at $10,000 it was the most expensive American car on the market, which reflected the fact that it was hand-built. Cunningham built just 26 C-3 chassis before closing down, but for many, the

Cunningham remains the ultimate American sports car. From 1997 the Cunningham Company, of Lime Rock Connecticut, offered a replica of the racing C-4R, with either modem running gear or a period Chrysler hemi engine.

DAVIS (1947–49)

One could concentrate on Davis of Richmond, Indiana, to recount the history

of Davis cars in the U.S.A., of which around 15,000 conventional fours and sixes were built in the 1920s, or the 1914 Davis cycle-car of Detroit. Far more interesting, however, is the Davis Motorcar Co. of Van Nuys, California.

Gary Davis designed a monstrous three-wheeler for which he made appropriately monstrous claims. He predicted the 46-bhp 135-ci (2212-cc) Hercules engine would deliver 116mph (187km/h) and 35mpg (12.3km/litre). This turned out to be as far-fetched as his claim that the 15ft (4.7-m) three-wheeler was stable enough to execute violent U-turns at 55mph (89km/h). In practice, the Davis could manage 65mph (105km/h) and 28mpg (9.86km/litre) and was less than stable.

Seventeen Davis prototypes were actually built, the later cars with 160-ci (2622-cc) Continental power units, but full production was never achieved. The enterprise came to a sticky end when Davis was sent to jail for finance irregularities.

DeLOREAN (1981–82)

It was like something out of a novel: a brilliant young engineer rises through the ranks of General Motors and becomes general manager of Chevrolet, overseeing record sales of over 3 million cars and trucks in 1971. In an apparent rejection of corporate mores, he grows his hair, ditches the suit and tie, and leaves General Motors. He also leaves his wife.

It seems he has a dream to build the world's first 'ethical' sports car, lighter and

more efficient than the products of
Detroit, and manages to raise $10 million
from investors and a further $138 million
from the British government, with a
factory built in a high-unemployment area
of Northern Ireland. Alas, the car proves
problematic, sales don't meet expectations
and the company slides into liquidation.
Our hero is finally arrested in a Los
Angeles motel room, accused of
involvement in cocaine smuggling. He's
acquitted, but that is the end of his dream.

Some day, someone will surely make a
movie about John DeLorean and the
stainless-steel gullwing sports car that was

his downfall. It seemed like a brave venture,
in tune with the times, but in reality the
DeLorean was heavy, handled badly and its
quality debatable. Its weight also blunted
the performance of its 183-ci (2999-cc)
Renault V6 engine, and sales were similarly
sluggish. After less than two years in
production, only a little over 4,000 cars
emerged from the Co. Antrim factory, many
of them sitting unsold on both sides of the
Atlantic. The end finally came when the
British government called in the receivers,
once financial irregularities had come to
light. DeLorean himself never returned to
Britain, facing arrest if he ever did.

DE SOTO (1923–60)

General Motors had Cadillac and Ford
had Lincoln, but De Soto was never
Chrysler's upmarket division, even before
Imperial filled that role from 1955.
Instead, it occupied the corporation's mid-
range, above Plymouth but below
Chrysler/Imperial, and was usually priced
just above or below Dodge. But because it
lacked a distinctive profile within the
Chrysler heirarchy, De Soto would
eventually find itself excluded from the
corporate pecking order altogether.

It was an all-new brand, launched
alongside Plymouth in 1928, the year

The car that launched a thousand dreams, or those of John DeLorean at least, plus the hope of jobs for 2,500 people in Northern Ireland. It was not to be, and the consequences followed John DeLorean to his grave. At the time of his death in March 2005, aged 80, he was still unable to set foot in Britain and Switzerland for fear of arrest.

Walter Chrysler purchased Dodge Brothers. In doing so, he underlined his determination to create a multi-division corporation to rival General Motors. As for the name, De Soto came from the 16th-century explorer, Hernando De Soto, who discovered the Mississippi in 1541; Chrysler possibly got the idea from General Motors, Cadillac having also been named after a European explorer of the New World.

The first De Sotos had much in common with the Plymouths and were even made in the same factory, though they were powered by a 176-ci (2884-cc) six-cylinder side-valve in place of Plymouth's 171-ci four. With the advanced feature of Lockheed hydraulic brakes, the first De Soto drove very well, and buyers had seven different body styles from which to choose, priced from $845, which bought a basic roadster, to $955 for a deluxe sedan. It was a hit, and just over 80,000 De Sotos were sold in the first 12 months.

A straight-eight was added in January 1930, claiming to be the world's cheapest at less than $1,000 for the basic model. Good performance was assured from the 209-ci (3425-cc) 70-bhp power unit, which was shared with the Dodge DC. But Chrysler chose De Soto, rather than Dodge, to share the new Airflow body in 1934. The Airflow was an advanced car for its time, with all-steel unitary construction and aerodynamic styling. The packaging was also new in that, for greater comfort, all its passengers were seated within the wheelbase.

This was all too radical for most American buyers and the Airflow was not a big seller, though it did fare better as a De Soto rather than a Chrysler, with 15,000 finding homes. It may have helped that the De Soto Airflow was cheaper than the Chrysler, due in part to its 243-ci (3982-cc) six-cylinder engine instead of the bigger straight-eight. Chrysler's response to disappointing sales was the less radical Airstream in 1935, and once again there was a De Soto equivalent which sold in greater numbers.

De Soto concentrated on more conventional cars through the late 1930s and early '40s, but there were several unusual features as well. The Skyview offered a sliding roof, while the 1940 convertible had a power-operated top. For 1942, features included retractable headlamps, air conditioning and a radio dial which changed colour according to the way it was tuned!

*This 1939 Dodge TC panel van used car
components and underlines the strength of
Dodge as a maker of commercial vehicles as
well as cars.*

own, this being a simple though up-to-date tourer aimed slightly upmarket of the Model T. It had a far bigger, more powerful four-cylinder engine of 213ci (3490cc) offering 35bhp, which was mated to a conventional three-speed transmission in place of the T's two-speed epicyclical. It also featured the world's first mass-produced all-steel welded body. Naturally, the first Dodge was a lot more expensive than a Ford, but it offered rather more, and 45,000 were built in 1915, with over 70,000 the year after, making Dodge the fourth best-seller in the country.

An all-steel closed sedan was added in 1919, which was another pioneer when others were relying on wooden frames. That year, over 100,000 Dodges were built, but disaster was about to strike. John died of influenza in early 1920 and a devastated Horace followed him by the end of the year. Four years later, their widows sold the company to the New York bank, Dillon, Reed & Co., for a record-breaking $146 million.

Without the Dodge brothers at the helm, the company seemed to lose

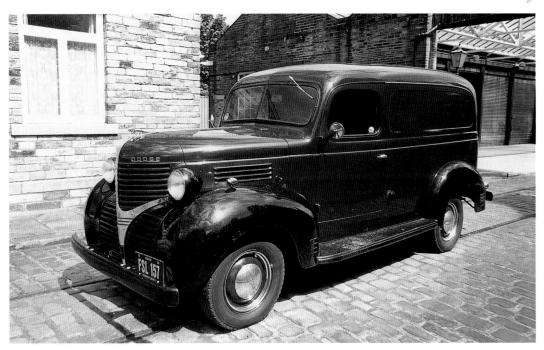

direction, and sales dropped through the 1920s despite more modern styling and the addition of 58- and 68-bhp straight-sixes in 1928. By now the Dodge was no longer the affordable car it once had been, the four now costing around twice as much as a Ford Model A.

However, a saviour in the guise of Walter P. Chrysler arrived, seeking to expand his fledgling corporation. In fact, Dodge was several times the size of Chrysler and he saw it as a hugely

significant acquisition. Almost as soon as Chrysler took over in July 1928, Dodge sales began to improve, increasing to over 120,000 in the 1928/29 model year. The four was dropped and in 1930 two new cars replaced the sixes. The 191-ci (3130-cc) DC6 and 222-ci (3638-cc) DC8 were relatively light and performed well, especially the straight-eight DCS, which weighed over 500lb (227kg) less than the Senior Six it replaced. Despite the Depression, which forced Dodge to drop

RIGHT
The humble Dodge pickup: the standard
workhorse of thousands of American
farmers. This 1952 example has been
customized, however.

BELOW
Police preferred a big sedan such as this
1957 Coronet.

BELOW RIGHT
More upmarket for 1957 was the Royal two-
door, the hemi V8 offering plenty of power.

the DCS after a few years, market share
continued to improve, and by 1933 the
company was back in fourth place and
the producer of a best-selling mid-range
of cars.

The straight-eight gone, Dodge was left
with one engine throughout the late 1930s,

though the side-valve six was enlarged to
219ci (3589cc), enough for 87bhp, while a
larger still 231-ci (3785-cc) was announced
for 1942. Meanwhile, technical advances
mirrored those of other Chryslers, with
hydraulic brakes, synchromesh, overdrive, a
hypoid rear axle and independent front
suspension all arriving in a steady drip-feed
of improvements. Compared with the
Airflow Chrysler and De Soto, these
Dodges were more conservative, which
didn't harm sales one little bit.

Mini Hemi
Dodge production ceased in February
1942, but when it resumed in late '45, like
the rest of Detroit, the cars had hardly
changed. This was because the industry
had been concentrating on satisfying a
public that had been starved of cars during
this time. New, restyled Dodges were
finally launched for 1949, the
Meadowbrook and Coronet replacing the
Deluxe and Custom. As well as the sedans,
there was the Wayfarer coupé and short-
lived Sportabout roadster. The following

year, continuing the Chrysler tradition of pioneering steelwork, saw the all-steel Sierra station wagon. For the time being, all these cars were powered by the pre-war side-valve six-cylinder engine, still at 23lci and now giving 105bhp with an optional fluid-drive automatic transmission.

The side-valve six was docile and reliable, but not quite the right power unit for a flagship in the early 1950s. In the immediate post-war years, the motoring public merely wanted personal transport and didn't care much about looks or performance. Now that need had been satisfied and incomes were rising, many were looking for something extra, to which Dodge replied with the Red Ram V8 in 1953. This was no more nor less than a smaller version of Chrysler's famous hemi, here measuring 243ci (3982cc) instead of the full 333ci (5457cc). But it did share the hemispherical combustion chambers, big valves and good breathing of the full-sized. The result was 140bhp, rising in just a few years to 260bhp from 315ci (5162cc).

Dodge had experimented with front-wheel-drive in 1949, but for the 1950s most customers were not interested in extreme innovations. They wanted power and style

ABOVE and PAGE 168
Welcome to the jet age! Dodge's performance image is apparent in this 1959 two-door model and confirmed by the respected hemi V8 beneath the hood.

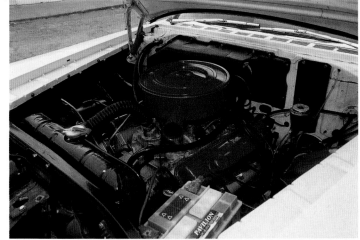

(2786-cc) form in the new Lancer for 1961. This really was a compact in the mould of the Plymouth Valiant, which had been sent to do battle with the Ford Falcon and Chevy Corvair.

The Ramcharger
While the six-cylinder range expanded, the full-sized V8s carried on gaining power in the early 1960s. Dodge had discovered that a performance image paid dividends, and while the first-generation hemi had been dropped, its place as horsepower flagship had been taken by the big-cube Ramcharger, all 426ci (6981cc) of it. Even with a single four-barrel carburetor it delivered 415bhp or 425bhp with two. It

LEFT
The NASCAR 1969/70, and Dodge fields the winged Charger to the delight of the crowds. Some Chargers even made it onto the street.

BELOW
More restrained is this example from 1966, though even the most staid Coronet sedans could be ordered with full-blown hemis.

from tried and tested layouts, and the new Dodge V8s provided both. Along with the Red Ram, the 1953 Dodges had new styling by Virgil Exner, the latest Coronet featuring an external spare wheel. For 1955, the whole range was again completely restyled, becoming longer, lower and wider than ever before. Three-tone paint, upmarket trim and upscaled models like the Custom Royal were unveiled, and Dodge sales boomed by over 160 per cent. Meanwhile, the Red Ram was fast establishing Dodge as the latest hot car: one sedan broke 196 AAA records at Bonneville Salt Flats in 1953, and was chosen as Pace Car for the Indianapolis

500 the following year.
The late 1950s were less happy times for Dodge as market share dropped to 3.1% by the end of the decade. Nineteen-fifty-nine saw the introduction of the new Dart. Not a true compact (it was only 4in/10cm shorter than the full-sized Dodges) the Dart was nonetheless cheaper than existing cars, intended to extend the division into Plymouth territory. It was powered by a new 226-ci (3703-cc) ohv slant-six, tilted towards the passenger side to give easier access to carburetor and spark plugs. This finally allowed the old side-valve six to be pensioned off, though the same engine was used in smaller 170-ci

was the most powerful production engine available. No wonder Dodge won the 1962 NHRA Championship and took the first three places in the Daytona 500 stock-car race in 1964.

The sedan range of Dart, Coronet and Polara, plus the Monte Carlo coupé, were all offered in 1965, but the following year the Charger was unveiled, this being a four-seater fastback based on the Coronet. This came as standard with the 318-ci (5211-cc) V8, though the second-generation hemi was an expensive option, chosen by a minority of buyers. This latest hemi, based on the same principles as the first, would become a performance legend in the late 1960s as the muscle-car boom gathered pace, ultimately delivering 500 horsepower.

OPPOSITE and THIS PAGE
This was the first Dodge Charger, really a fastback version of the Coronet, with standard V8, bucket seats and extra instrumentation.

PAGE 172
A 1966 Coronet, modified for drag racing.

PAGE 173
The 1959 Dart was smaller than the full-sized Dodges but not a true compact. That was on the way.

A new rebodied Charger arrived in 1968, now with the choice of five V8s, the most powerful of which were the 426-ci (6981-cc) hemi at 425bhp and the 440ci (7210-cc) Magnum with 375bhp. Either way, the Charger R/T ('Road and Track') was a seriously fast muscle car, capable of over 150mph (240km/h) and sprinting to 60mph in less than five seconds. Those on a more limited budget may have preferred to look at other members of what Dodge termed the Seat Pack; the Super Bee and Dart GTS were existing Dodge hardtops with extra power, stripes and other go-faster goodies.

But the Charger R/T was still the ultimate muscle car for many, especially as the 1970 Daytona. With its aerodynamic

OPPOSITE and THIS PAGE
Dodge's Super Bee offered buyers of muscle cars exactly what they wanted, which was an affordable basic package with plenty of sporty options. This is an example from 1969.

OPPOSITE and LEFT
The Challenger was restyled for 1970, this
R/T ('Road and Track') being a good
example. It is not exactly as it left the
factory!

droop-snoot and massive rear spoiler, it was simply a means of qualifying the winged Charger for NASCAR racing, and only 505 cars were built. The Daytona looked dramatic and epitomized its time, but a price tag of nearly $9,000 and its way-out looks deterred many buyers; some Daytonas had to be converted back into standard Chargers before they could be sold. In any case, the early 1970s was seeing the end of the muscle-car boom, and though the new-for-1970 Challenger could be had with the same high-horsepower engines as the Charger, it wasn't a great success and lasted for only four years.

The full-sized Polara and Monaco, plus the intermediate Coronet, all continued into the 1970s, but all of them were downsized in terms of length, weight and engine size. The Aspen was the 1976 replacement compact for the Dart, though even this could be had with an R/T package that included a 360-ci (5899-cc) V8. More radical, in American eyes at least, was the subcompact Omni, launched in 1978. Like the Chevrolet Chevette, this

OPPOSITE
The Charger went through several incarnations, the name being synonymous with the golden era of muscle cars.

ABOVE
A 1970 Coronet coupé. Headlights hidden behind the grille were a popular feature of the time.

A Charger 440 Magnum of 1972. The '440' refers to the cubic inches.

was a U.S.-built version of a European-designed car, in this case the Chrysler/Simca Horizon. At first, it was powered by a 105-ci (1721-cc) four-cylinder engine, though it became 136-ci

(2229-cc) in 1982, by which time the Omni had been joined by the 024 Charger coupé. Chevy's Chevette had rear-wheel-drive, but the Omni was front-driven and began a gradual transition that would see

Dodge's entire range becoming front-wheel-drive by 1990.

Excellent though the Omni was, it failed to transform Dodge's fortunes, but the Aries, which followed in 1981, certainly

1972 was the final year of the old-school muscle car, of which this Charger was one.

did. This larger front-driven sedan was Dodge's take on Chrysler's K-car, powered by the company's own 136-ci or a Mitsubishi unit of 157ci (2573cc), both of four cylinders. Dodge was now co-operating with the Japanese concern, which would see Mitsubishi Colt hatchbacks being badged as subcompact Dodges. The Aries, in coupé and convertible forms on slightly stretched chassis, were badged as 400s in a numerical system used on the 1983 600 sedan.

That same year, the front-driven Charger was offered in Shelby form, now with 107bhp, indicating that Dodge was

The Charger 500 (opposite) shows a clean profile, while the hood scoops on the Super Bee (above) can he attributed to the influence of NASCAR racing on aerodynamics.

ABOVE
A 1998 Intrepid ESX – a Dodge for the 21st century?

ABOVE RIGHT
A 1999 Dodge Avenger coupé.

RIGHT
The Dodge Neon, seen here in R/T form.

returning to its old obsession with performance. The Daytona name was revived in an Aries coupé, offered with a 142-bhp turbo engine, while even the Omni received its own performance variant, the GLH. In spite of this. Dodge sales fell by 15 per cent in 1986 though they recovered slightly the following year when the division sold just over half a million cars, the Aries proving the most popular model. The Aries and Omni were dropped in 1990, the Diplomat, the last of the rear-driven Dodges, having gone the previous year. This left the Shadow, Lancer and Dynasty as the smaller Dodges in the early 1990s.

These were all replaced by the Neon and Intrepid, members of Chrysler's 'cab forward' family and came with 202-ci

(3310-cc) or 216-ci (3540-cc) V6s – driving through the front wheels, of course. Both cars were Dodge-badged versions of standard Chryslers, as was the Stratus (based on the Chrysler Cirrus), equipped with the corporation's 149-ci (2442-cc) four or a 153-ci (2507-cc) Mitsubishi V6, Chrysler and Mitsubishi by now having a co-owned plant in Normal, Illinois. Other notable Dodges of the 1990s were the Caravan MPV and Durango SUV.

But perhaps the most notable of all, at least for enthusiasts, was the Viper V10 sports car, launched in 1992, though it had been unveiled nearly three years earlier as a concept car. The Viper sought to recreate the spirit of the legendary Shelby Cobra, with two seats, rear-drive and a V10 engine of 490ci (8030cc) derived from the power

LEFT
The Dodge Viper V10 astonished the motoring world in 1993.

BELOW
The 2006 Charger Daytona RT. Dodge understood the value of ancient hot-rod badges.

PAGE 186
By 2006, the Viper was still going strong, having earned its place as an evergreen classic.

PAGE 187
A 2007 Dodge Avenger.

ABOVE
The 2011 Dodge Nitro SUV.

RIGHT
The 2010 Dodge Journey crossover.

OPPOSITE
2010, and the Dodge Charger's body shape has changed dramatically since the mid-2000s.

unit of a truck. With 400bhp, the Viper could top 167mph (269km/h) and confirmed, in no uncertain terms, that the performance car was back. Dodge sold fewer than 9,000 Vipers in the first five years, but the car's commanding power made it worth its place as the company's image-builder. It was followed by the hardtop GTS. The Viper is still going strong in the early-21st century, as is the badge affixed to its front end.

Today, with more than nine decades of fine history and a superb pedigree, the famous American Dodge brand also enjoys a strong fan base in many parts of

the world outside the U.S.A. Among the world's great automotive companies, Dodge is set to boldly go into international markets, while staying true to its core values of providing cool, powerful, spirited, boldly-styled yet affordable vehicles, and attracting a whole new generation of consumers for whom the brand continues to exert a unique attraction.

DORT (1915–24)
Joshua Dallas Dort was a successful manufacturer of horse-drawn carriages

and buggies and a partner of William C. Durant, who went on to found General Motors. Dort, however, stayed in the business he knew best for several years after his erstwhile partner had transferred to the booming car industry. But he finally took the plunge and launched his own car in 1915, the Dort Four. Interestingly, it was designed by the French-born Etienne Planche, who was also responsible for the first Chevrolet.

The first Dort came with a four-cylinder Lycoming engine of 166ci (2720cc), driving through a three-speed gearbox. It

was highly conventional, the Dort's only individual feature being that the footbrake and clutch were combined on the same pedal, the other one acting as an emergency brake. Tourer was the only body style offered until 1917, when it was joined by a sedan and roadster. The following year was Dort's best, when just over 30,000 cars were sold, and saw the larger Lycoming 193-ci (3163-cc) unit adopted.

A six-cylinder Falls engine was offered in 1923, but the Dort was now on a downward slope with fewer than 6,000 cars sold that year. Rising prices had by now removed it from the Ford/Chevrolet bracket, but without a perceived move upmarket. Consequently, Joshua Dort ceased production of his car at the end of 1924.

A 1929 Duesenberg Model J, the first upmarket car from the Duesenberg brothers.

DUESENBERG (1919–37)

'He [She] Drives a Duesenberg', went the advertising for the cars of Frederick and August Duesenberg from 1934 onwards. What makes it remarkable is that the publicity doesn't show a car at all, but an elegant yachtsman or woman, the implication being that their eight-cylinder town car is parked somewhere just out of sight. It says much for the Duesenbergs that the right image was conveyed simply by using a good-looking picture together with their name.

In a way this is odd, as they didn't produce a car bearing their name until 1919, well after other superior marques, such as Packard and Pierce-Arrow, had been well-established. But it was not as odd as one might think, for the Duesenbergs

already had a good track record in high-horsepower engines by that time. Born in Germany, they were taken to the U.S.A. when they were 12 and five. As young men they built bicycles, and in 1905 Frederick (always known as Fred, his brother as Augie) designed a two-cylinder car.

The Mason Motor Car Co. of Des Moines, Iowa, was formed to produce it, and both brothers worked for the company through to 1913, when it went into receivership. Part of Fred's work at Mason's had involved designing a new four-cylinder engine with horizontal valves operated by long vertical rocker arms, this being nicknamed the 'walking beam' engine. It proved to be a successful racing engine, used by many different manufacturers, though only from 1914, with Mason now defunct, could the Duesenbergs use their own name, both on the walking beam motor and on racing cars.

That same year, they demonstrated their versatility by designing a 3,000-ci (50-litre) straight-twelve engine producing 800hp. It was intended for a racing hydroplane, the Disturber IV, which used two of these monsters to make it the first boat to exceed 60mph (l00km/h). Other, more modest marine engines of six and eight cylinder followed, which attracted both private and military customers. During the First World War, a large factory was erected at Elizabeth, New Jersey, to build Bugatti-designed 16-cylinder aero engines, but when the war ended, so too did the venture itself.

Meanwhile, Fred Duesenberg sold the rights to the four-cylinder walking beam to Rochester Motors, while he and his brother applied themselves to an all-new car for peacetime. This was the Duesenberg Model A, powered by a single-ohc straight-eight engine producing 100bhp from its 261ci (4277cc). With the first American-built straight-eight, plus hydraulic four-wheel brakes, the first Duesenberg was an advanced machine, which is probably why dealers didn't receive the first production cars until late in 1921, over a year after the official launch in New York. During 1922, around 150 cars were built, all of which had coach-built bodywork, the Duesenbergs having no facilities to build their own, which was possibly why the car cost $1,000 more than a Packard Twin Six. With fine handling and good performance, the Duesenberg was one of America's exceptional cars, though only 600 were sold in four years of production.

In fact, they became progressively more difficult to sell; what had been advanced features in 1921 (eight cylinders and hydraulic brakes) were rapidly becoming standard fare among quality American cars.

Things came to crisis point in 1926 when sales were down to a trickle and the company was running out of money, which might have spelled the end had not Errett Lobban Cord appeared in the nick of time. At the time, Cord had been running Auburn but really wanted to build a top-class car, and with Duesenberg in

difficulty and now up for sale he grasped the opportunity. Once in charge, Cord gave Fred Duesenberg a free hand to design the ultimate car, one that would outshine everything else on the market. It was a designer's dream.

The Model J

The famous Model J was the result. Once again it was a straight-eight, but any resemblance to the Model A ended there. The 422-ci (6915-cc) engine had twin-overhead camshafts and four valves per cylinder, features unheard of on a large touring car. It is thought that Fred Duesenberg's claim of 265bhp at 4250rpm had been a little optimistic, but even a more realistic 250bhp made the Model J the most powerful production tourer in the world. With this sort of power available, it had brakes to suit and hydraulic drums measuring 15 x 3in (38 x 8cm). Even these weren't deemed sufficient, however, and a vacuum booster was added the year after the Model J's 1928 launch.

As before, there were no factory-built bodies, but Gordon Buehrig designed some standard types which were built for Duesenberg by Derham, Brunn or Murphy, and seven body styles were listed in all. Not that these made the Duesenberg any more affordable, as even the bare chassis was $8,500, with finished cars costing anything up to $14,000 in 1929. Of course, it was possible to spend a great deal more on a one-off custom body; in fact, the one built by Bohman & Schwartz on an extended 178-in (4.5-m) wheelbase

cost its owner, the evangelist Father Divine, a reputed $25,000.

Even in the depths of the Depression there were still a wealthy few who could afford a Duesenberg, and the car attracted some big Hollywood names, such as Mae West and Gary Cooper, not to mention Jimmy Walker, the mayor of New York City, while an Indian maharajah and a sprinkling of European royalty were other Duesenberg customers. It was an impressive list, but as the Depression began to bite, so the numbers of the super-rich began to dwindle, or at least fewer were willing to flaunt their wealth when times were hard.

Undaunted, Fred Duesenberg began to think that the Model J needed more power, and decided it should be supercharged. Adding a supercharger to the dohc straight-eight produced a claimed 320bhp and a top speed of over 130mph (210km/h), given a suitable body, and resulted in the SJ, the most exclusive Duesenberg model of all, of which only 36 were produced, some being modified Model Js. The last five cars had 'ram's horn' inlet manifolds, which boosted claimed power to over 400bhp.

None of this, however, could prevent Duesenberg sales and production from slowing to a trickle in the early 1930s. Three hundred and sixty cars were sold in the first three years, but E.L. Cord's plan to build a first batch of 500, with more to follow, never happened. More Model Js were completed over the next few years, the last one built in 1935. Some must have

been hanging around the factory unclaimed, as a number were sold the following year, and the Model J was still listed for 1937, when the entire Cord enterprise closed down.

Duesenberg, however, was still a legend, so it is not surprising that attempts were made to revive the name. In fact, this was tried three times. In 1947, Marshall Merkes bought the remains of the company and hired August Duesenberg to design a new car, but the enterprise soon came to nought. Twelve years later, Mike Kollins also tried, transferring an original but modified Duesenberg straight-eight into a Packard chassis with a two-seat sports-car body, only one of which was built.

A similar fate befell the 1966 Duesenberg Model D, though Fred F. Duesenberg, August's son, was mainly responsible for this. It was a striking four-door sedan styled by Virgil Exner and built by Ghia of Italy on Chrysler running gear. With a 400-bph Chrysler V8, it would have been fast, but the Model D cost $19,500 and only one prototype was ever built. But that wasn't the end of the Duesenberg family's attempt at a revival. Harlan and Kenneth were nephews of Fred and August, and in 1978 offered a Cadillac-based sedan bearing the family name, though at $100,000 a time there were to be no takers. In the end, it wasn't new Duesenbergs that succeeded but replicas of the 1930s originals. So in one sense, the Duesenberg did rise again.

DU PONT (1920–32)

The Du Pont car was certainly exclusive, with only a little over 500 of various types built in 12 years. E. Paul Du Pont, whose industrial dynasty included textiles, chemicals and munitions, formed a company to build marine engines for the U.S. Navy in 1917, but when that market declined after the end of the First World War, he decided to build a luxury car instead, bringing in experienced men from the motor industry to help him do so.

At a time when six cylinders were *de rigueur* for most American cars, short of the Model T, and with straight-eights on the horizon, the Du Pont Model A made do with only four, its 251-ci (4113-cc) side-valve unit producing 55bhp. Even so, the cheapest of four body styles (tourer, roadster, sedan and suburban sedan) still cost $4,000, the most expensive being $5,600.

Only 188 of these four-cylinder Model As were built before they were replaced by the six-cylinder Model C. This used a proprietory power unit from Hershell-Spillman, of 290ci (4752cc), but despite the extra cylinders and a much lower price (the cheapest Model C was about half the price of its predecessor) only 48 cars were sold

Frank later converted it to a four. With the added advance of pneumatic tyres, this was far superior to the first car, underlined by the fact that it won the Times-Herald race held in Chicago in November 1895.

Frank's third prototype also won a race, this time organized by Cosmopolitan magazine and run from New York to Irvington. It was actually the only car to finish, which proved its reliability; it was used, as a result, as the basis of the production Duryea. The Duryea Motor Wagon Co. was formed late in 1895 and

cars were produced up to 1898, while Frank went on to build the Hampden car.

Meanwhile, Charles had been a partner in this first production venture, even though he had played no active part. It was 1898 before he began making his own cars, the first being a three-wheeler with three-cylinder engine and epicyclical drive. It also had tiller steering, in which Charles was a firm believer. The advantage over a wheel, in his opinion, was that it required only one hand, the other left available to hold a good cigar,

an umbrella or one's passenger's waist. The three-cylinder engine, with water-cooled cylinder heads, offered 15hp, though a 25–30-hp version was later added. Named the Duryea Trap, this two- or four-seater car proved quite enduring in both three- and later four-wheel forms, and 370 were built before Charles' company went into receivership in 1907.

Charles began again the following year with the Buggyaut, which would look decidedly old-fashioned next to a Model T, with its solid tyres, tiller steering and direct

A 1995 Eagle Talon race car.

drive. Charles, nevertheless, built it in two different forms for six years. Between 1914 and 1916 Charles made limited numbers of three- and four-wheeled cycle-cars – vehicles that marked the end of the pioneer era.

EAGLE (1987–1998)

'Eagle' is probably the most popular name of all as far as American car-makers are concerned, with the definitive *Beaulieu Encyclopedia of the Automobile* listing no fewer than eight, from the Eagle Auto Company of Buffalo, New York, to Chrysler's Jeep-Eagle division, though none of the first seven lasted more than a couple of years. In addition to these are the sprinkling of 1970s and '80s kit cars that used 'Eagle' as part of their name, as well as the Eagle-Macomber car (1916–18) and the 1914 Eaglet cycle-car.

The most enduring Eagle of all was offered by American Motors from 1987 onwards. AMC had used the name before, on the 1952 Willys Aero Eagle and on its own range of four-wheel-drive cars during 1980s, but in 1987 it was launched as a new marque. AMC already sold the Renault 25 as the AMC Premier, but following Chrysler's takeover in 1987 it became the Eagle Premier, joined by the Medallion, which was really a Renault 21.

Neither sold well, and from 1989 the Chrysler connection brought a range of Mitsubishis to be sold under the Eagle name These were first imported and later assembled at the Diamond Star factory in Normal, Illinois, which was a joint

LEFT
The 1995 Eagle Vision.

BELOW
The 1998 Eagle Talon was the most successful of the Jeep-Eagles.

ABOVE
The 1903 Ford Model A was a breakthrough in the history of the automobile and a commercial success.

RIGHT
Earlier still, Ford himself had a brief flirtation with racing. He is seen here with driver Barney Oldfield.

William Clay Jr., a fourth-generation Ford, is at the head of the company today.

Henry was born in 1863, the son of a farmer fleeing the potato famine, who had arrived on a boat from Ireland in the mid-19th century. By the time the first of six surviving Ford children had been born, his parents were farming several hundred acres in Dearborn, Michigan. But while Henry would later keep his nostalgic longing for a simple, rural way of life, a life, it has to be said, that the Model T and mass car ownership did much to destroy,

he had no ambition to take over the family farm. The sight of a steam traction engine when he was young encouraged his natural aptitude for mechanical things, and he went straight from school to a machine shop in Detroit, eventually becoming chief engineer at the Edison Illuminating Co.

Most of Henry's fellow pioneers were young men, but Ford was in his 30s when he built his first car, and 40 when he finally settled down to series production. The first car was the quadricycle, a simple two-cylinder machine driving through a two-speed epicyclical transmission (a type Ford would use for the next 30 years) and chain drive. The quadricycle was built in his spare time in a workshop behind his house on Bagley Avenue, Detroit. Famously, it turned out to be too large to get through the workshop door, and Ford had to take a sledgehammer to a wall to get it out.

The quadricycle turned out to be a practical proposition, capable of 20mph (32km/h) on the roads around Detroit, but Ford soon sold it and built a more sophisticated car, now with proper financial backing and a view to putting it into production. But the Detroit Automobile Co. was a flop, Henry fell out with his backers, and in 1901 the company was wound up. Soon afterwards, he tried again with the Henry Ford Company, this time concentrating on a racing car. The famous 999 broke several records, and Henry himself drove it to 91.37mph (147.04km/h) over a mile on a frozen Lake St. Clair. Once again, disagreements with his backers ended in failure.

The breakthrough came in 1903 when local coal merchant, Alexander Young Malcolmson, agreed to finance Henry's third venture. This time it worked, with

By 1906, Ford's new factory on Piquette Avenue, Detroit, was churning out 100 cars a day, the range still running to three models. The Model F was the final two-cylinder development of the C, but Ford's future lay in the Model N. Despite having an 18-bhp four-cylinder engine of 150ci (2458cc) it was actually less than half the price of the F (even before the famous T arrived, Henry's aims were clear). By contrast, the big six-cylinder Model K did not accord with Ford ambitions. It was an expensive luxury car, being a hangover from the Malcolmson days; Henry had to make his dealers take one for every ten of the popular Model Ns they ordered. Less than 600 Ks were sold in two years, and the experience led to the avoidance of six cylinders for many years. More in keeping with the Ford philosophy were the smaller Models R and S.

The Model T

But all of these were dropped in October 1908 in favour of the car that would make Ford a multimillionaire: the Model T. There was nothing radical about the T's engineering. The new 178-ci (2917-cc) four-cylinder engine had a detachable cylinder head but was otherwise conventional, driving though the same two-speed epicyclical transmission as every other Ford. There was a choice of body styles, from a two-seater runabout ($825) to a seven-seater town car ($,1000) and the Model T quickly proved to be the most popular Ford yet, with over 10,000 sold in its first year. But the first Model Ts looked

Model Ts were not the only ones to be piled high and sold cheap, there were also Fordson tractors, seen here on the assembly line at Dearborn.

another simple chain-driven car with epicyclical transmission and a 101-ci (1655-cc) flat-twin engine mounted under the seat. It was actually quite similar to a Cadillac recently in production by the Henry Ford Co., which was hardly surprising since Henry designed them both.

The Model A was composed of bought-in parts – even the engines were supplied by Dodge – which led to Ford's censure by the Association of Licensed Automobile Manufacturers (ALAM). Fred L. Smith, treasurer of Oldsmobile, had dismissed Ford's as 'nothing but an assemblage plant'. Suitably stung, Ford refused to pay the royalties which ALAM demanded from all non-members, took the cartel to court, and won his case.

Ford's early customers didn't seem to care whether the Model A was an assemblage or not, as 670 of them were

sold over the next 15 months, and may have been even more, but it placed Ford on a firm financial footing, whatever the figure. In late 1904 the Model A was dropped in favour of a range of three cars. The Model AC was quite similar to the original, but with a larger 121-ci (1983-cc) engine, while the Model C added a front hood and vertical radiator. The Model B was quite different, being a reflection of Alexander Malcomson's ambition for a larger, more expensive car. It was a 285-ci (4670-cc) four-cylinder tourer with a price tag of $2,000, and Henry didn't like it one bit, in that his aim, as would be the case for the rest of his life, was to build cheap cars and as many of them as possible. It remained a bone of contention between the two, solved only when Henry managed to elbow his partner out of the company.

record profits. So $5 a day was something of a double-edged sword where the workforce was concerned, though for most it was a fair price for a life governed by the production line.

The other side of these savings was a lower sticker price on the cars. By 1915 the Model T tourer was only $440, when in 1908 it had been listed at $850, the latter being far better equipped with previous extras such as windshield, headlamps and speedometer all made standard.

This was the key to Henry Ford's pile 'em high, sell 'em cheap philosophy: he could have kept prices as they were, made even bigger profits and to hell with expanding the market. But that wasn't the Ford way. By continually cutting prices, and to an extent that no rival could meet

OPPOSITE
A procession of restored Model Ts.

LEFT
The car that changed the world: the Ford Model T.

BELOW
Britain also made Model Ts, and quite a few of them at that.

like expensive limited-editions compared with what would come in future.

Henry Ford wasn't the sole owner of his rapidly-growing enterprise, though that would come, but he was in full control, the ace up his sleeve being the massive new factory at Highland Park, outside of Detroit. It was here, from August 1913, that Model T production was organized on moving assembly lines, dramatically boosting productivity and slashing costs at one fell swoop. In the first year, just over 200,000 Model Ts were built, and in 1914, with the lines operating at full speed, the figure exceeded 300,000. Two years on and it was an incredible 738,811, when Ford's

nearest American rival, Willys-Overland, was making only one-fifth as many.

So great were the savings made by mass-production that Ford was virtually able to double his workers' wages, right across the board. The famous Five Dollar Day gave Ford huge publicity and led to crowds of job-seekers converging on Highland Park from all over the country. Of course, the pace of work, now dictated by the speed of the line, was a punishing one, and contemporary accounts of working for Ford emphasize the sheer exhaustion that came from earning that $5. Meanwhile, Ford shareholders voted themselves far greater dividends based on

*OPPOSITE, TOP FAR LEFT and
BELOW LEFT
Not all Model Ts were simple workhorses,
as this special-bodied example shows,
though it was no more sophisticated beneath
the skin.*

*LEFT
Henry Ford has a right to look happy: this
was the 20-millionth car to bear his name.*

in the 1920s, he was making the Model T
more accessible to more people. So in
1923 the Model T had its best year, with
over 1.8 million built. The result? In 1924,
the cheapest T cost only $260, or little
more than half the price of the equivalent
Chevrolet. Advertising seemed superfluous
with the car selling so well, and there was
none at all for some years, which, of
course, saved more money still.
Henry Ford became more and more
obsessed with cutting costs to the bone,
reducing R&D and white-collar staff to
the bare essentials.

This was all very well in the early days
when the public was happy to buy any car
as long as it was cheap enough, but as the
1920s progressed it was clear that changes
were afoot. Buyers were becoming more

affluent and more demanding: they now required four-wheel brakes, a six-cylinder engine and even a choice of colours. Up-and-coming companies, such as Chevrolet, recognized this fact, gave the public what it wanted and began to catch Ford up. Meanwhile, the Model T retained its 20-bhp four-cylinder engine, its two-speed transmission and choice of any colour as long as it was black right to the end, though in its final year, colours were finally offered. Typically, this was because new technology had brought quick-drying paint to the fore, where before only black had been fast-drying enough to keep up with the production lines.

Henry's son, Edsel, had been arguing for change throughout the 1920s, which Henry ignored. The fact that Edsel had been president of the company since 1918 made no difference, Henry still being firmly in charge of the enterprise he had founded. But even Henry had to admit the Model T could not last forever, and in May 1927 the tireless production line finally stopped. Over 15 million Model Ts had been made in the U.S.A. and Canada, though many more had emerged from plants all over the world.

A new car was coming, according to the company, though it wasn't ready yet. It was seven months before the all-new Model A was finally launched, a fatal seven months in which Chevrolet was finally to overtake Ford and put thousands of Ford staff out of work into the bargain. But few cared when the Model A was unveiled in December 1927.

OPPOSITE and THIS PAGE
Model Ts come in all kinds of guises, including commercials, conventional tourers and even the special-bodied racer shown opposite.

Yet another variation of the Model T was the Wagonette, the closest thing to a station wagon in its day.

This, the first new Ford for nearly 20 years, caused such excitement, especially outside Ford showrooms in Cleveland, that mounted police had to be called in to control the crowds.

All Change

The Model A certainly was an improvement on the boxy, utilitarian T. Influenced by Ford's upmarket car, the Lincoln, it was quite an elegant little car, and within a couple of years the range had

'Henry's made a lady out of Lizzie' was the cry when the new Model A – updated, slightly more elegant and with twice the power – was launched in 1927.

been extended to 18 styles, including bodies by Briggs and Murphy. A station wagon for 1929 was something of an innovation, which other manufacturers were quick to copy.

Under the skin, the A had plenty of worthwhile improvements. There was not the straight-six that some had predicted, but the 202-ci (3310-cc) four produced 40bhp, twice that of the T. The ancient epicyclical transmission, easy to use though it was, was finally abandoned in favour of a conventional three-speed sliding gear unit, and there were four-wheel brakes at last.

Ford had nearly half a million orders for the new car even before the December announcement, and in 1929 over 1.3 million were sold. Nevertheless, Ford was still affected by the Depression, and sales in 1931 slumped to fewer than those for 1929. Henry responded by laying off tens of thousands of workers and temporarily closing his factories. Meanwhile, even the Model A was suffering the effects of competition, specifically from the excellent-value Chevrolet six, to which,

OPPOSITE and LEFT
A 1956 Thunderbird. This was Ford's
'personal car', offering a more civilized
alternative to the Corvette.

once again, Henry made a forthright response: Ford would leapfrog its rivals with a cheap V8.

It wasn't the first time Ford had considered an eight: an unusual X8 had been studied as a possible successor to the Model T, but the simpler, easier-to-make V8 won the day. With 65bhp from its 222ci (3638cc), it gave the 1932 Ford Model 18 striking performance, the new car weighing little more than a Model A. The

mechanical drum brakes and transverse leaf suspension made the V8's 80mph+ quite a handful, but with prices starting at $460 it sold by the thousands and Ford had done it again. The famous flathead (side-valve) V8 also proved responsive to tuning, inspiring a whole generation of hot-rodders, and would see Ford right through the 1930s.

There was a half-hearted attempt to make a four-cylinder Model 18 to replace

the Model A, but this Model B was dropped after only seven months, the American public having seemingly quickly outgrown fours. Yet despite having the V8 which Chevrolet lacked, Ford was still overtaken by Chevy in 1936. Once again, it was falling behind: hydraulic brakes weren't offered until 1939 and independent front suspension until '48, over a decade after it had been adopted by most mainstream American cars. There were

ABOVE
Mercury was the slightly upmarket Ford favoured by customizers.

ABOVE RIGHT
A 1959 Ford station wagon, seen as the age of compacts was beginning to dawn.

OPPOSITE
The Fairlane was the intermediate Ford sedan in 1958.

attempts to offer a cheaper alternative to the V8 in the form of a smaller 137-ci (2245-cc) V8 and a 227-ci (3720-cc) straight-six, but neither was successful.

Ford emerged from the Second World War in disarray. Edsel Ford had died of cancer in 1943, when an increasingly frail Henry, then in his 80th year, took the reins once more. It was now a sprawling empire with little leadership or financial control. Things began to change when Henry Ford II, then aged 26 and fresh out of the navy, took over as president in late 1945. He was a quick learner, bringing in a group of high-flying business brains from the air force (the 'whiz kids'), who helped to bring the business back to profitability.

As for the cars, the only improvement that was seen for 1945 was a larger version of the flathead V8, new with 240ci (3933cc). The genuinely new Fords didn't arrive until 1948, when as well as new styling they finally received coil-sprung independent front suspension. The company also needed a new overhead-valve V8 to keep up with the competition, though that didn't arrive until 1954 in 241-ci form. There was a new intermediate Fairlane for the following year, a good-looking car, but most exciting for 1955 was the two-seater Thunderbird.

This was Ford's response to the Chevrolet Corvette, in many ways a more complete car, with a standard V8, manual

transmission and interior comforts such as wind-up windows. The T'Bird wasn't an out-and-out sports car like the Corvette – Ford termed it a 'personal car' – but the 198-bhp V8 gave it respectable performance and the styling was neat and distinctive. The Thunderbird outsold the more specialized Corvette in huge numbers, and was even more popular in its 1958 four-seater form, though enthusiasts mourned the trim little original.

Power Plus
Like the rest of Detroit, Ford was caught up in the 1950s power race and boosted the V8 to 312ci (5113cc) for 1956, adding supercharging for 1957 to give 300bhp.

A 1959 Edsel, one of Ford's rare mistakes (see Edsel).

The year after, the famous 'FE' big-block V8s arrived in 332-ci (5440-cc) and 352-ci (5768-cc) forms. These would stand Ford in good stead as the power race gathered pace through the 1960s, in bigger 390-ci (6391-cc) and ultimate 427-ci (6997-cc) forms. The 427 was really designed for racing, giving up to 425bhp with two four- barrelled carburetors; in conjunction with the heavy but aerodynamic Galaxie fastback, it allowed Ford to dominate NASCAR through the early 1960s.

By then. Ford had a new compact addition to its line-up in the neat and simple Falcon, with 145-ci (2376-cc) six-cylinder engine and a spacious interior. The Falcon was good value for money and easily outsold its main rivals, the Chevy Corvair and Chrysler Valiant. It was also given a V8 option as the 1960s progressed. With compact Falcon, intermediate Fairlane (now renewed), full-sized Galaxie and a grown-up Thunderbird, Ford seemed to have the conventional car market sewn up, even though it was about to blow it apart with the Mustang.

The Mustang created a new class of machine, the 'pony car', having four seats (preferably for a family with children instead of four large adults), sporty looks and a strong image. It was a winning combination, especially when the Mustang used so many Falcon and Fairlane parts, which kept costs to a minimum. Another Mustang secret weapon was the wide range of engines (from a 101-bhp six to a 271-bhpV8), transmissions and other options, widening its appeal to a multitude of buyers. Men, women, the young, middle-aged and old – everyone loved the Mustang – and half a million were sold in the 18 months following its late-1964 launch.

Lee Iaccoca is usually seen as the inspiration behind the Mustang. He was a super-salesman and marketeer who joined Ford as an engineer, transferred to sales, then rapidly rose through the ranks almost to the top of the company. He eventually fell out with Henry Ford II and was sacked in 1978. As for his baby, the Mustang grew bigger and heavier in 1967 to accommodate the big-block V8s and compete in the increasingly ferocious muscle-car wars. The Shelby Mustangs were uncompromising and well-regarded, at least at first (later Shelbys were more cosmetic), with Ford producing its own low-volume Mustangs such as the Boss 429. Cars like this were unable to survive the first oil crisis, with the result that the all-new 1974 Mustang II was smaller, lighter and with a mere four cylinders. Enthusiasts howled in pain, but the new-generation Mustang was hugely successful; within a few years, it even had a V8 option as well.

This was a new era of smaller Fords, the subcompact Pinto having been announced in 1970 to rival the Chevy Vega. The four-cylinder engines came from Ford of Britain and Germany (99ci/1622cc and 123ci/2016cc respectively) and there was also a V6 of 171ci/2802cc). The Pinto sold well until cases of ruptured fuel tanks necessitated a recall. The compact Maverick was launched the same year as the Pinto, intended to replace the Falcon as a two- or four-door sedan with a 171-ci six or a bigger V8. It was supplemented in 1975 by the Granada, related to the European Granada and filling the slot between Maverick and the intermediate Torino. The Maverick was dropped in 1978 in favour of the Fairmont, another

The 1959 Galaxie, a big four-seater convertible which would soon become the province of the Thunderbird.

thoroughly conventional rear-wheel-drive Ford, though it had been designed with fuel economy in mind, the base engine now being a 140-ci (2294-cc) four, the same that was used in the base Mustang, though a six and V8 were also offered. As for the full-sized Fords, the Galaxie had given way to the LTD, which would retain its large dimensions until 1979, and the big Thunderbird was replaced by a downsized version in 1977 and again in 1980. The following year, its base engine had a mere six cylinders.

The Era of Front-Wheel-Drive

But the big news was the arrival of the front-wheel-drive Escort in 1981. This was Ford's 'world car', intended to be as appealing to Americans as Europeans. The CVH 98-ci (1606-cc) four-cylinder engine was the smallest ever seen in a U.S. Ford, and seemed to be exactly what the buyers wanted. The Escort rapidly became not only the best-selling Ford but also the best-selling car in America. It was joined in 1982 by the EXP two-seater coupé, based on the same parts.

But it was not a happy time for Ford: over 70,000 jobs were lost between 1979 and 1981, and losses of billions of dollars were being regularly posted. Nevertheless, enthusiasts did have something to cheer about as the 1979 Mustang became a true performance machine during the 1980s with the return of a V8 option and power increasing almost year on year, eventually equalling muscle cars of the 1960s. The year 1983 also saw the return of the convertible, while rather more sober was the front-driven Tempo with a choice of

ABOVE
The original pony car: a 1965 Mustang coupé.

ABOVE RIGHT
A fastback joined the coupé and convertible in 1966.

RIGHT
Bigger and wider for 1967, the later Mustang offered bigger V8s and more power.

This 1926 Franklin is air-cooled despite its impressive radiator grille, as were all its predecessors.

responded with drastic price cuts of $1,000, and over $400 was cut from the price of the six. The company tried hard to offer a more affordable car, launching the Olympic sedan in late 1932. This was actually the Reo Flying Cloud, powered by Franklin's air-cooled six, with prices starting at $1,385.

But it was not enough, and sales dwindled to only 360 in 1934 when Franklin shut up shop. However, the name lived on, thanks to a couple of company engineers, who bought the factory to make air-cooled aero engines.

GARDNER (1919–31)

Russell E. Gardner was the largest maker of horse-drawn buggies in the U.S.A., and in 1913 decided to diversify into cars. At first Gardner and his sons, Russell Jr. and Fred, built bodies for Chevrolet, then complete Chevys under licence before selling that side of the business to General Motors during the First World War. But Gardner wanted to produce his own car, and prototypes were running by late 1919, with production starting early in 1920.

The Gardner Light Four was powered by Lycoming, a make of engine the company would be loyal to almost until the end, in this case a simple 193-ci (3163-cc) unit equipped with side valves and thermosyphonic cooling. There was a tourer, sedan or roadster, prices starting at $1,125, and over 6,000 cars were built in the first year. That total halved in 1921 when Gardner suffered the effects of the

post-war slump, but output rocketed to 9,000 the following year.

Prices were cut for 1923, despite an improved 215-ci (3523-cc) Lycoming four with five main bearings. The big news came in 1925 with Gardner's new 'Eight-in-Line'. As the name suggests, power came from a Lycoming straight-eight of 278ci (4556cc) and 65bhp. Meanwhile, the Light Four was replaced by a six, which didn't sell, Gardner bringing in a smaller eight of 227ci (3720cc) to replace it.

In spite of stylish looks and reasonable prices, Gardner sales were well past their peak, the company never having surpassed its 1922 record, and talks with Sears, Roebuck & Co. to sell through its mail-order house came to nothing.

Gardner's response was the big front-wheel-drive sedan, which abandoned Lycoming in favour of a Continental six. It was a handsome car, long and low with a streamlined grille, but did not sell well. Unable to survive on its own, Gardner considered a merger, but in the end closed the business before it got further into debt.

GAYLORD (1956–57)

Not to be confused with the earlier Gaylord, a conventional four-cylinder car built in Gaylord, Michigan, between 1910 and 1913, this company was named after its designer, Ed Gaylord. The plan was to produce a top-flight American sports car, and the prototype, styled by Brook Stevens, was certainly striking, if not good-looking. Powered by a Chrysler V8

with four-speed automatic transmission, the Gaylord Gentleman coupé also featured a retractable hardtop and variable-assisted power steering. It was also something of an international effort in that the first all-metal prototype was built by Spohn of Germany, while the three production chassis were also made in Germany, this time by Zeppelin The plan was to use a Cadillac V8, but only one chassis was fitted with a body before the project came to a halt.

GRAHAM-PAIGE (1928–40)

The three Graham brothers, Joseph, Robert and Ray, were born entrepreneurs. Their first venture transformed the small-scale Lythgoe Bottle Company into a viable industrial concern. After selling that, they went into the truck business, making the 'Truck-Builder' conversion for the Ford Model Ts. That led to the Graham Speed Truck, using Dodge components, which so impressed the Dodge brothers that it was sold through their own dealers. Eventually, the Grahams sold their truck business to the Dodges in 1926.

They expanded into automobiles the following year by purchasing the Paige-Detroit Co. Within six months, their new Graham-Paige car was ready to go, in a range of four six-cylinder cars and a single straight-eight. The three sixes measured 176ci (2884cc), 208ci (3408cc) and 290ci (4752cc), all with side valves, on a choice of four wheelbases, from a compact 111in (2.8m) to a limousine-like 129in (303m). As for the eight, that was a 324-ci (5309-cc)

unit, the Model 835 it powered having a 135in (3.4-m) wheelbase. Whether it was this full range of cars or the handsome styling or the standard four-speed gearbox on all but the cheapest cars, the Graham-Paige was an instant success, selling 73,000, a record for a new marque in its first year.

The cars were updated with hydraulic brakes and automatic chassis lubrication in early 1930, but in the wake of the Wall

Street crash, the honeymoon couldn't last forever, and sales halved that year. Graham-Paige found itself in the position of every other manufacturer of luxury cars in a world where few people could afford its products. The company tried to respond with a cheaper eight, the Special 820 and the Prosperity Six, but it wasn't enough to turn the tide.

Even the sleek new Blue Streak for

1932, with raked styling by the talented Amos Northup that set new standards, failed to have an effect, and the following year Graham-Paige built only 11,000 cars. But no one could accuse the brothers of not trying. For 1934, they tried supercharging, using a centrifugal unit to boost the power of the eight to 135bhp. At $1,245, it was cheap for a supercharged car, and the later Special Eight ($1,045) was even better value. For 1936, the eight having been dropped, a supercharged six was launched which was cheaper still, due in part to the use of the Reo Flying Cloud body. The brothers also ventured down-market, launching the Standard Six that same year at $595, and sales finally began to creep up.

But it was too late to save the original line, and the Grahams sold their tooling to Nissan, though they returned to car production for 1938 with the 'Spirit of Motion' six. This had unusual styling with an imposing front end, but the public weren't impressed and the Spirit never saw 1939. In that year, Joseph Graham agreed a deal with Norman DeVaux to build a car using the Cord 810 body shell under both Graham and Hupp badges. But only 2,000 Graham Hollywoods and just over 300 Hupp Skylarks were built before production ceased in September 1940. Graham-Paige didn't resume business after the Second World War, and the brothers sold what was left to Kaiser-Frazer.

HAYNES-APPERSON/HAYNES (1897–1925)

Elwood Haynes was a skilled metallurgist,

A mildly-customized Hudson tourer from 1935.

more interested in the minutiae of research than marketing or business management. So his first automotive ambition was not to make a fortune or change the world but to design a car for his own use. He bought a single-horsepower Stintz marine engine in 1893, turning to Elmer and Edgar Apperson to build the car.

The Apperson brothers were established engineers and agreed to build the car to Haynes' design, finishing it in July 1894. The two-speed single-horsepowered car was able to run, but proved underpowered, so Elwood bought a 2-hp Stintz, which still wasn't good enough. In any case, Haynes had higher ambitions, having learned that the *Chicago Times-Herald* was holding a race for horseless carriages and offering $5,000 as a prize. A two-cylinder Haynes-Apperson was built, but it skidded early in the race, shattering a wheel.

Undaunted, the three of them formed the Haynes-Apperson company in 1898 and began building 5-hp cars in a new factory. The cars did well in racing and endurance events, but the partners quarrelled. The Appersons left, but Elwood Haynes continued to build two- and soon four-cylinder cars, dropping the Apperson name in 1904.

A six followed in 1913 and a V12 three years later, its 358-ci (5866-cc) ohv power unit built in-house. The Light Twelve would be in production for five years, but only around 650 were produced, the company's main income

coming from the more conservative Light Six. For 1924 Haynes offered a cheaper six-cylinder, the Model 60, at $1,295 in tourer form, but the company was by now in severe financial trouble. It was wound up later that year by the U.S. District Court.

HENRY J (1950–54)

Long before the Detroit Big Three finally began to make compact cars, other American manufacturers were producing them. The Henry J was one such, built by the Kaiser-Frazer company, which had ambitions to beat the Detroit big boys at their own game. On paper, it all looked good. The Henry J, named after Henry J. Kaiser, was a modern-looking two-door sedan, with the choice of 135-ci (2212-cc) four or 162-ci (2655-cc) six-cylinder

engines. Both were built by Willys, the four being straight out of the Jeep, though with 68 and 80bhp respectively the lightweight Henry J was by no means underpowered.

Its price was its downfall. Despite a very basic specification (at first, there was no trunk that opened) and poor quality, the Henry J was still too expensive at $1,363 for the four, when a full-sized Ford coupé with a cylinder engine was $1,324, while the Henry J six came in at $1,499. The company still managed to build over 130,000 Henry Js in four years (a limited number were sold through Sears, Roebuck as the Allstate) but production ceased in 1954. The fate of Kaiser-Frazer and its Henry J demonstrates how impossible it was to break the stranglehold of Detroit's Big Three.

A 1929 Hudson dual-cowled phaeton tourer.

HUDSON (1909–57)

The eventual fate of Hudson shows how difficult it was for an independent manufacture to crack the domination of the Detroit Big Three, or even to co-exist with them after the Second World War. Despite healthy sales in the 1920s, when it was fourth in the production pecking order for a while, Hudson was too small to survive on its own. It was forced to merge with Nash, though the name disappeared a few years later.

The men who formed Hudson were all experienced in the car industry in that Roy Chapin, Howard Coffin, Frederick Bezner and Joseph L. Hudson, who financed the enterprise, had all worked for Oldsmobile. Their first car was the Model 20, and very successful it was. In fact, sufficient of these four-cylinder roadsters were sold at $900 to place the new company 11th nationwide, and a tourer was soon added.

The company would become famous for its sixes, and was early in the market for them with the Model 54 in 1912. The side-valve engine was a big one, at 423ci (6932cc), and Hudson was soon claiming to be the world's biggest maker of sixes. The Model 54 was followed by the smaller Super Six in 1915, this 269-ci (4408-cc) unit being Hudson's first in-house engine. Racing driver Ralph Mulford set a new record in a Super Six at a time when transcontinental records were being regularly set and broken.

Launching the lower-priced four-cylinder Essex (see Essex) set Hudson on the path to success, showing that it was possible to produce closed sedans for less than the price of an open tourer. Meanwhile, the Super Six had been coaxed up to 92bhp for 1927, thanks to a new inlet-over-exhaust valve arrangement.

With remarkable foresight, Hudson managed to downsize its cars for 1930 in the aftermath of the Wall Street crash, making them lighter and cheaper. It also launched a low-priced straight-eight of 215ci (3523cc), developed from the Essex six and starting at just over $1,000. But it failed to deliver the goods and Hudson was hit as hard by the slump as everyone else. Hudson cut prices again in the summer of 1930, this time by a drastic 15 per cent, but sales did not begin to recover until 1934. Fortunately, the fat years of the 1920s had given Hudson some financial muscle, and it was able to ride out the storm.

During the 1930s, Hudson had more in common with the cheaper Terraplane,

The familiar Hudson six and eight now offered up to 100 and 124bhp respectively, but with Terraplane as part of Hudson territory, the company launched the Hudson 112 as a low-priced model to compete with Chevrolet and Ford. Starting at less than $700, it was reasonable value, considering the standard 176-ci (2884-cc) six, though it was not well-equipped. The mid-range Hudsons now started with the Traveler series, updated with a new front end, while an all-new body appeared for 1941, though was short-lived, when war work called a temporary halt to civilian car production.

In common with most American manufacturers, Hudson reintroduced its 1942 models in 1945, now called the six-cylinder Super or eight-cylinder Commodore, both based on the same 121-in (3-m) wheelbase. They were replaced by an all-new car in 1948, featuring step-down chassis, its low floor allowing passengers to step down into the car. And while the old side-valve straight-eight – splash lubrication and all – carried on, it was joined by an all-new six of 263ci (4310cc) with modern full-pressure lubrication and 121bhp.

These were good times for Hudson as the public flocked to buy the new cars, and

ABOVE
A 1937 Hudson coupé, now sharing a body as well as chassis with the Terraplane.

RIGHT and OPPOSITE
The 1946 Hudson convertible kept buyers happy until the all-new unit-constructed car was ready for 1948.

which replaced the Essex in 1934. It adopted the Terraplane's lightweight chassis and from 1936 the two ranges shared a body shell as well, newly styled by Frank Spring, Hudson's individualistic designer who ate health foods and practised yoga long before it was fashionable. As for the cars, these were updated during the rest of the decade, with hydraulic brakes arriving the same year as the corporate restyle. For customers suspicious of the new-fangled hydraulics, Hudson provided a Duo-Automatic system that would apply the parking brake if the hydraulics failed. The cars still didn't have true independent front suspension, but Baker Axleflex, a more basic type, was optional from 1934, with a proper set-up finally arriving in 1940.

sales peaked at 143,000 in 1950. They were boosted that year by the smaller Pacemaker, with shorter 119-in wheelbase and a 233-ci (3818-cc) version of the successful six. For 1951, the six was taken up in size for the Hudson Hornet. Now measuring 310ci (5080cc), it proved an impressive performer, especially when equipped with the optional Twin H-Power (twin- two-barrelled carburetors), and became a popular NASCAR competitor.

This post-war success faltered in 1953 when Hudson launched the new Jet. Styled once again by Frank Spring, it was the company's bid for a place in the new market for compact cars, already exploited by imports and American cars such as the Henry J. It was awkward in appearance, Spring having been ordered to base it on the 1952 Ford, and despite offering a standard six-cylinder engine, sales were poor. Attempts to inject some glamour, with a Twin H-Power option and the leather-lined Jet Liner, failed to have much impact.

It was the expense and failure of the Jet that spelled the end of independence for Hudson, together with the fact that the unit-construction step-down design was expensive to restyle. The company simply couldn't afford a new body style or the ohv V8 that it so badly needed. In 1954 it merged with Nash to form the new American Motors Corporation.

Hudson's distinctiveness was rapidly dissipated in the name of rationalization when, for 1955, it adopted the Nash Airflyte body shape, albeit with Hornet or Jet engines, though a Packard V8 was also offered in the Hornet. AMC announced its own ohv V8 of 251ci (4113cc) the following year, which appeared in the Hornet Special; but the V8 Hornet was the sole Hudson for 1957, and even that had disappeared by the following year.

HUPMOBILE (1908–40)

'In Hupmobile, exterior beauty and interior luxury are built upon the swift smoothness, the sparkling performance and the ease which you can expect only from a fine straight eight.' So went a 1927 advertisement for the Hupmobile Distinguished Eight, built by a company whose cars had little to distinguish them, certainly at first. Hupmobile was also a company that reached its peak a year after the above appeared, making a record number of cars and a profit of $8 million. Yet only seven years later it was a million dollars in debt and on the brink of ceasing production.

Robert Craig Hupp founded the Hupp Motor Car Company in November 1908 in Detroit, which even then was a centre of the rapidly developing U.S. car industry. Hupp was no dreamer, however, having already worked for Oldsmobile, Regal and Ford, though it was his first attempt at building a car of his own. Technically, it was simple and unambitious, being a two-seater roadster with a 172-ci (2818-cc) four and a two-speed gearbox where most contemporaries would have had three or four. But at $750, however, it was relatively cheap.

That alone seemed enough to endear it to the public, and Hupp's Model 20 sold over 1,600 in 1909, its first year, with over 5,000 finding buyers in 1910 and 6,000 the year after. By this time it had been joined by a four-seater tourer and for 1912 by the larger Model 32. This had a longer 106-in (2.7-m) wheelbase, though it kept the four-cylinder engine of 183ci (2999cc). With more room and more power, the Model 32 broadened the Hupmobile's appeal, despite its odd styling, and over 12,500 cars were sold in 1913.

The Model K that appeared in 1915 with the same size of power unit, had a more conventional appearance, and was sold alongside the Model 32 until both were replaced by the Model N the following year. This was larger all round, with a 245-ci (4015-cc) engine, still with four cylinders, and a wheelbase of up to 134in (3.4m); unlike previous Hupmobiles, it was offered as a limousine, whose standard equipment included a smoking set and flower vase. The Model N was also relatively popular, selling over 27,000 in two years. But its replacement, the 1918 Model R, saw a return to basics, with a 183-ci engine and shorter wheelbase, plus simple roadster or tourer bodies; the expensive limousine had not sold well, but the Model R sold fast enough to push Hupmobile into the top-ten manufacturers.

Until now, Hupmobile had ignored the trend towards six cylinders, but like Henry Ford overcame this by going straight to an eight. Launched in January 1925, the Model E was powered by a 248-ci

1946 Hudson sedan. The company enjoyed a few years of post-war success before succumbing to the power of Ford, General Motors and Chrysler.

Looks familiar? This 1931 Imperial GC Roadster was really a luxury Chrysler (See also pages 136 and 137.)

(4064-cc) eight of 60bhp. It also offered the advanced feature of four-wheel hydraulic brakes, though all this technology was reflected in a top price of $2,595; even with improved styling the eights made up only 16 per cent of Hupmobile production in 1927.

But overall, the company was riding high. Nineteen-twenty-eight, of course, was the record-breaking year, when over 65,000 cars were made, and all Hupmobiles now had elegant new styling by Amos Northup. Now cash-rich, the company bought the Chandler-Cleveland concern, but the Wall Street crash hit only weeks later, leading Hupmobile to sell the Chandler factory. Meanwhile, it persevered

with the eights through the Depression, but overall sales were barely 10,000 in 1933, only a fraction of their 1928 peak. But the cars had reached a new level of stylishness, redesigned in fashionable aerodynamic form by Raymond Loewy and Amos Northup, with faired-in headlamps and streamlined rear ends. Not everyone agreed, however, and the sleek Hupmobiles were outsold by the more conventional types by more than two to one in 1934. There were three engine choices that year: sixes of 225ci (3687cc) and 247ci (4048cc) plus a 305-ci (4998-cc) straight-eight.

Hupmobile was in deep trouble by late 1935: not only had it run out of money

but its new president, Archie M. Andrews, also had a poor reputation in the industry, so potential backers were reluctant to get involved. There was no alternative but to suspend production, though some cars were produced sporadically through 1938 and up to May 1939. Hupmobile's one last hope was to build cars using the Cord 810 body tooling, though it lacked the money to do so and Graham built them instead. Only 319 Hupmobile Skylarks had been made, however, before the project folded in July 1940.

IMPERIAL (1955–75)

There were several Imperials built in the U.S.A. from 1900 onwards, and some unconnected companies were actually in business at the same time. But it is odd that such a regal name should have had such apparent appeal in one of the world's largest republics! The longest-lived and most recent of all those Imperials was the Chrysler division announced in 1955.

Chrysler had been using the Imperial name for its flagship cars as far back as 1926, but the 1955 launch set it up as a separate division for the first time, giving it a considerable degree of autonomy. The reasoning was simple: Chrysler needed a separate marque, rather than a model badge or level of trim, that could outclass a Cadillac or a Lincoln.

The first product of this new division, the 1955 Imperial came as two-door hardtop, four-door sedan or limousine and used Chrysler's biggest 331-ci (5424-cc) V8, here in 250-bhp form. Automatic

transmission, power brakes and power steering were all standard, with a power seat in the limousine. Air conditioning was among the options and free-standing tail-lights featured on both 1955 and '56 Imperials, with a larger 356-ci (5834cc) V8 in the latter year. In fact, Imperials were always to use the biggest Chrysler V8 available, up to the 442-ci (7243-cc) unit from 1966 onwards. Later Imperials also began to look more like Chryslers.

This went against the trend at a time when Ford and General Motors were trying to align the styling of their cheaper cars with that of the top marques. The traditional full-sized Imperial was never going to survive the crisis-ridden 1970s unscathed, and again in 1990 there were two attempts to revive the name, as a badge rather than a division, but neither was a roaring success.

INTERMECCANICA (1960–)
If Automobili Intermeccanica doesn't sound like a bona fide American car manufacturer, it's because it started life in Turin, only moving to California in 1975. Even before then, however, the firm, started by Hungarian-born Frank Riesner, had had plenty of stateside connections. The Apollo GT, for example, was a prototype sports car with a Buick V8, and the company later built a Ford Mustang station wagon for Bob Cumberford, who intended to put it into production. The Griffith was another sports car, this time powered by a Ford V8, and around 500 were built under various names. Other one-offs which never saw production were the Corvair-powered Fitch and Ford V8-engined Murena sports station wagon.

But Intermeccanica entered a new phase when Frank Riesner moved to the West Coast, planning to build a development of the Griffith. That didn't work out, so he went into the VW car kit business instead, with a Porsche Speedster replica sold either partially or fully assembled. That was followed by the LaCrosse, a generic 1930s-style car based on Checker running gear and the Ford 350-ci (5735-cc) V8.

Intermeccanica was back in the Porsche replica business in 1982, the Roadster RS aping a 1959 Convertible D. Originally based on the standard VW floorpan, this popular car kit later acquired its own tubular frame, able to take Porsche 911 running gear. In 1999, the company, now run by Henry Riesner, the founder's son, revealed a prototype VW Kubelwagen replica.

INTERNATIONAL (1907–11, 1956–80)
The International Harvester Company (IHC) is best known for its trucks and tractors, but the company also made excursions into car manufacture. From 1907, it built a simple car using its own 14/16-hp flat-twin engine, with two-speed friction transmission and chain drive, in a choice of two- or four-seater versions. Two new cars were offered from 1910, a two-cylinder 18/20-hp roadster and a four-cylinder 26/30-hp tourer, but these were dropped the following year.

After that, International Harvester concentrated on commercial vehicles, though it did make a limited number for passengers based on a pickup chassis. It wasn't until 1956 that the company returned to series car production with the Travel all station wagon, based on its half-ton truck. More popular was the Scout four-wheel-drive, with a choice of four-cylinder or V8 engines, which exploited the growing market for leisure 4x4s. It was replaced by the Scout II in 1971, once again with four-cylinder or V8 power units. There were plans for a Scout III, but International Harvester's financial problems prevented this and the last Scout was built in October 1980.

JACKSON (1903–23)
Jackson, of Jackson, Michigan, must surely be the only American manufacturer to have offered both a steam and gasoline car in its first year. Both were designed by Byron F. Carter, who set up the Jackson Automobile Co. with George A. Matthews and Charles Lewis in 1903. But the three-cylinder 6-hp steamer didn't last a year, leaving Carter's single-cylinder gasoline car to carry on alone. He added a 16-hp twin the following year, and the 18-hp Model C in 1905.

The following year, the single was dropped and a four-cylinder 40/50-hp announced. Jackson lost no time offering a straight-six, and the Sultanic was launched in 1913 with a 40-hp Northway engine. It was also early in the V8 market, though the car it offered from 1916 to 1918 was actually less powerful than the Sultanic,

ABOVE
*The 1974 Cherokee, a two-door version of
the Wagoneer.*

ABOVE RIGHT
*Meanwhile, the Wagoneer soldiered on: this
is a model from 1978.*

RIGHT
The 2001 downsized Jeep Cherokee

Wagoneer V8 hung on, renamed the Grand Wagoneer, while the CJ5 was heavily revised as the Universal in 1985 when the V8 option was dropped.

Meanwhile, AMC, under Renault ownership since 1978, was nearing its end, and in 1987 the company was bought by Chrysler, having now emerged from near-bankruptcy under the energetic leadership of Lee Iaccoca. Chrysler wanted AMC so that it could obtain Jeep, and the AMC car range was soon dropped. Under Chrysler, a new Grand Cherokee was announced in 1991, replacing the Grand Wagoneer, now with a 244-ci (3998-cc) six or 320-ci (5244-cc) V8. The baby Cherokee now came only in five-door form, the basic Jeep (now Wrangler) seeing gradual updates

ABOVE LEFT
The 2002 Jeep Liberty Sport has a strong family resemblance to the original.

ABOVE
In 2004 it was still possible to have a traditional Jeep in the Wrangler Sport.

LEFT
The 2004 Grand Cherokee headed the line-up of Jeep's SUVs.

OPPOSITE
2005 swa the appearance of the special-edition Jeep Rubicon.

LEFT
The 2005 Cherokee continues as the entry-level Jeep SUV.

ABOVE
2008 Jeep Wrangler JK Unlimited Sahara.

ABOVE RIGHT
2009 Jeep Wrangler Unlimirted X.

RIGHT
2010 Jeep Wrangler Mountain Unlimited.

OPPOSITE
New shape and styling for the 2011 Jeep Cherokee SRT8.

throughout the 1990s. Now something of an off-road icon, the ex-Second World War Jeep was still selling strongly 65 years on.

Another new Grand Cherokee appeared in 1999, now Jeep's best-seller, with a smaller but more powerful 230-bhp V8, plus a five-speed automatic transmission, while European buyers had the option of a 190-ci (3113-cc) five-cylinder turbo diesel. It was the smaller Cherokee's turn in 2002, when it was replaced by a new model complete with round headlamps and slightly retro styling making it perfectly clear that Jeep was actively exploiting its heritage.

JORDAN (1916–31)
'Somewhere west of Laramie, there's a bronco-busting, steer-roping girl who knows what I'm talking about. She can tell what a sassy pony, that's a cross between

greased lightning and the place where it hits, can do with eleven hundred pounds of steel and action when he's going high, wide and handsome. The truth is, the Playboy was built for her.'

Ned Jordan, the author of these lines, will probably be remembered more for his advertising copy than his cars. A natural-born salesman, he realized that the key to selling cars in an increasingly affluent market was not the boring details, like the number of cylinders and cubic inches, but image. The story goes that he was on a train in Wyoming when he spotted a woman on horseback, and inspiration struck.

Jordon's lyricism extended beyond the advertising: his cars didn't come in 'green' or 'blue', but 'Venetian Green' and 'Liberty Blue'. Like the Playboy roadster for which the Laramie girl would gladly have dismounted, the cars had names that suggested speed and freedom – the 'Speedway Ace', 'Cross-Country Six', and 'Silhouette' being only a few.

But what of the cars themselves? Well the truth of the matter is that there was nothing remarkable about them, apart from being well-built and reasonably priced; there was nothing else to justify that extravagant prose. But then, the advertising of automobiles has always contained fanciful images, anything to make the dullest of cars seem sexy. The first Jordan 60 was launched in 1916 in roadster and tourer forms, both powered by a 302-ci (4949-cc) Continental six. Sales were encouraging and a whole range of body styles was added in the following year.

Then came the Model C Sport Marine, the Silhouette and, of course, the Playboy, the latter two with the same 120-in (3-m) wheelbase chassis and 223-ci (3654-cc) six. The sixes were joined by a straight-eight Jordan in 1925, and by the following year the smaller cars had been dropped, while Jordan production peaked at over 11,000.

But a return to six cylinders with the Little Custom in 1927 did nothing to attract sales, neither did the Cross-Country Six the following year. With Ned Jordan now in poor health, the company was beginning to lose its direction, though in 1930–31 it did offer the 100-mph (160-km/h) Speedway Ace roadster and Sportsman sedan, both with 125-bhp Continental straight-eights and four-speed transmission. But there were few takers, at a list price of $5,500, and Jordan closed in 1931. But some great lines were left behind.

KAISER (1946–55)

The Kaiser-Frazer Corporation was yet another example, along with Studebaker, Nash and several now-defunct names, of the difficulties facing independent car manufacturers in the U.S.A. after the Second World War, especially those with designs on the mass car market. But for a few years, Kaiser-Frazer did well, selling nearly three-quarters of a million cars in all, making it one of the top ten marques in America, despite its lack of a track record in car production.

Kaiser-Frazer owed its early success to two men. One was Henry J. Kaiser, the wealthy industrialist with a fine record in

shipbuilding. The other was Joseph W. Frazer, who was a foil to Kaiser's dynamism and had experience of the motor industry, having worked at Chrysler and Graham-Paige. Therefore, when the first Kaiser-Frazer cars were launched in 1946, they were able to steal a march on the competition.

The Detroit Big Three (Ford, Chrysler and General Motors) reintroduced their 1942 cars after the Second World War in an attempt to meet the huge demand for cars as quickly as possible. But the Kaiser-Frazers were freshly designed, with smooth, full-width styling by Howard 'Dutch' Darrin and Robert Cadwallader that distinguished them from the pre-war lines of the others.

There were, in fact, two cars, a base-model Kaiser and more plush Frazer, both with the same 227-ci (3720-cc) 100-bhp six and rear-wheel-drive layout. The

Kaiser was originally envisaged with front-wheel-drive and torsion-bar suspension, but these innovations were wisely omitted from the production car. Despite moderately high prices that started at $1,868, these were more comparable to eight-cylinder mid-range cars than the Ford and Chevy sixes, but they sold well, finding nearly 145,000 buyers in 1947 and over 180,000 the following year, and enabling even Kaiser-Frazer to make a profit.

The honeymoon period ended in 1949, however, when the Big Three announced their all-new cars with modern full-width styling. Kaiser-Frazer sales slumped to fewer than 60,000, indicating that the healthy first couple of years had been due to the company's unique position which was now no more. In 1949 it responded with three niche models, a four-door convertible (the first such post-war car in America), a four-door hardtop named the Virginian, and an intriguing hatchback called the Kaiser Traveler or Vagabond. Unfortunately, all of them were too expensive to sell in sufficient numbers.

What Kaiser-Frazer really needed was new models, but it didn't have the money. A lifeline appeared in the form of a $69 million loan from the Government-backed Reconstruction Finance Corporation, which financed the launch of the compact Henry J in 1950 (see Henry J) and a new Kaiser for 1951.

The latest Kaiser was quite distinctive, with its low waist and large area of glass, but was hampered by the ancient side-valve six-cylinder engine (once a Continental, now built in-house) at a time when the rest of the industry was progressing to powerful overhead-valve V8s. The company tried to spruce up its sedans with special editions and fancy trims, such as the Dragon, with optional padded vinyl roof. A braver move was the Kaiser Darrin 161 sports car, unveiled in 1952. Designed, as the name suggests, by 'Dutch' Darrin, the glass-fibre open-top was based on a Henry J chassis with a Willys 161-ci (2638-cc) four-cylinder engine. With 90bhp, it was no road-burner, and even such individual features as sliding doors could not attract the buyers. Only 435 were sold, Dutch Darrin himself buying the last batch of 50 unfinished cars and fitting them with Cadillac V8s.

As for Kaiser, sales continued to slide, to 32,000 in 1952 and a mere 22,000 the following year, with a little over 7,000 in 1954. Merger was the only way to survive, and Kaiser amalgamated with Willys-Overland that year, selling its huge Willow Run factory to General Motors and moving car production to Willys' Toledo plant, though Kaisers were only made until early 1955. So ended Kaiser-Frazer, an enterprise which historian Richard Langworth referred to as 'The Last Onslaught on Detroit'.

KELLISON (1959–72)

Kellison was one of the largest makers of kit cars in the 1960s. Jim Kellison made his name with a series of roadsters and coupés designed to fit the chassis either of full-sized American sedans or that of the VW Beetle or MG. These were the J-4 coupé (only 39in/1m tall), the K-3 coupé and the J-2 and K-2 roadsters. He later added his own chassis to the range.

As is often the way, in 1965 Kellison sold the production rights to another company and moved on to something else. In his case there were several projects, including the Dagger, a coupé that fitted a shortened VW floorpan, and the Can-Am, a one-off coupé designed for a racing car. He also sold kits for dune buggies, and was one of the first to offer a Ford GT40 replica, based around either a V8 or the ubiquitous VW. Plenty more Kellison replicas followed, based on the Jaguar D-Type and XKE as well as the Corvette Stingray and Lotus Elite.

Jim Kellison left the company in the late 1960s, going on to build kits under the Kelmark name and the Stallion, a replica of the AC Cobra.

KELSEY (1921–24)

Kelsey cars first entered production in 1921, though Cadwallader Washburn Kelsey had made forays into the car-making business more than 20 years earlier, first with a single-cylinder three-wheeler and a four-cylinder car in 1902. Neither got beyond the prototype stage.

The new six-cylinder Kelsey of 1921 was unusual for its friction drive, though was otherwise fairly conventional, with a range of sedan, tourer or runabout body styles. A new Gray-powered four-cylinder car, also friction-driven, was added the following year, but sales were slow and it was only when Kelsey introduced a four-cylinder with conventional transmission – this time, Lycoming-powered – that they began to pick up. In fact, Kelsey did quite well for a short time, and had a substantial order book by early 1924. However, in June that year, the company was forced into bankruptcy (by illegal methods, as it turned out), which meant the end of car production for Kelsey.

KING MIDGET (1947–69)
An appropriate name for a tiny but surprisingly long-lived micro car, the first King Midgets used a 6-hp Wisconsin single-cylinder engine and had zero weather protection, but the redesigned model of 1951 had a more conventional two-seater bodywork and an 8.5-bhp engine. Not that conventional, however, as it wasn't until 1958 that doors joined the options list! In 1967 a 12-hp Kohler engine made it the most powerful yet, but the King's days were clearly numbered when small cars like the VW Beetle –

economical, practical and weather-tight, with the bonus of four seats – became available. There were plans for a fibreglass replacement along the lines of a dune buggy, but a factory fire destroyed everything in 1969 and that was that.

KISSEL (1906–31)
Brothers William and George Kissel were of German stock and used various company names, including Kisselkar, Kissel Kar and plain Kissel in 1919. They built their first four-cylinder prototype in 1906 and limited production followed, but it received a significant boost when an order for 100 cars was received from a Chicago merchant.

Unlike the earliest Kissels, the 1909 cars used in-house engines with cylinders cast in pairs: two fours of 243ci (3982cc) and 288ci (4719) plus a 432-ci (7079-cc) six. These were superseded by a single-block six in 1916, a 52-bhp unit that was in production for five years, though Kissel turned to Weidely for its short-lived V12, offered only in 1917–18. A new sense of style was injected with the Silver Special

Speedster, seen at the New York show in 1918, which entered production as the 'Gold Bug' roadster (actually a nickname).

Kissel managed to keep up to date in the 1920s with automatic lubrication and four-wheel hydraulic brakes, while Lycoming now supplied straight-eight engine blocks, topped with Kissel's own aluminium head. The Kissels were imposing cars, but sales were dwindling through the late 1920s and the company went into voluntary liquidation in 1930.

KURTIS (1932–63)
Frank Kurtis built racing cars in the 1930s but had previously been rebodying Fords and Buicks, going on to build a number of road cars. The most intriguing of these was the 1949 sports car, a sleek machine that resembled a Jaguar XK120 with most of the curves removed. Power came from the Ford flathead V8, but only 38 were built before Kurtis sold the project to Earl Muntz, who stretched it to four seats, fitted a Lincoln or Cadillac V8 and named it the Muntz Jet.

Meanwhile, Kurtis was now in the market for kit cars, building a road version of his pre-war K500 Indy race chassis, which was able to accept a number of bodies and had torsion-bar suspension at both ends. These came both as kits and fully assembled, and 35–40 were sold. The 500M of 1955 mounted a full-width fibreglass body on the same chassis, but production ended after only 25 had been built. Later, Frank's son, Arlen, began to build replicas of the Kurtis 500S racer.

A later Kissel 6-45 Speedster.

This 1927 La Salle convertible coupé was aimed at buyers who set their sights above a Buick but couldn't afford a Cadillac.

LA SALLE (1927–40)

A glance at a list of Detroit-based car manufacturers and the unitiated could be forgiven for thinking there were a host of competing makes, when in fact Buick, Cadillac, Plymouth, Mercury and most of the others were simply divisions of the Big Three – General Motors, Chrysler and Ford. La Salle was just another of those divisions, though as the upmarket name suggests, it was aimed more towards the Cadillac end of the market than the Chevrolet.

In fact, in the early 1920s La Salle was conceived as a means of filling the gap in GM's range between Buick and Cadillac. Steps were taken to create this new car marque in 1924, and promising young stylist Harley Earl was brought in from California. Earl, of course, would shortly be in charge of General Motors styling across the corporation, and was arguably the most influential designer the American motor industry has ever produced.

For the first La Salle, he took as his inspiration the Hispano-Suiza, the result being graceful and elegant with 11 body styles, all with dual colour schemes. Prices started at $2,495, but buyers could spend rather more on the Fleetwood coach-built bodies costing up to $4,700. Under the skin, naturally, the La Salle used plenty of General Motors parts, the 305-ci (4998-cc)

261

The sleek special-bodied La Salle. Sadly, the marque would not survive beyond 1940.

V8 being simply a smaller version of the existing Cadillac unit.

The La Salles were a huge success, actually outselling Cadillac in their first two years and selling another 60,000 in 1929–31. Although it was in a lower-priced band than Cadillac, the La Salle shared some new Cadillac features as they arrived, such as safety glass and a synchromesh transmission in 1929. The line was dropped in 1933, partly due to a slump in sales during the Depression, but a new La Salle appeared the following year, now with a straight-eight, and the Fisher all-steel turret-top body was adopted in 1935.

La Salle was back with a Cadillac V8 for 1937, a year in which sales climbed to over 30,000, the marque's best yet. But they halved the following year and General Motors could not fail to notice that price cuts to the Cadillac in 1939 left little reason to buy a La Salle. Consequently, the badge was dropped altogether in 1940, leaving Cadillac as the car to which millions of Americans would aspire.

LINCOLN (1920–)

Lincoln's progenitor was not Henry Ford, though it was his flagship marque for over 80 years. Neither was his son, Edsel, who was the brains behind some of Lincoln's

appearance did not live up to its engineering until Leland commissioned coach-builders Brunn and Judkins to supply more elegant bodywork. Even so, sales were way below target, sending the

Leland Lincoln into receivership. This was when Henry Ford stepped in and offered to buy, promising the Lelands full control. They accepted, but left within months, when it became clear that Henry was not keen on having an independent marque within his empire.

Lincoln cars, however, now under the discipline of Ford management, saw increasing production and falling costs, with nearly 8,000 cars sold in 1923. Edsel Ford had been made president when the Lelands left, and this proved another boost

most beautiful cars. Originally, Lincoln had nothing to do with the Ford empire, though it was set up by Henry M. Leland, who had been an early partner of Ford back in 1902.

The Lincoln Moto Co. was established during the First World War to make aero engines, but when it ended, Leland and his son Wilfrid launched their first Lincoln car. It had much in common with the contemporary Cadillac (another Leland-established marque) with the additional refinement of full-pressure lubrication in its 360-ci (5899-cc) V8 and thermostatically-controlled radiator shutters. Unfortunately, the Lincoln's

to the division. Nominally president of the entire Ford empire. Edsel had no real power with Henry still firmly in control, but his position allowed him to give rein to his considerable artistic talent. He decided to broaden the car's appeal by commissioning well-known coach-builders, such as Fleetwood and Le Baron, to supply batches of special bodies. Thus Lincoln buyers had a choice of 32 body styles by 1926, and at a reasonable cost.

That first Lincoln was replaced by the Model K in 1931, with the same V8; but its real significance was the availability of a 450-ci (7374-cc) V12 in the same chassis from 1932. The V8 was dropped and smaller V12s added, but Lincoln sales were suffering as the Depression squeezed sales of big luxury cars. There was even talk of closing down the division.

Edsel's reply was a smaller, cheaper mid-range car, but keeping a V12 engine, albeit a cheaper unit derived from Ford's own flathead V8. With 110bhp, this 269-ci (4408-cc) pushed the new Zephyr up to 90mph (145km/h). Edsel worked with the young stylist Bob Gregorie to produce a sleek and distinctive body shell. Who cared that it rested on Ford's primitive transverse leaf-sprung suspension, with mechanical brakes? Launched in 1935, the new Zephyr offered the Lincoln badge, good performance and the cachet of a V12 for only $1,275 for the two-door sedan.

Lincoln sales rocketed as a result, with over 28,000 Zephyrs sold in 1937. The following year, the 90-mph car was given hydraulic brakes, while the V12 was

OPPOSITE and THIS PAGE
Who cared about the mechanical brakes, leaf-sprung front end or even that the engine had been derived from Henry Ford's flathead V8, when the Lincoln Zephyr was a genuine V12 for less than $1,300?

enlarged to 294ci (4818cc) in 1940, producing 120bhp. Meanwhile, the big Model K V12 was selling in fewer numbers by the year and was dropped in 1939.

The Continental

One of the perks of running a successful car company is to have personal special editions created at company expense. That is what the Lincoln Continental was, at first, when Edsel Ford commissioned Gregorie to produce a Zephyr cabriolet specially for him. Lowered, smoothed out, and with a European-style external spare wheel, the Continental certainly turned heads when Edsel took it on his Florida vacation in 1939, So much so that it was decided to put the coach-built Ford into production, with a convertible and a coupé

ABOVE
The 1940 Lincoln Continental coupé was based on Zephyr mechanicals but with more graceful bodywork.

RIGHT
Ownership of a Continental came at a $1,000 premium, so not many were sold; but it did give Ford a flagship automobile.

offered for 1940. based on Zephyr running gear. Prices started at $2,747 (around $1,000 more than the regular Zephyr) and in the best year (1941) only 1,200 or so Continentals were sold, though they were stylish flagships for Ford. It is said that Ford never made a profit on the Continentals, but it still revived the model in 1946, along with the Zephyr. However, together with most of Detroit, these pre-war models were merely treading water in the first post-war years until the new generation was ready. In Lincoln's case this meant forsaking its trademark V12 for a 338-ci (5539-cc) V8 of 152bhp, which may not have had the glamour of the 12 but was just as powerful. Moreover, by abandoning

ABOVE LEFT
The 1956 Lincoln Continental MkII, still with the trademark external spare wheel.

ABOVE
1960 Lincoln Continental MkV.

FAR LEFT
1961 Lincoln Continental convertible.

the transverse leaf-sprung suspension for a modern independent set-up, a real, if belated, step forward had been made. The basic line-up of sedan, coupé and convertible shared styling with the equivalent Mercury, but there was also a notchback or fastback six-seater sedan unique to Lincoln.

Styling took another step closer to the standard Fords and Mercurys in 1952, though the following year there was a new ohv V8 of 205bhp. In fact, in the years that followed, Lincolns increased in weight, horsepower and cubic inches, culminating in those of 1958–60 that were 19ft (6m) long, weighed 5,450lb (2472kg) and required a 432-ci (7079-cc) V8 of 375bhp to push them along. But there was already reaction against this kind of

OPPOSITE and THIS PAGE
There was no doubt about it, a Continental was designed to make its owner feel very special indeed. This is a 1960 MkV.

excess, and Lincoln sales more than halved in the late 1950s. In response, the 1961 Lincoln was 15in (38cm) shorter, and would shed weight as the 1960s progressed, though it still used the same V8, which was enlarged to 464ci (7604cc) in 1966.

Ford had resurrected the Continental name in the mid 1950s as a separate division, though it lasted only a few years (see Continental). The badge returned as a

Lincoln model for 1968, this time as the MkIII four-seater coupé with the characteristic external spare wheel. Unlike previous Continentals, this was a big-seller, with over 20,000 sold in 1970, making up one in three Lincoln sales. The name became a fixture in the Lincoln line-up, later applied to sedans as well as coupés, which retained the numerical designation up to the MkVIII of the 1990s.

Meanwhile, all Lincolns were downsizing for the 1970s, and in a more purposeful way than ten years earlier. This time the V8s became smaller, and by 1980 the choice was between 304ci (4982cc) and 353ci (5785cc), with a V6-powered Lincoln of only 233ci (3818cc) for 1982. This smallest-ever motor only lasted a year and was back in the new 1988 Continental, which even had front-wheel-drive. The

OPPOSITE
1965 Lincoln Continental 430.

BELOW
1975 Lincoln Continental Mark IV.

standard Lincolns were now more rounded and aerodynamic, though the Town Car retained its conservative, square-rigged lines.

The three-car range from the mid-1990s (Lincoln sedan, MkVIII) coupé and Town Car) all used Ford's modular 283-ci (4637-cc) V8, the Town Car in single-ohc guise with 210bhp. The demise of the MkVIII came in 1998, but a new Lincoln was also launched that year, the LS sedan, offered with the choice of high-tech V6 or V8 power units. By then, the range had expanded with the Navigator, a loaded SUV that was really a Ford Explorer with new badges and grille.

Lincoln was one of the Premier Automotive Group brands from 1998 to 2002, but was pulled out due to Ford's new marketing strategy of separating its import brands from its domestic marques. In

OPPOSITE
1978 Lincoln Continental MkVI.

ABOVE
2003 Lincoln Town Car.

recent years the company had fallen behind Japanese, European and American competitors for a lack of new models. The company has reacted to remedy this, however, by sharing parts and platforms with other Ford divisions worldwide in an attempt to bring more new models to market faster. The result is the introduction of several new models, starting with the 2006 Mark LT pickup (later replaced by the Platinum trim version of the Ford F-150), Zephyr (upgraded and renamed Lincoln MKZ for the 2007 model year) and the MKX Crossover SUV. Subsequent model launches were the MKS sedan in 2009 and the MKT 'Touring' crossover for the 2010 model year.

OPPOSITE
2005 Lincoln Aviator. By this time, a short-based luxury pickup had joined the line-up.

ABOVE
2005 Lincoln LS sedan.

LEFT
2005 Lincoln Town Car.

A Lincoln Zephyr is still available for 2006
though not with a V12.

LEFT
2008 Lincoln Town and Country.

BELOW LEFT
2010 Lincoln MKZ.

BELOW
2010 MKX crossover.

LOCOMOBILE (1899–1929)

Locomobile was in the business of
producing cars for 30 years, making it
long-lived compared with many
contemporaries. Yet it remained a minor
player in the luxury sector, of which it was
a part, never quite achieving the success of
Cadillac or Packard.

It started life, unlikely as it may seem,
as an offshoot of the Stanley steamer. In
1899, publisher John Brisben Walker
persuaded the Stanley brothers to sell their
complete steam-car business – factory,
tooling, patents and all – in a deal
financed by businessman, Amzi Lorenzo
Barber. A new factory was built at

Bridgeport, Connecticut, to unite Stanley's
scattered production, and the new
Locomobile Company was now in
business, building a lightweight steamer to
a Stanley design.

Despite improvements to the steamer,
sales began to slide, and the company, now
run by Barber, Walker having left earlier,
looked at the possibility of gasoline cars.
Engineer Andrew Riker designed the
prototype, which first ran in 1902, going
into production late that same year. It used
a 253-ci (4146-cc) four-cylinder engine,
with water-cooling and a T-head layout.
The first gas Locomobile wasn't cheap at
$4,000, though it was billed as 'Easily the
best-built car in America'.

A cheaper two-cylinder car lasted only
a year and by 1905 Locomobile had settled
on a range of 20- to 40-hp fours. Steam
cars were still being built in small numbers,
but they were dropped altogether that year.
A Locomobile won the Vanderbilt Cup

race in 1908 and in 1911 the company
launched its first six, the Model M or 48,
its 431-ci (7063-cc) capacity mounted on a
bronze crankcase. Within three years,
Locomobile was making nothing but sixes.

Upmarket cars, like the Locomobile,
needed to look stylish as well as be well-
built, and Frenchman J. Frank de Causse
was headhunted from coach-builder
Kellner et Fils of Paris to inject some style.
His stately, imposing designs were
produced by coach-builders such as
Holbrook and Demarest mounting on
Locomobile chassis.

Locomobile, however, began to
experience uncertain times from 1919:
Hare's Motors took the company over but
soon collapsed; Locomobile escaped, still
independent, but itself was in trouble
within months. Only when William Crapo
Durant bought the company in July 1922
was Locomobile back on a firm footing.
He commissioned a new car, the Series

VIII, to run alongside the ageing 48, this 528-ci (8652-cc) six being followed in 1925 by the smaller Junior Six and Junior Eight, though the former never reached production. Later that same year, the 374-ci (6129-cc) six-cylinder 90 replaced the faithful 48, though it was still available on special order.

Within three years of the Durant takeover, Locombile had a completely renewed range and things were looking up, with 3,000 cars built in 1926. But Billy Durant had many other enterprises to look after and decided to take a back seat, with the result that Locomobile seened to lose direction. There was a new 8-70 and 8-80 in 1928, and a rebodied 8-88 in January 1929, but sales were falling fast and production ceased in March that year.

LOZIER (1905–18)

Henry Abraham Lozier did nothing by halves. He made his fortune in the bicycle and sewing-machine businesses before selling up for $4 million and putting the money into the Lozier Motor Co. to make marine engines for the wealthy. When he decided to go into the luxury car trade, Lozier refrained from jumping straight in. In 1902 he sent company engineer J.M. Whitebeck to Europe to study the best practices in modern car design, while another engineer, named John G. Perrin, did the same at home, concentrating on imported cars.

Lozier died in 1903, but his son Harry took over the business while Whitbeck and Perrin were occupied with their first car. Launched at the 1905 New York Automobile Show, it was a 30/35-hp, with four-cylinder engine, four-speed transmission and chain-drive. Unusually, the tourer bodywork was of aluminium, the $4,500 Lozier car being directly aimed upmarket.

Production was very limited, with only 56 cars sold in 1906, despite the addition of 40- and 60-hp engines plus landaulet and limousine bodies. The company's first six-cylinder car, the 50-hp Type I, was launched in 1908 when the whole range was given shaft-drive. Within two years production had broken the 500 barrier. A new factory was built in Detroit to build the less expensive Type 77, though this was not finally announced until September 1912. By now, Harry Lozier had been elbowed out by new management, which failed to impress the staff. Some of the best brains resigned, and the company went into decline; in 1914, sales were down to 250 and the company was in receivership by the end of that year. Production was briefly revived, and small numbers of the Type 84 four and Type 82 six were built until mid-1918.

MARMON (1902–33)

The young Howard C. Marmon was in a good position to build his own car. Not only had he studied engineering at the University of California, but he was also vice-president and chief engineer of the family firm, his father having been a successful maker of milling machinery. So it was quite a simple matter for Howard to

begin experimenting with motor cars in a corner of the factory, which, from 1898, was exactly what he did.

He wouldn't actually reach series production until 1909, but before then was able to produce a string of advanced prototypes, all with air-cooling, including a V6 and V8. The first car was a V-twin of 90ci (1475cc) with the advanced feature of full-pressure lubrication. The drive was by shaft, rather than chain, via a three-speed gearbox, and the entire power unit was mounted in a suspended subframe.

This was followed by an air-cooled V4 with many of the same features, and Marmon actually sold six copies of it in 1904, with a further 25 the following year. The V6 was tried and rejected before Marmon showed his air-cooled V8 at the

The four-cylinder Marmon Wasp. This is the car that won the first ever Indianapolis 500 in 1911.

New York show in 1906, but at $5,000 there were no takers.

That was the end of Howard Marmon's air-cooled era, and from 1909 more conventional water-cooled cars would see him finally enter full-time production. Now with a four-cylinder T-head engine, the Marmon 32, soon renamed the Wasp, won the inaugural Indianapolis 500 in 1911 and was destined to stay in production for seven years. The range was then expanded in both directions with the six-cylinder Model 48, starting at $5,000, launched in 1913, and the smaller four-cylinder Model 41 the following year.

Howard Marmon had always been a fan of aluminium and went further than ever to exploit its use in his next new car, the Model 34. The 34's 342-ci (5604-cc) six was made almost entirely of aluminium alloy: only the crankshaft, the valves and the cast-iron cylinder sleeves and heads were made of other materials. This and the

innovative chassis, which did away with body sills, was in a car that weighed 25 per cent less than the opposition, so its 75bhp was enough for sparkling performance. But buyers were somewhat deterred by this radical approach and for 1920 the Model 34 was substantially redesigned, the result being heavier but reliable. It remained in

production for eight years.

But financial stability still eluded Marmon's new president, George M. Williams, who initiated a change of strategy with a new line in lower-priced closed sedans. At first it seemed to work, with sales up by two-thirds in 1925, but Williams' second phase, the straight-eight Little Marmon of 1927, was not a success. Williams was convinced that salvation lay in a line of cheaper eights, and followed the Little Marmon with the Models 68 and 78, with prices starting at $1,395, while an entry-level Marmon, the Roosevelt, was launched for 1930 at less than $1,000. The cheaper eights had already helped to boost production to over 22,000 in 1929, which would turn out to be Marmon's best year.

Meanwhile, the company was not unmindful of the luxury market and unveiled the Big Eight alongside the Roosevelt, but this would mark the beginning of the end for the Marmon eights. It had the credentials of a luxury car, with a 125-bhp side-valve straight-eight of 317ci (5195cc) and a four-speed gearbox, but 1930 was not a good time to launch a car such this, and sales of all Marmon eights began to slide: all were dropped in 1932.

Undeterred, Howard Marmon persevered with the development of his most ambitious design yet, but one that would turn out to be his swansong. In the face of an increasing world Depression, he unveiled his Marmon Sixteen, powered by a high-compression V16 engine of 494ci (8095cc) and 200bhp at 3400rpm. The

Sixteen was a big car, on a 145-in (3.7-m) wheelbase with styling from the studio of industrial designer Walter Dorwin Theague. At over $5,000, the Marmon Sixteen didn't stand a chance, especially as Cadillac had been selling a V16 for over a year, so the novelty value had already been dissipated. Less than 400 Sixteens were built and the company went into receivership in May 1933. But the name lived on: Howard's brother Walter was in the truck business, and the Marmon Motor Co. continued to build trucks until 1997.

MATHESON (1903–12)
The Matheson was only made in small numbers (900 cars in nine years), though it seems that brothers Charles and Frank Matheson had no ambitions to rival Henry Ford. Their venture was partly financed by New York businessman, Henry U. Palmer, and Charles A. Singer, who undertook to buy the entire Matheson output. It was an enviable situation for any fledgling car manufacturer, though it did not save Matheson from bankruptcy in the end.

The first Matheson was a chain-driven machine powered by a 24-hp four-cylinder engine, and at $5,000 was aimed at the very top of the market. Its quality justified the price and by 1907, installed in a new factory, the company turned out 300 cars. The range was now led by a 60/65-hp four-cylinder tourer, the asking price for which was $7,500. A six-cylinder car was launched for 1909, when the Matheson also switched to shaft-drive.

But despite being early in the market with a six, the company was heading for trouble, and went into receivership in July 1910. It was soon up and running again, but the organized Matheson only lasted two years before receivership was on the horizon yet again.

MAXWELL (1904–25)
At one time Maxwell seemed set to establish itself as one of the biggest U.S. motor manufactures of all, alongside Ford, Chevrolet, Buick and the rest. In 1910 it was the third best-selling make and in 1917 over 100,000 vehicles, both cars and trucks, were sold. And yet it had had two brushes with receivership and was only saved when Walter P. Chrysler was brought in as trouble-shooter. But as part of Chrysler, and what would become Plymouth, it could be said that Maxwell really did fulfill its early promise.

The name Maxwell came about more by accident than design. Benjamin and Frank Briscoe supplied sheet metalwork to Olds, but wanted to build their own car. They knew that machinist, Jonathan Maxwell, was capable of designing one, and persuaded him into the enterprise by promising to name the car after him. Maxwell agreed, and the Briscoes were as good as their word.

The Maxwell-Briscoe Motor Co.'s first car, that appeared in 1904, was a simple little twin, with two-speed planetary transmission in two-seater tourabout or five-seater tourer bodies. Just ten of them were built in the first

year, which increased to over 800 in 1905. By 1909, when a four-cylinder car was being sold alongside the twin, production had rocketed to over 9,000, with over 20,000 sold the following year.

Sales manager C.W. Kelsey was a key part of this early success, recognizing in those early days that much of the public still had to be convinced of the automobile's toughness and reliability. So in the name of publicity, Maxwell cars took part in stunts, driving up and down the steps of public buildings and Alice Ramsey, accompanied by three friends, agreed to be the first woman to drive a Maxwell across the American continent in 1909.

But Maxwell was about to become entangled in company politics. Benjamin Briscoe had ambitions to develop an automotive giant, but merger talks with Ford, Olds and Buick came to nothing. Instead, he started the United States Motor Co. in 1910, consisting of Columbia, Brush, Stoddard-Dayton, Alden-Sampson and Maxwell. In a little over two years the combine had run out of money and only Maxwell survived, now run by ex-Ford man, Walter Flanders, and with production concentrated in Detroit.

At first, all seemed well with the reborn Maxwell. Although the twins had been dropped and the 379-ci (6211-cc) six was short-lived, the four-cylinder Maxwell continued to sell well, now in 187-ci (3064-cc) form. Seventy-five thousand were sold in 1917 when Maxwell merged with Chalmers, offering the opportunity for increased production. But the post-war boom didn't happen, and sales slumped to a little over 34,000 by 1920. This was when the banks summoned Walter Chrysler to sort things out. Chrysler soon fixed Maxwell's problems (traced to a troublesome rear axle) and did such a good job that 67,000 Maxwells were sold in 1922. He wasn't enamoured of the name, but appreciated the car and its following, and in 1925 brought Maxwell and his own Chrysler six together in the new Chrysler Corporation. Within a year, the Maxwell name had disappeared, but its legacy formed the basis of one of Detroit's Big Three.

McFARLAN (1910–28)

Built in Connersville, Indiana, the McFarlan was an attempt by the McFarlan Carriage Co., a builder of horse-drawn carriages, to diversify, and so successful was the car that within three years the carriages had been dropped altogether. In terms of limited production, this was success indeed, 3,600 cars having left the works in 19 years.

The company never made a car with fewer than six cylinders, its early models using sixes from a variety of sources, of which Buda and Continental were the best-known.

Bigger Teetor-Hartley sixes were adopted from 1916, which were needed as McFarlans grew bigger and heavier with the passing years. Typical was the 1922 TV (Twin Valve), which was based on a 140-in (3.5-m) wheelbase and even in seven-seat

tourer form weighed 5,000lb (2268kg), the closed sedan tipping the scales at even more. To propel this substantial piece of metal-work, the six-cylinder Teetor-Hartley developed 120bhp at 2400rpm, facilitated by the triple-ignition system which used three spark plugs per cylinder. Not surprisingly, the McFarlan TV wasn't cheap at up to $9,000 depending on bodywork, though that would not have fazed the typical customer, which included boxer Jack Dempsey, band leader Paul Whiteman and at least two state governors.

Unfortunately, there weren't enough governors to go around, and in its best year only 235 TVs were sold. McFarlan's attempt to offer a less expensive six, the $2,600 Wisconsin of 1924, met with little success, and was replaced two years later by the new Line-8, which cost only a little more but offered 79bhp from its Lycoming engine. McFarlan ceased production of both the Line-8 and the TV in 1928.

MERCER (1910–25)

Before the Dodge Viper, the Corvette and many other post-war American sports cars, that were either made in tiny numbers or never actually got as far as production, there was the Stutz Bearcat and the Mercer Type 35 Raceabout. But although the stark, exciting Raceabout would be the most famous Mercer of all, it made up only a tiny proportion of the firm's output.

Mercer was established in about 1910 when the wealthy Roebling family of contracting engineers decided to back another car to replace the Roebling-

Planche, which had been their first automotive project. The very first Mercer, with Beaver engine and shaft-drive, was probably part-designed by Etienne Planche, who had been part of the previous set-up and would shortly design the first Chevrolet. Planche soon left, and his replacement, Finlay Robertson Porter, designed a 302-ci (4949-cc) T-head four-cylinder engine, fitted with toy tonneau or raceabout bodies.

The Raceabout, of course, captured all the attention. Its appearance confirmed that it was a racer for the road, with skimpy bodywork, two seats and zero weather protection. A little monocle screen for the driver was optional, but as observed by historian, Nick Georgano, a good pair of goggles would probably have given more protection. The lightweight Raceabout could top 75mph (121km/h), and many were raced successfully: driven to the circuit in the days before regulations had been imposed, they were raced and driven home again. There were, of course, less glamourous Type 35s than the Raceabout, including a taxicab, tourer and runabout, all with the luxuries of windshield, doors and folding top.

Washington A. Roebling, the driving force behind the Raceabout, was lost on the *Titanic* in April 1912. By 1914, the other Roeblings were convinced the Type 35 needed replacing, but were unable to convince Finlay Porter, who left the company. His replacement, Erik H. Delling. designed a new L-head four of 297ci (4867cc) which, despite a long stroke, produced 72bhp, significantly more than the old T-head. The 22/70 was the new car to go with it, and once again came in a variety of forms, including a raceabout, though now with such refinements as a windshield and electric start.

Mercer was sold to Emlen Hare in 1918, after involved members of the Roebling family had died. Hare had unrealistic expectations as far as Mercer production was concerned, aiming at 50,000 a year when the total had been less than 900 in 1919, and quickly sold the company to the Kuser family. The cars continued, though the Raceabout became further removed from the raw original and Mercer's own four-cylinder engine gave way to a bought-in six. By now the company was struggling, and fewer than 300 cars were built in 1925, the final year.

Ex-Chevrolet manager, Harry M. Wahl, bought the name, and got as far as showing two new Continental-powered Mercers in New York in 1930, which came to nothing.

MERCURY (1938–)

Lincoln, Plymouth, Buick and Cadillac are all parts of giant corporations as divisions with their own identity and following. The same cannot be said of Mercury, Ford's upper-middle marque designed to fill the gap between plain Ford and the aristocratic, high-priced Lincolns.

Although there were times when Mercury had something of an upmarket identity, closer to that of Lincoln than Ford, for most of the marque's existence it

has been regarded as little more than a fancy Ford. It may have more equipment, a different badge and grille, but underneath a Mercury is a Ford, unlike a top-spec Buick, which isn't seen as a superior Chevrolet. Since the mid-1970s, that perception has become firmly entrenched as Mercury lost its own bodyshells and become a simple case of rebadging.

Mercury, launched in 1938, was the project of Edsel Ford. He understood, far more so than his father, Henry, that people didn't only buy cars because they were cheap. Since the 1920s, American buyers had also been looking for status, prestige

and extra equipment in their automobiles, if only to differentiate them from the Ford or Chevy standing in their neighbour's suburban driveway. With Lincoln, Edsel had done a good job in establishing an upscale Ford division, especially with the relatively affordable Zephyr V12 launched in 1935. The trouble was, there was still a large price gap between the Zephyr and the Ford V8; the income of plenty of people had outgrown their flathead Ford, but it still didn't run to a Zephyr and they bought a Buick instead. Edsel's plan was to keep them in the Ford corporate fold with a new mid-range division. There were

A 1938 Mercury Eight. This was intended for those who had outgrown their flathead Ford but couldn't yet afford a Lincoln.

OPPOSITE and LEFT
A 1940 Mercury. Power still came from the familiar Ford flathead V8, albeit in uprated 95-bhp form. The combination of unique styling and proven mechanicals proved highly successful.

over 100 suggestions for the all-important name, which had to be upmarket but not too pompous or stodgy. Edsel himself chose the name, Mercury. A group of engineers and stylists got to work, led by Bob Gregorie who had been behind the 1930s Lincolns. When it was launched in late 1938, the new Mercury certainly looked the part. Although there were Ford overtones, its front-end was more like a Zephyr, and all its body panels were unique. Underneath, there were plenty of Ford components, but the Mercury had an

extra 4in (10cm) in the wheelbase, all of it given to the passengers, while the familiar flathead V8 was bored out from 222ci (3638cc) to 240ci (3933cc), which boosted power from 85 to 95bhp. Available as two- or four-door sedan, as a coupé or convertible, the Mercury cost $167 more than the equivalent Ford in four-door sedan form but $40 less than the cheapest four-door Buick.

The work of Edsel and his new division seemed vindicated when over 70,000 cars were sold in the first year, and

for 1941 a four-door convertible was added to the line, along with a longer wheelbase and new styling. Engine power was up to l00bhp for the final pre-war year (1942) and Liquimatic auto transmission was also offered. Mercury returned in 1946 with the same formula and over 86,000 cars were sold that year, with marginally fewer in 1947.

Post-War Optimism
The 1948 Mercury didn't get much of a look-in as the '49 was unveiled in the April

This was the first genuinely new post-war Mercury, with all-new bodywork and independent front suspension. It was wildly successful.

of 1948. Along with the mainstream Fords, it was completely restyled and re-engineered, transformed overnight from a clear pre-war leftover to a car for the new era. It now had more in common with Lincoln than Ford, using some Lincoln panels and reflecting the fact that a separate Lincoln-Mercury division had

been established in 1947. With no new overhead-valve V8 the old flathead was coaxed up to 110bhp, due to a capacity increase to 255ci (4179cc). Moreover, the new-era Mercurys were given two much-needed updates along with the Fords, including independent front suspension and a hypoid rear axle.

The public loved the new-look Mercury, thought by some to be one of the best-looking Detroit cars of its time. Over 300,000 were sold in the 1949 model year extending over 17 months, but it confirmed that Mercury was a potential good-seller in its own right. A two-speed Merc-O-Matic appeared for 1951, the

unsuccessful Liquimatic having been abandoned after the war, and there was a complete restyle for 1952. Sharing features with Lincoln once again, the Mercury had frenched headlights, a one-piece curved windshield and wraparound rear window. Again, the ohv V8 wasn't in place, though it had been planned for this car, and the 255 flathead soldiered on, though with higher compression to produce 125bhp. This didn't prevent Ford from selling over 150,000 1952 Mercurys, however, and the Lincoln-Mercury division now had four new assembly plants to keep up with demand.

The next big change came for 1954 when the new V8 finally arrived. Shorter-stroked and harder-revving than the old side-valve, it offered considerably more

The year 1953 saw the end of the flathead V8, while the Mercury offered a one-piece curved windshield and wraparound rear window.

power (161bhp at 4400rpm) from virtually the same capacity. Having got wind of the new Chevy V8 for 1955, Ford quickly beefed up its own that year, taking it up to 292ci (4785cc) and 188bhp, or 198bhp with the 8.5:1 compression. A new feature for 1954 had been the Sun Valley option, replacing the front half of the steel roof with tinted plexiglas, which was a nice idea but turned the car into a greenhouse on a hot day and was soon dropped.

As the 1950s progressed, the Mercury became larger, with more girth and chrome, as was the case with virtually every other Detroit car. In 1957, the line-up comprised the Monterey and Montclair lines, both offered as sedan, coupé or convertible, with a base 312-ci (5113-cc) V8. New for that year was the 368-ci

OPPOSITE and LEFT ABOVE & BELOW
The 1956 Mercury Montclair, now with Ford's overhead-valve V8 providing power to match its looks. The arrival of Chevrolet's small-block V8 prompted Ford to offer extra power in 1955 and in the following two years.

ABOVE
The 1957 Mercury Monterey, available as a sedan, coupé or convertible.

(6030-cc) V8 with 290bhp, and the gadget-laden Turnpike Cruiser with retractable rear window, air ducts on top of the windshield, and the Seat-O-Matic power-operated seat. But the market was changing, and though Mercury broke the 300,000 barrier again in 1955, sales were fewer than half they had been in 1958.

The answer was to go compact, and a few months after the Ford Falcon was announced late in 1959, the Mercury equivalent followed. Although it was a standard Falcon under the skin, with the same 145-ci (2376-cc) six, it was styled to resemble the bigger Mercurys, offering an extra 5in (13cm) of wheelbase in sedan and station-wagon form. It did much to help Mercury sales recover in 1960, adding over 116,000 cars to the total sold. Like the

OPPOSITE and LEFT
Mercury's Mustang. The Cougar was based closely on Ford's pony car but with its own external panels and a more luxurious interior.

BELOW LEFT
1964 Comet. This was Mercury's version of the compact Ford Falcon, which, though it had a longer wheelbase, was mechanically similar.

Falcon, the Comet offered powered-up V8 versions within a few years, and the sporty S-22 and Cyclone fastback with bucket seats gave Mercury dealers something to sell against the Corvair Monza. But the Comet hinted at the way things were going in 1966, dropping its own bodyshell to share that of the Ford Fairlane and losing its compact size as well as some of its Mercury identity.

Meanwhile, the full-sized Monterey and Montclair endured through the 1960s, joined by the top-line Park Lane for 1964, the latter being no larger than the others, with the same engine options but a more luxurious interior. The latest big-block V8 of 390ci (6391cc) was now standard on

OPPOSITE and FAR ABOVE & BELOW
A Comet convertible, shown here in base six-cylinder form, though it followed the Falcon by offering a V8 option later on.

BELOW
The 1964 Marauder, one of Mercury's full-sized sedans.

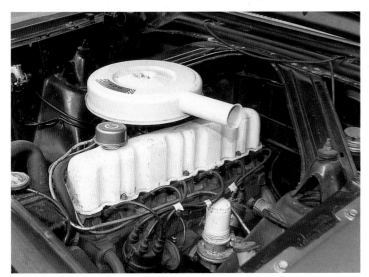

293

A 1967 Cougar. The Cougar never sold as strongly as the Mustang, but Mercury's pony car was popular all the same. After a break in the early 1970s, it would return in 1979 as the Capri.

both the Monterey and Park Lane, in 250- and 300-bhp forms respectively. The Park Lane was replaced by the Marquis in 1969.

A Luxury Mustang?
It took Mercury three years to acquire its own pony car, but when the Cougar for 1967 did arrive, it was more than a simple case of rebadging based on the now-familiar stretched Mustang platform, albeit with an extra 3in (8cm) in the wheelbase.

Softer and with more luxury trim than the original pony car, the Cougar could also be had with all the same performance options, including the 428-ci (7014-cc) V8. The Eliminator, from 1969, was the sportiest Cougar, offered with the Boss 302 or 351 V8s as well as the big-block 428. This was true muscle-car material, but the Eliminator had come late to the scene and was dropped after a couple of years, the highly-tuned 400-hp V8 unable to make it

through the new emissions regulations. More relevant to more Cougar buyers was the XR-7, which added a leather interior and mock-walnut dashboard, outselling the Eliminator by nearly ten to one in 1970.

But the distinctive Cougar didn't last much longer. The Mustang-based car was dropped in 1974 in favour of a coupé version of the Montego sedan, and by 1977 the name was applied to the whole range of intermediate Mercurys and it was a luxury muscle car no more. As the 1970s progressed there were more signs that Mercury would be used for badge engineering. For 1971 the Comet name returned as Mercury's version of the Ford Maverick, though there was little difference visually, one writer describing it as 'a Maverick with make-up'. The engine options, two sixes and a V8, were also the same. It was joined by the Monarch in 1975, a 'precision-sized luxury car', according to Ford, about the same size as the Comet but with better trim. This was really a U.S. Ford Granada with Mercury badges and trim. Similarly, the Mercury Bobcat was an upgraded Ford Pinto in hatchback or station-wagon form.

Mercury's intermediate car was still the Montego, which lasted until 1977 in sedan, coupé and station-wagon forms, with engines extending to the 428-ci V8. The following year, the Maverick-based Comet was replaced by the Fairmont-based Zephyr with four-, six-cylinder or V8 options. Weighing 300lb (136kg) less than the car it superseded, this latest Zephyr was a clear indication of the trend towards

Where else but Pikes Peak! Parnelli Jones power-slides a Marauder up the famous tree-lined turns.

This coupé from 1972 tends towards a mild muscle car, but even the hottest Mercurys were more restrained than their Ford counterparts.

downsizing that was affecting Mercury as much as every other U.S. car-maker. The base engine was a 140-ci (2294-cc) four mated to a four-speed gearbox.

The same fate befell the full-sized Marquis for 1979. It lost 800lb (363kg) in weight and 17in (43cm) of length, with engine choices restricted to 302ci (4949cc) or 35lci (5752cc): the big 400 and 460 V8s had gone. Another new-era Mercury that year was the Capri. It was a slightly different version of the new aerodynamic

FAR LEFT
More recently, Mercurys have lost their distinctive styling. This is a 1995 Mystique LS.

BELOW LEFT
1998 Mercury Tracer Trio.

BELOW
1998 Mercury Villager. This is a rebadged Nissan Quest.

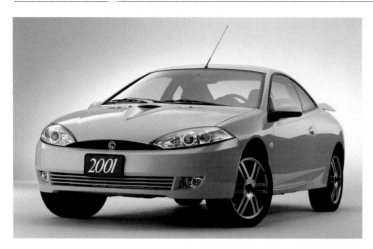

OPPOSITE
2004 Mercury Marauder.

ABOVE LEFT
2001 Cougar. This returned in 1999 with front-wheel-drive.

ABOVE
2003 Grand Marquis, a traditional Mercury sedan.

LEFT
2004 Monterey people carrier.

and lightweight Mustang launched that year, coming with exactly the same four-cylinder V6 or V8 options. The Mercury Capri was quite a good-seller, though it was dropped in 1986. But the four-cylinder Capri and Zephyr weren't the smallest Mercurys by any means, for 1981 saw the arrival of the Lynx, based on the Ford's front-drive Escort world car. It replaced the now slow-selling Bobcat, with a base engine of 98ci (1606cc), and for three years was joined by the LN7 coupé version, though it was not a great success.

Having an entirely Ford-based range meant the Mercury line-up was wider than ever, from the Escort-based Lynx to the full-sized (though downsized) Grand

Marquis. The Lynx would last through to 1987 in three-door and five-door hatchback forms, while the LN7 coupé was no more, but the hatchback could be had in sporty XR3 form. Base engine was now a 113-ci (1852-cc) gasoline with a 121-ci (1983-cc) diesel option.

Underlining the trend towards front-wheel-drive, the rear-drive Zephyr was replaced by the front-drive Topaz (really the Ford Tempo) for 1984. Gone were the straight-six and V8 options and Topaz buyers could choose between four-cylinder gasoline or diesel. Similarly, for 1986, the rear-drive Marquis gave way to the front-drive Sable, a Ford Taurus, appropriately rebadged, with four-cylinder or V6 engines in sedan or station-wagon forms. Meanwhile, the Cougar was back as a proper coupé; it stayed with rear-wheel-drive by cloning the Ford Thunderbird, which had happened since 1983 in both V6 and V8 forms. The Cougar would run through to 1997, miss a year, then return for 1999 as a front-drive four-seater coupé based on the Mystique. The latter was launched in 1998 as Mercury's version of the Ford Contour or European Mondeo, though it only lasted until 2000.

The Grand Marquis was still rear-wheel-drive, based on the Ford LTD and powered by the modular 281-ci (4605-cc)

V8. Other, less traditional Mercurys of the 1990s and beyond were the Tracer hatchback (a Mazda 323), the Merkur XR4Ti and Scorpio from Germany, together with the Villager MPV (Nissan Quest). It's not clear what Edsel Ford would have made of all this, but it looks as though Mercury will be part of the Ford line-up for some time to come.

Last Revival

During the mid-2000s, after relative stagnation, the Mercury range was targeted for major updates to attract new (primarily, younger) buyers. The full-size 2004 Montego, a clone of the Ford Five Hundred, was introduced as the (intended) replacement for the Grand Marquis while

ABOVE
Inevitably, Mercury had to have its own SUV. This is a 2006 Mariner Hybrid.

FAR RIGHT
But one could still have a conventional three-box sedan, like this 2005 Monterey.

the mid-size 2005 Milan, a clone of the Ford Fusion and Lincoln MKZ would become the Sable replacement. The 2003 Monterey and 2005 Mariner were both introduced as badge-engineered Fords as well. However, the Grand Marquis remained in production; in contrast to the Dodge Charger selling nearly as well as its

Chrysler 300 counterpart, the Montego sold only a fraction in comparison with its Ford Five Hundred counterpart and was also outsold by the Grand Marquis as well. Unlike Ford's 'F' model naming scheme, reaction to Mercury's 'M' naming scheme was less extreme, as it had been in use since the 1950s.

Traditionally, Mercury was given a counterpart to most Ford platforms. During the 2000s, Ford focused on making its cars more luxurious, meaning Mercurys were less distinctive from other Ford nameplates. The exception was the Grand Marquis, which had all but replaced the civilian Crown Victoria; the latter was

discontinued from retail sale after 2007. While Mercury had reached the minivan and SUV segments before a number of other foreign or domestic brands, by the time Mercury received a more competitive entry (the Monterey, its version of the Ford Freestar), the minivan segment was in decline. The Mariner crossover SUV debuted in 2005, four years after its Ford Escape twin. Mercury also had no version of the Ford Focus or the Ford Edge.

Discontinuation

On 2 June 2010, Ford officially announced the closure of the Mercury line by the end of the year. In terms of sales, Mercury represented only 1% of North America's automobile market, while Ford has a 16% share. The Ford Motor Company has stated that additional Lincoln models will be introduced to help replace any shortfall from the discontinued Mercury brand. At the time of the announcement of Mercury's closure, Mercury was selling fewer than 90,000 units a year, which is less than both Plymouth and Oldsmobile right before they were phased out.

Many industry observers questioned whether Mercury would survive in the long term, since Ford insisted that there was no intention of letting the brand die until recently. The Mercury Mountaineer was discontinued in the 2010 model year, with the remaining Mercurys following suit after the 2011 model year.

ABOVE LEFT
2008 Mercury Sable.

ABOVE
2007 Mercury Mariner.

LEFT
2006 Mercury Montego.

MILBURN (1914–23)

Milburn electric cars were used by President Wilson's secret service, perhaps because of their silent approach. The Milburn Wagon Co. had been attracted to car manufacture when the Ohio Electric Car Co. leased to it part of its factory. Milburn's own electric car was launched late in 1914 as a coupé, roadster and delivery van. As with other later electric cars, Milburn tried to mimic gasoline cars as the taste for electrics diminished, giving the Model 36L limousine a gasoline-like hood in 1919.

A serious fire almost destroyed the company later that year, and by the time things had settled down, most of Milburn's business was subcontracted, building bodies for Oldsmobile. General Motors bought the factory in 1923, which was the end of Milburn's electric cars.

MITCHELL (1903–23)

Mitchell was another maker of horse-drawn wagons which diversified into car production, though in this case via bicycles and a prototype motorcycle. The first Mitchell car of 1903 was a small, single-cylinder machine of 4hp, with two seats and chain-drive. Bit it was shortlived, superseded by a 7-hp version the following year, along with a 16-hp four – a five-seater tourer with a three-speed gearbox replacing the previous epicyclical type.

Only 82 cars were built in 1904 but there were nearly 1,400 by 1907, the company having standardized water-cooling and shaft-drive. The cars had also grown,

with 20-, 24-/30- and 35-hp models offered that year as tourers or runabouts. These all had four cylinders, but Mitchell's first six, developed from the fours, was launched in 1910 and had 428ci (7014cc). A new range of T-head fours and sixes was announced for 1913, and Mitchell seemed to be riding high as the biggest car manufacturer in Wisconsin. Sales plunged to 2,253 in 1914, only to make a spectacular recovery after the company was reorganized, with sales hitting nearly 11,000 in 1917, and this despite an unsuccessful foray into V8s which lasted only a year.

But in spite of the good sales and the wide range of bodies on conventional six-cylinder cars on offer, Mitchell was without the resources to compete with bigger rivals: the end came when Nash took over its factory in 1923, Mitchell having built only 713 cars that year.

MOHS (1967–78)

Mohs had been successful building seaplanes, to which it added an eccentric sideline in four-wheeled flights of fancy. The Safarikar was an odd-looking convertible with sliding doors and padded bodywork, and a few of these were sold. But that looked positively conventional when compared with the clownish Ostentatienne Opera sedan. Based on an International Harvester truck chassis, it was without conventional doors, the passenger entering through a large single door at the back. Nitrogen-filled tyres, velvet trim, and a price of $25,000 were its other attributes. It is believed that only one was built.

MUNTZ (1950–54)

The Muntz Jet was a continuation of the Kurtis sports car though it was more successful in terms of numbers. Earl 'Madman' Muntz bought the whole project from Frank Kurtis in 1950, and restarted production in Illinois after redesigning the car to accommodate four seats and a Cadillac V8, though a Lincoln V8 was fitted later. In 1951 Muntz ditched the aluminium panels for steel, though never offered a soft-top, only a removable hardtop. The Muntz Jet cost $5,500, ready to roll, so it was really too expensive to have more than rarity appeal, and even at that price Muntz lost money on every car. He ended the project in 1954, having built less than 400.

MURRAY (1916–31)

The Murray Eight started well. Launched at the New York Show in December 1916 and powered by a Herschell-Spillman V8, it attracted much attention, especially the following year when a whole range of body styles (roadster, town car, sedan and coupé) were made available, starting at $2,500. But the publicity failed to generate many sales and Murray went into receivership after fewer than 200 cars had been built.

John J. McCarthy bought the company and moved it to Boston, Massachusetts, but it is not clear how many cars he actually built, and whether his promotion of the car was based on fact or fantasy. The indications are that he built cars on an ad hoc basis, with specification and engine type varying according to what was to hand. McCarthy wasn't shy of promoting the car. In 1929 he distributed a list of famous Murray customers in an attempt to attract new finance, but the list turned out to be ten years old. He continued to promote the car until 1931, though whether any Murrays were actually built after 1928 is not known.

NASH (1917–57)

Many American independents had roller-coaster careers, with wildly fluctuating profits and sales, but not Nash. The Nash Motor Corporation was fairly consistent throughout the 1920s and '30s, though it was never a match for the Detroit Big Three: it even continued to make money in the depths the Depression!

It owed this stability largely to its founder, Charles W. Nash, whose own early life had been anything but. Born in 1864, he was effectively orphaned at the age of six when his parents split up, neither caring to look after him. Young Charles was palmed off on a local farmer, who forced him to work for up to 20 hours a day. But he escaped at the age of 12, worked for another farmer, then a carpenter, all the while saving hard. By the time he was 18, Charles owned his own hay-baling machine, which he hired to farmers and later, while working as a clerk, he met and duly impressed William Crapo Durant.

Starting in Durant's blacksmith's shop, he rose rapidly through the ranks, and by his early 30s was vice-president of the Durant Dort Co. In 1910, Durant was ousted from his recently formed General

Motors by the banks, who asked Nash to take his place as manager. He left General Motors in 1916, and together with banker, James Storrow, bought the Jeffrey Motor Co. Within a year, the six-cylinder Jeffrey was renamed the Nash and Charlie had settled on the company that would occupy the rest of his working life.

The first proper Nash car was a conventional six-cylinder machine of 250ci (4097cc), offered in five body styles and reasonably priced at $1,295 for the tourer. Over 10,000 were built in the first year. The company grew fast, selling over 35,000 cars in 1920, and was able to take control of its body supplier, the Seaman Body Co. The range was expanded in both directions, with a four-cylinder version of the existing six, the Model 41, and the luxury Lafayette, though the latter only lasted a few years, with fewer than 2,000 built.

With sales exceeding 85,000 in 1925, Nash was determined to expand still further by making a cheaper car, and launched the Ajax that same year. Powered by a 171-ci (2802-cc) side-valve six, the Ajax started at $865, with a closed sedan at $995. Over 22,000 were sold in the first year, when it was renamed the Nash Light Six and continued as the company's cheapest car. It was joined by the 209-ci (3425-cc) Special Six and 285-ci (4670-cc) Advanced Six, while sales continued to climb steadily, exceeding 138,000 in 1928 when twin ignition (two spark plugs per cylinder) was introduced.

Like several American manufacturers, Nash managed to launch a big car in the

aftermath of the Wall Street crash, but the 100-bhp straight-eight was reasonably priced, starting at $1,625; thanks to Charlie Nash's careful management, the company managed to make a profit in 1932 (the only manufacturer to do so, apart from General Motors), despite sales slumping to only 20,000. The company responded with the cheaper Lafayette for 1934, a 75-bhp side-valve six, with eight body styles from $585 to $715. Meanwhile, the bigger Nashes were restyled by Russian émigré Count Alexis de Sakhnoffsky, with new or updated models including the 400, Ambassador Six and Ambassador Eight.

Airflytes & Ramblers

Charlie Nash retired in 1936, his place taken by George Mason, who presided over a continued sales recovery through the late 1930s (almost 86,000 by 1938), helped by innovations such as reclining front seats, restyling with faired-in headlights (1939) and independent front suspension (1940), while the 600 was a new model for 1941. Nash was a strong exporter, with around 10 per cent of its output going abroad, the pre-war Ambassador being available with a six-cylinder Perkins diesel engine in the U.K.

Nash got off to a good start immediately after the Second World War, so much so that it outsold many traditional rivals to command third place in the domestic pecking order. As the big guns of Detroit cranked their lines back up to full speed, however, Nash reverted to its customary place just outside the top ten and was placed 11th in 1947. But the company was hoping for great things from its new Airflyte body for 1949, a startling design nicknamed 'the bathtub' for its rounded, jelly-mould shape. Offered as the 600 and Ambassador, the new car was the most aerodynamic of its day, yet was fairly conventional beneath the skin, with 173-ci (2835-cc) or 236-ci (3867-cc) sixes. That year, Nash sold a record 142,592 cars.

The Rambler, the first post-war compact, was unveiled the following year, with a wheelbase of 100in (2.5m) but sharing the full-sized 600's 173-ci six. The initial convertible was soon joined by a station wagon and country club coupé, and buyers seemed to like the new approach to American compact motoring: Nash enjoyed another record-breaking year in 1950, with the Rambler contributing 20,000 sales. Nash also unveiled America's first domestic subcompact that year, a little two-seater that was a miniaturized version of the big cars. The prototype used a Fiat 500 engine, but when the little Nash Metropolitan finally entered production in 1954, it came with an Austin four-cylinder unit of 74ci (1213cc) with 9lci (1491cc) later on. In fact, the entire car had been built at Austin's factory in Birmingham, England, 97,000 of which were sold over seven years.

Cars like this emphasized George Mason's determination to offer a different challenge to the Big Three rather than try to meet them head-on. Another example was the Nash-Healey, an Anglo-American hybrid sports car using Healey

body/chassis and Nash engine and transmission. Over 500 were built in four years. The baby Nashes, by contrast, were successful, but George Mason realized the company could not survive on its own, and negotiated a merger with Hudson in 1954 to form American Motors. He died shortly afterwards and was replaced by George Romney.

By the mid-1950s Nash badly needed a V8, the old straight-eight having failed to survive the war, so it acquired a 322-ci (5255-cc) unit from Packard before its own 250-ci (4097-cc) V8 was launched the following year. For 1956, the Rambler was restyled and extended, now with a longer wheelbase and wider choice of engines: ohv 197-ci (3228-cc) six and the 250-ci V8, plus a new 327-ci (5358-cc) version. The following model year was the final one for the Nash badge, as the Rambler name was used on all AMC cars. Thanks to consistent management and some innovative cars, Nash had survived some hard times, but it wasn't to be a part of AMC's future.

NATIONAL (1900–24)
National built only electric cars in its first three years, though the company went on to produce its own gasoline engines, and came very early to the American market with both a straight-six and a V12. The range of electrics included a lightweight runabout, named the Electromobile, and the far more exclusive-sounding Stanhope. Prices went from $900 to $1,750, but the company could see that the future of the automobile lay in gasoline. (Arthur C.

Newby, in particular, who would be part-owner of the Indianapolis Speedway, went a long way to promote gas.)

The result was an 8-hp twin-cylinder car and a 16-hp four in 1903, though National continued to build electrics, and would do so for another three years. These were followed, in 1905, by a bigger 35/40-hp four and 50/60-hp six. At this point, National bought its engines from outside suppliers, but in 1907 the company began to make its own power units, which by the following year included fours of 40 and 50hp and a 50- or 75-hp six. Nationals were raced successfully, one actually winning the 1912 Indianapolis 500, while sales crept to a peak of over 1,800 in 1915.

The company reverted to a bought-in Continental engine for its new, cheaper six of 1916, but also built its own V12 to power the new Highway Twelve. Incredibly, this was actually cheaper than the six it replaced and at $1,990 for the tourer, only $300 more than that new 'cheaper' six. But this was the zenith of National design, for it was taken over that same year and designed nothing more. The Twelve lasted for three years, and the six-cylinder National Sextet was offered from 1920–22. Under new ownership again in 1922, the National badge was applied to other cars, such as the Dixie Flyer, but sales dwindled and 1924 was the marque's final year.

OAKLAND (1907–31)
Had things been different, General Motors' mid-range division for the 21st

both smaller and larger versions, though for 1915 the range was simplified to a Light Four and Light Six.

In 1916 Oakland was quick to follow Cadillac into the V8 market with a 348-ci (5703-cc) unit that offered 71bhp, though it only lasted a couple of years. Also in 1916 came a more sober 178-ci (2917-cc) six-cylinder car, aptly named 'the Sensible Six'. In fact, Oakland liked to imbue its cars with rationality rather than glamour: one advertising slogan described it as 'the car with a conscience'. Whatever its name, the little six was a survivor, and was part of the Oakland range for several years; in fact it was the sole model until 1923, in spite of which, over 50,000 were sold in 1919, which made it Oakland's best year yet. Although it soon switched from side-valves to ohv, gaining 6bhp in the process, the six later reverted to side-valve, which made it cheaper to produce. Perhaps the marque was already under pressure from the management of General Motors to cut costs.

Nineteen-twenty-four was a significant year, not only due to the adoption of four-wheel brakes, but also because Oaklands were now painted in Duco nitro-cellulose, which cut drying time by nearly two-thirds and had a dramatic effect on production rates. But despite this, and selling over 37,000 Oaklands that year, Alfred P. Sloan thought the cars weren't selling fast enough, and that their price range didn't fit the General Motors family. It also had idle production capacity. So he brought in a new manager, whose first job was to

Oakland could have been General Motors' mid-range marque had the popularity of Pontiac not consigned the name to history.

century would not have been Pontiac but Oakland. In 1924, General Motors president, Alfred P. Sloan, was keen to fill the gap between Chevrolet and Oldsmobile, and Oakland didn't fit the bill. Starting at nearly $1,000, its cars were far too expensive and also clashed with those of Olds. A successful new range of sixes was launched to remedy this, but Sloan badged them Pontiacs instead. The new name eclipsed the old, and in less than a decade the Oakland name had gone. This is ironic, for when Oakland was first launched in 1907, the directors' first choice had been Pontiac, but the name had already been used by another car-maker.

The first Oakland was a 20-hp twin-cylinder machine with planetary transmission and shaft-drive, designed by

Alanson P. Brush, who had been instrumental in setting up Cadillac. Unusually for a small twin, the Oakland came in a choice of body styles (tourer, landaulet, two-seater and taxicab) but was eclipsed in 1909 by a new four-cylinder car of 320ci (5244CC) and 40hp.

That same year, Oakland was taken over by William Crapo Durant's General Motors, and in 1910 added a 30-hp four, which was most successful, boosting production to over 4,000 in its first year. By 1912, with a three-car range and sales of over 5,800, Oakland was one of the top-ten American manufacturers, building on its success with its first six in 1913. Available with full electric lighting, starting and ignition, the new car's engine came from Northway and was soon joined by

The Oldsmobile Pirate, a racing car from 1903, when Olds was already the largest car manufacturer in the world.

launch a new line of lower-cost cars, called Pontiacs, to use this capacity and fill the gap between Chevrolet and Olds.

Meanwhile, the Oakland six continued, though with capacity boosted to 186ci (3048cc) in 1925 and a new 213-ci (3490-cc) variant powered the All-American Six to distinguish it from the smaller Pontiacs. In Oakland terms, the All-American was a roaring success, selling over 60,000 in the 12 months from June 1927. The trouble was that over twice as many people bought Pontiacs, and once it had overtaken its junior partner, Oakland's days were surely numbered.

The range was expanded in 1930, with an 85-bhp 252-ci (4129-cc) V8 offered in the All-American chassis. But it was to no avail, for the All-American's reign of popularity was fading fast and fewer than 25,000 of these V8s were sold in its first year. The plain fact was that Oakland now shared many Pontiac parts, and all that really distinguished it was a slightly longer wheelbase and a synchromesh gearbox – and, of course, a higher price. Fewer than 13,000 were sold in 1931, so maybe it came as no surprise when the V8 was rebadged Pontiac from January 1932. Thus Oakland survived, but as Pontiac.

OLDSMOBILE (1897–2004)

Oldsmobile was a true pioneer of the American motor industry. Ransom Eli Olds built a one-off three-wheeled steam car as early as 1886, and by 1897 was building gasoline-engined cars for sale to the public. In 1903, when Henry Ford was finally starting series production, Oldsmobile was churning out 4,000 Curved Dash machines. At that time, it was the largest car-maker in the world, yet only a few short years later, sales had slumped, and had Olds not been taken over by General Motors, it might even have gone bust and become a mere

FAR LEFT
The popular Curved Dash, the best-selling car on the planet in 1903.

LEFT
1932 Patrician sedan.

BELOW LEFT
An F-series six-cylinder Olds with sports coupé body.

footnote in the history books today. As it is, the division has been in the car business for well over 100 years and is still producing cars today.

Unlike Henry Ford, Ransom Olds was born into an engineering family, going to work in his father's machine shop in 1883. P.F. Olds & Son built steam engines, which is how Ransom's first steam car came about. But gasoline power was the future and Ransom, together with Madison F. Bates, were awarded a number of patents for their internal combustion engine in 1895. By the summer of the following year, the engine had been installed in a four-wheel carriage, going into production the following year, with Ransom firmly in control of the Olds company. The first production cars were four-seaters of 5hp, able to rattle along at up to 18mph (29km/h).

Olds lacked the capital to take the company forward on his own, so a new one was formed, bankrolled by businessman Samuel L. Smith, who had made his fortune in mining. At first, the Olds Motor Works operated in Detroit, where land and labour were more plentiful, but the new factory burned down and the company returned to small-town Lansing, Michigan, where it had begun life.

With a new, much larger factory, Sam Smith as president, and Ransom his deputy, Olds could finally proceed with the business of building cars. These, of course, were the famous Curved Dash models, so-named for the graceful shape of the dashboards. The Curved Dash had a 96-ci (1573-cc) single-cylinder engine beneath the seat, driving through an epicyclical transmission. Final drive was by chain, and although the basic car was a little bare (fenders cost $10 extra) it was offered at $650.

It has been argued that although the first Olds were not made on a moving, Ford-style production line, they were nevertheless mass-produced, and the figures appear to confirm this. In 1901, 425 Curved Dashes left the factory, rocketing to over 2,000 the following year and doubling the year after. By 1905, 6,500 Oldsmobiles had been built, the car was being exported to Europe and Russia, and despite its lightweight looks it was tough enough to undergo epic journeys on the rough roads

RIGHT
The eight-cylinder Oldsmobile was offered for only $50 more than the equivalent straight-six.

CENTRE RIGHT
The 1937 Business Coupé had the automatic transmission that Olds did much to promote.

BELOW RIGHT
Ready for the big trip? A 1940 'woody' station wagon.

of the day the first Olds in New York was actually driven there, covering the 632 miles (1017km) in seven days.

So far so good, but the Curved Dash was becoming rapidly outdated as motor technology progressed. The Smith family, which owned most of the company, wanted to build bigger, more modern cars, but Ransom Olds disagreed and left in 1904. He went on to form Reo, the name being his initials, which for a few years actually outsold Olds cars.

Now the Smiths were free to expand, though things didn't go according to plan. There were a couple of variations on the Curved Dash before it was dropped in 1906, replaced by a 20-hp twin, then joined the following year by a conventional 28-hp four with front-mounted engine. But the new cars were facing stiff competition, the four being twice the price of a Model T, though it did offer more power. As a result, Olds sales slumped to only 1,200 cars in 1907. The end came the following year when the new six-cylinder Model Z was a flop.

Saved by Durant

A saviour arrived in the form of William C. Durant, already involved with Buick, who bought Oldsmobile in what would prove be the first building block of General Motors in 1908. The Olds line quickly benefited, its new four-cylinder Model 20 for 1909 being an enlarged Buick that sold for only $1,250. Sales began to pick up. Durant did not shy from big cars, and for 1910 unveiled the 507-ci (8308-cc)

six-cylinder Limited, with 42-in (107-cm) wheels and a price tag of up to $5,800. This increased to $7,000 in 1911, when engine size was upped to a truck-like 710ci (11635cc). In fact. Olds seemed to have a line in 'big bangers'; the four-cylinder cars sold alongside the Limited and included the 473-ci (7751-cc) Autocrat.

The installation of Charles W. Nash as manager of Olds saw a return to the small-car philosophy, and the Model 42, or Baby Olds, was launched in 1914. This 193-ci (3163-cc) four was a great success, boosting overall sales to over 7,000 in 1915 and over 10,000 the following year. It was soon complemented by the Model 44 V8,

FAR LEFT
The 1952 Oldsmobile four-door coupé. By now, the entire range was powered by V8s.

BELOW LEFT
The 1948 Olds 88 the year before the Rocket V8 arrived to involve Olds in Detroit's horsepower war.

OPPOSITE and LEFT
Relatively restrained by the standards of the
time, the 1958 Oldsmobile Dynamic was the
base model that was topped by the Super 88
and the 99.

whose Northway-built motor measured 247ci (4048cc) and produced 40bhp. This soon outsold even the Baby Olds and in 1917 over 22,000 cars left the works, with more than 39,000 two years later. Nineteen-twenty-one brought a new, bigger four (225ci/3687cc) and a smaller V8 of 235ci (3851cc), both of which were replaced by a 171-ci (2802-cc) six in 1923. This was the Model 30, which benefited from General Motors' Duco quick-drying paint in 1925 and four-wheel brakes a couple of years later, together with a bigger engine in 1927. It was replaced by another six of 198ci (3245cc), which proved just as successful, helping Olds to break the 100,000 sales barrier in 1929 when the company returned to the realms of the top-ten manufacturers.

After several years of offering only a six, Olds again decided to try a V8 in 1929, the car badged as the Viking. But this was not a good time to launch any sort of car, and Viking sales failed to match the dynamism of its name. According to historian Dennis F. Casteele, 'by 1930 the Viking was just a bitter-tasting memory'.

OPPOSITE and THIS PAGE
A 1964 Oldsmobile Cutlass, with many
sporty features including bucket seats, T-bar
floor shift and a tachometer. By the
standards of the time, however, it was still
very restrained.

The Viking was replaced by the L-32, actually no more than the F-series six-cylinder chassis fitted with an 87-bhp eight. At only $50 more than the six, the L-series was good value and sold well, enabling Olds to recover well from the Depression, with the result that General Motors abandoned plans to merge or close Buick, Oldsmobile and Pontiac.

Through the late 1930s, Oldsmobiles received the same updates as every other General Motors car, which enabled the corporation to stay one step ahead of Ford. There was independent front suspension in 1934 and Fisher's new 'turret-top' body in 1935, with its all-steel roof. Engines grew in size and power, up to

The 1971 Olds 442 was still offered as a model in its own right. The numbers indicate four-speed gearbox, four-barrel carburetor and twin-outlet exhaust.

95-bhp (six) and 110-bhp (eight). Clutchless gear-changing was something of an Olds speciality, first offered with the Safety Automatic Transmission for 1937, which was really a column-change semi-automatic. The real breakthrough was Hydra-Matic, offered from 1940 for a trifling $57, which was a genuine two-pedalled, fully automatic system. Within a year, nearly half of all new Oldses were ordered with Hydra-Matic, the figure slowly increasing to 90%.

Meanwhile, Olds was enjoying the zenith of a pre-war boom before American history changed as a result of the Japanese attack on Pearl Harbor. The company sold over 270,000 cars in the 1941 model year, the range now consisting of four models – 60, 70, 80 and 90 – powered by a 239-ci (3916-cc) six and 258-ci (4228-cc) eight.

Like other American manufacturers, Olds ceased production in early 1942 and resumed with 1946 models that were simply warmed over '42s, though the company was quick off the mark. New Olds mobiles were back in American showrooms while Hitler was still cowering in his Berlin bunker. But they didn't get a real update until the 1948 model year, with new Futuramic styling for the 98 series as two-or four-door sedans and convertibles.

V8 Revolution

The cheaper 60 and 70 series adopted this styling the following year, but the big news for 1949 was an all-new overhead-valve V8 named the Rocket. With a 7.25:1 compression ratio and 135bhp, the Rocket gave Olds a real advantage: Ford still depended on its side-valve V8 and Chevrolet wouldn't get a V8 of any sort until 1955. Only Cadillac had a new V8 that same year.

This gave the 98 series suitably rocket-like performance, by the standards of the day, but the Rocket was even more effective when it was fitted to the smaller 76 series, which weighed 3-400lb less than the 98. Now renamed 88, it was good news for hot-rodders, capable of 100mph (160km/h) straight out of the showroom, and more still when it had been worked upon. The Olds 88 proved very effective in NASCAR, winning six of the nine races that year, and easily won the 1951 championship. To look at, the 88 sedan station wagon and convertible didn't appear that special, this being long before the era of spoilers, wide wheels and rally stripes, but it was the 'hot one' of its time, six years before Chevrolet coined that particular phrase.

With such runaway success (almost 100,000 88s were sold that first year) it is not surprising that Oldsmobile dropped the ageing straight-six for 1950, expanding

Downsized in the uncertain 1970s, this is a 1976 Olds Cutlass, America's best-seller that year.

the V8 line for 1951 instead. A new 160-bhp version of the Rocket V8 was fitted to the range-topping 98 and the new Super 88 immediately eclipsed the old and over 150,000 were sold, compared with a 'mere' 34,000 plain 88s. Olds had cottoned on very quickly to Detroit's horsepower race, and power was boosted again for 1953 to 150bhp for the base 88 and 165bhp for the top. There was a complete restyle the following year that included the first signs of tailfins, plus a wraparound windshield. The Rocket, meanwhile, had been upsized to 326ci (5342cc), taking power to 170bhp and 185bhp, the latter

due to a Carter four-barrelled carburetor and 8.25:1 compression ratio.

There seemed no end to this almost annual growth in horsepower and cubic inches in the late 1950s, and even the base 88 was not ignored. It was offering 185bhp in 1955, 230bhp in '56 and for 1957 had climbed to 277bhp plus 400lb ft, due to yet more cubic inches, now standing at 373ci (6112cc). The 88, Super 88 and 98 all used the same unit that year, though choice returned for 1959. The 88 (now the 'Dynamic 88') used a slightly detuned 373-ci Rocket for 270bhp, while the Super 88 and 98 offered a biggest-yet 394-ci

(6456-cc) version with 315bhp. The first signs of change came in 1960, when tailfins flattened out, chrome receded a little and there were no step changes in power or size. But real change came for 1961, when Olds launched its F-85 compact. This was a sister car to the Pontiac and Buick compacts and quite advanced beneath the skin, with unitary construction and coil springs all round. The engine was a new 216-ci (3540-cc) unit with aluminium block and a 155bhp – useful when you consider that the F-85 sedan weighed 1,500lb (680kg) less than the full-sized 98.

The F-85 was a success, selling more

than 76,000 in its first year, and was soon joined by a convertible. For 1964 the car gained 11in (28cm) in length, taking it into intermediate territory with a choice of 225-ci (3687-cc) six (155bhp) or 210-bhp 330-ci (5408-cc) V8 engines. Of more interest to aficionados of hot cars was the new 4-4-2 option, standing for four-barrel carburetor, four-speed gearbox and twin exhaust pipes, and proving a real hit; so

successful was it that it became one of the legendary muscle cars. Olds made the 4-4-2 a model in its own right, its engine peaking at 370bhp from a 455-ci (7456-cc) V8 in 1970. Only when the demand for muscle cars receded was the 4-4-2 relegated to the status of an option.

The 4-4-2, and in fact all Oldsmobiles up to the mid-1960s, were conventional rear-wheel-drive cars, but the Toronado,

announced for 1966, was something new. Styled by David North, this large, long-wheelbased coupé had front-wheel-drive, its 427-ci (6997-cc) V8 mounted alongside the transmission. With 385bhp and an all-up weight of 4,366lb (1980kg), the Toronado broke front-wheel-drive records, yet handled well and despite a price of $4,585 was very popular, selling over 40,000 in its first year. It also endured: the

OPPOSITE and BELOW LEFT
The 1971 442 was a good-looking car in fastback coupé form. But within a few years, the rapid decline in the popularity of muscle cars would see this legendary number disappear.

Toronado as a big front-drive coupé became a permanent part of the Olds range, redesigned and downsized from 1979 but still a Toronado.

Thank You, Chevrolet
Meanwhile, the F-85 had split into base and Cutlass lines, with a 250-ci (4097-cc) six of 155bhp and V8s of up to 350ci (5735cc) and 250bhp, while the full-sized 88 and 98 sedans continued alongside the gargantuan Vista Cruiser station wagon. The basic F-85 was now restricted to a

single two-door coupé. But for 1973 Olds made a fresh bid for the new-generation compact market, though the new Omega wasn't that fresh, using the Chevy Nova body that had been around since 1968. There was only one engine, the 250-ci six giving 100 net horsepower, whether it be in sedan, coupé or hatchback forms. There were still smaller cars for 1975, and again Olds looked to Chevrolet for help. General Motors was putting renewed efforts into encouraging divisions to share parts and save costs; consequently, the new

subcompact Starfire bore a strong resemblance to Chevy's Monza and the Buick Skyhawk. It came only in two-door coupé guise, with a 231-ci (3785-cc) V6. But as the fuel crisis began to bite, Olds fitted smaller engines, notably a 10-ci (2294-cc) four to the Starfire and the 231-ci V6 to the Omega.

The Cutlass, which had begun as an upscaled F-85, had developed into a range of its own, and a complex one at that, with sub-lines of Supremes, Broughams, Salons and Calais coupés. But the effort paid off,

V6 offering 115bhp. Olds' front-drive revolution then gathered pace with the subcompact Firenza sedan and hatchback, launched for 1982, alongside an all-new downsized Cutlass Ciera which used General Motors' semi-wedge-shaped A-body. This came with four-cylinder or V6 engines, but the intermediate Cutlass Supreme was still available, with everything from a 231-ci V6 gasoline to the 350-ci V8 diesel. Traditionalists would have been pleased to see that the 98 badge had now returned alongside the 88, both on full-sized rear-drive sedans, though with similar engine options as the smaller Cutlass. They were finally dropped in 1985, when the 88/98 took on General Motors' front-drive C-body, though the Custom Cruiser station wagon hung on

OPPOSITE and THIS PAGE
Olds was still offering traditional
intermediates like the Cutlass/442 in 1971,
but more compact cars were on the way.

the Cutlass becoming America's favourite car in 1976, helping Oldsmobile to third place in the industry rankings. Never before did Olds have so many cars, neither had it reached the top three. As for the Cutlass, it had come a long way since its compact/mid-sized origins, and was nearly as large as the full-sized 98, which was dropped in 1976. It was now subjected to downsizing from 1977, the largest V8 now being a 307-ci (5031cc).

Oldsmobile's other reaction to the uncertain 1970s and its own specialist niche within General Motors, was the production of diesel engines. It was the first time an American manufacturer had attempted to offer diesels to the public on a large scale, and General Motors hoped

that Olds' 350-ci (5735-cc) V8 and later 264-ci (4326-cc) V6 would allow traditional buyers to keep their big cubes with acceptable fuel economy. Both engines were based on existing units but proved unreliable in service, and no amount of extended warranties could convince a skeptical public otherwise. Despite promising initial sales (Olds built nearly 280,000 engines for itself and General Motors in 1980 alone) this experiment with diesel died a death in the early 1980s.

The rear-wheel-drive Omega was dropped in 1980 to make way for a front-drive replacement, which was the division's take on the General Motors X-car, with a base 90-bhp four of 15lci (2474cc) and an optional 173-ci (2835-cc)

until 1992 as Oldsmobile's final rear-wheel-drive car of the old generation.

By then, the Omega X-car was long gone, and the subcompact Firenza was dropped in 1988. Olds' only true compact was the Cutlass Calais, which had been introduced in two-door coupé form in 1985. By the end of the decade, it came as a four-door sedan with a choice of three four-cylinder units: 15lci (2474cc) with 110bhp and 2351b ft; 138-ci (2261-cc) dohc 16-valve in 160- or 180-bhp forms, all of them fuel-injected. By 1990, General Motors was heading for the growing MPV market, Olds' version being the Silhouette, with a 192-ci (3146-cc) V6 driving the front wheels. Another General Motors corporate move was the Olds Bravada, announced the same year, which consisted of Olds badges on a Chevrolet Blazer 4×4 SUV.

The following year saw a short-lived return to rear-wheel-drive, with the station wagon-only Cruiser, derived from the Chevrolet Caprice and Buick Roadmaster. It was a big car with a 307-ci (5031-cc) V8, but there had been a shift from big traditional station wagons to SUVs and MPVs and the Cruiser lasted only three years. The future did include cars like the compact Achieva, however, which replaced the Cutlass Calais in 1992, now with four engine options, three of them the 138-ci four plus a 205-ci (3359-cc) V6 of 160bhp. The 1990s equivalent of the muscle-car driver could still opt for the high-revving, high-compression 180-bhp four.

It was replaced in 1998 by the similar Alero, again with four-cylinder and V6 options and four-door sedan or two-door coupé bodies. The mid-range was still covered by the Ciera and Cutlass Supreme, the former with a four or V6, the latter V6 only, while the big sedans, now smoothly aerodynamic, continued the 88 and 98

OPPOSITE
ABOVE LEFT
1995 Oldsmobile LSS.

ABOVE RIGHT
The Ciera came with four-cylinder or V6 engines.

BELOW LEFT
The Achieva replaced the Cutlass Calais. This is a 1996 SL.

LEFT
The Intrigue, one of the last cars to bear the Oldsmobile badge.

badges, albeit with V6 engines. But Oldsmobile had made a return to V8s with the Aurora, a front-wheel-drive luxury sedan that did not actually wear Olds badges. The dohc 32-valve Northstar V8 measured 245ci (4015cc) and offered 253bhp. The Aurora was very well received, winning numerous awards and outselling all its rivals.

With a string of strong cars such as these in the line-up, Oldsmobile

celebrated its 100th anniversary in 1997, the first American marque to have achieve such longevity.

In spite of Oldsmobile's critical successes since the mid-1990s, however, a reported shortfall in sales and overall profitability prompted General Motors to announce in December 2000 their plans to phase out the Oldsmobile brand. The announcement took place just two days after Oldsmobile unveiled what would be

its last new model ever, the Bravada SUV, which became, somewhat ironically, another critical hit for the division.

The phaseout was conducted on the following schedule: Mid-2001: the 2002 Bravada, the company's last new model, hits Oldsmobile showrooms. June 2002: production ends for Intrigue and the Aurora V6 sedans. March 2003: Aurora V8 sedan production ends. January 2004: Bravada SUV production ends. March

ABOVE
Alero came in sedan form as well as coupé,
with four-cylinder or V6 options.

ABOVE RIGHT
The Bravada – a compact SUV.

RIGHT
The sleek Aurora was aimed at the
shrinking market for big sedans.

2004: Silhouette minivan production
ends. April 2004: Alero compact car
production ends. The final 500 Aleros,
Auroras, Bravadas, Silhouettes and
Intrigues produced received special
Oldsmobile heritage emblems and
markings which signified 'Final 500'. All
featured a unique Dark Cherry Metallic
paint scheme. Auroras and Intrigues
would be accompanied by special Final
500 literature.

The final production day for
Oldsmobile was 29 April 2004. The
division's last car built was an Alero GLS
four-door sedan, which was signed by all
of the Olds assembly line-workers. It is on
display at the R.E. Olds Transportation
Museum located in Lansing, Michigan.

OVERLAND (1903–26)

One would have thought that with a name like Overland the company would have had a natural advantage in the growing SUV market of the 1990s, but the badge had already long since died. It was another of America's early car-makers that had shown promise, having been second only to Ford between 1912 and 1917, but had slipped and become only a minor player.

The Standard Wheel Co., part of America's huge carriage and wagon industry, decided to diversify into automobiles in 1903. Its first product was fairly conventional, except that its single-cylinder 5-hp engine was mounted in the front, under the hood, when it would have been more usually under the seat. Designed by Standard's Claude E. Cox, the little two-seat runabout was built in limited numbers, joined by a similar two-cylinder version in 1904, while 1905 saw a 16-hp four with a four-seater tourer body and shaft-drive.

Despite the growing model range, and investment by buggy-maker, David M. Parry, who took over the business, production was still on a cottage scale, with only 47 cars built in 1906. All of these were bought by John North Willys, a New York dealer, who was so impressed that he ordered 500 cars for the following year, secured by a deposit of $10,000. Willys was an extraordinary man, saving the company in a way that owed more to Hollywood than real life.

By the due date, however, he hadn't received a single car, and he arrived at Parry's Indianapolis factory to find out what was going on. He was aghast to find his $10,000 gone and Parry bankrupt, having lost his house as well as his factory. There were only 15 men left on the payroll, no complete cars, though there were the parts to build two or three. Willys didn't hesitate. Even though he lacked a factory, he resumed production in a circus tent, where in 1908 he produced 465 cars. The following year he had abandoned the tent for bricks and mortar, having bought a large factory in Toledo, Ohio.

At first, the new Willys-Overland Co. built conventional four-cylinder cars, 20/24-hp machines costing $1,250, the new factory producing nearly 5,000 of them in 1909 and three times that number the following year. Production and sales rocketed, giving Overland second place in the industry, and in 1916 over 140,000 cars were built. Most of the range still consisted of fours (30- and 35h-p in 1915) though a 40/45-hp six was added later.

John Willys was determined to take the coveted top spot from Ford and planned to sell the 1919 Overland Four for $500, undercutting the Model T. But production was seriously delayed, and by the time the Four reached production, the price had jumped to $945, so Henry Ford was hardly quaking in his boots.

The delay caused Willys to lose control of his company, but he was back in 1921, and after the experience of the Four launched larger, more expensive cars such as the Bluebird and Redbird. The bird motif was appropriate as Overland had risen phoenix-like from the ashes to sell 50,000 cars in 1921 and 150,000 by 125. The company followed up with another six in 1926, but Willys decided to drop the Overland name. In 1927 the existing cars were replaced by the Whippet and, apart from a brief appearance in 1939 as a model name, that was the end of Overland.

PACKARD (1899–1958)

Ferruccio Lamborghini, long before he went into the sports-car business, was a producer of farm tractors. He owned a Ferrari, and was so unhappy with it that he took it back to Enzo Ferrari himself to complain in person. The great man was dismissive, telling Lamborghini he should stick to tractors. Suitably stung, Lamborghini began to build fast cars instead, determined to have his revenge. According to legend, this is also how Packard came into being. James Ward Packard took his Winton back to its maker, to be told that if he was so smart he could build a car himself. So he did.

Somehow or other, the brothers managed to acquire two engineers from Winton, and in November 1899 built their first car. The Model A was along conventional lines for the time, though at 143ci (2343cc) considerably larger than contemporaries such as the Oldsmobile. In fact, Packard's early years are distinguished by large cylinders, the Model B that followed in 1900 being a 185-ci (3032-cc) single. Both used an epicyclical transmission and chain drive, but the B

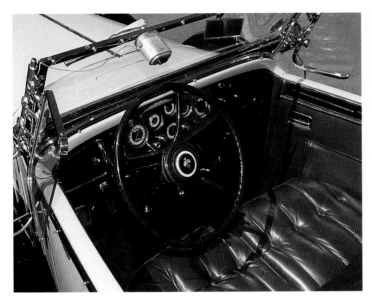

had the added refinement of automatic ignition advance, while the bigger Model F also offers a three-speed sliding gear transmission. The F also gained a distinct advantage in 1903, when it was driven from San Francisco to New York in 61 days, beating the previous record set by a Winton. Better still, one of Packard's growing list of wealthy clients was William D. Rockefeller, who abandoned Winton to buy a Packard.

This was all very well, but James was beginning to show a tendency that later afflicted Henry Ford and Ransom Olds – refusing to believe that tried and tested cars could be improved. Packard was even loath to use a two-cylinder engine, remarking, 'Two cylinders in a Packard would be like two tails on a cat – you just don't need it.' Fortunately, he was persuaded otherwise, though the 1902 Model G used two of the F's large cylinders, making it a 370-ci (6063-cc) engine. Better balanced, and far more advanced, was the Model K announced later the same year, with a 253-ci (4146-cc) four, four-speed gearbox and shaft-drive, though the smaller, cheaper Model L which followed it a year later was more successful. This became Packard's staple product, growing as the 267-ci (4375-cc) Model N, 352-ci (5768-cc) Model S and

434-ci (7112-cc) Model U, or Thirty. The Eighteen, launched in 1909, was around $1,000 cheaper, and found fewer buyers, though Packard built both cars until 1913.

Given Packard's original reluctance to use more than one cylinder, the company later seemed to be making up for lost time. By now, it was under the management of Henry B. Joy, who had refinanced the company in 1902, the Packard brothers now taking a back seat. So it was 1911 when Packard unveiled its first six, a large car offered in 13 body styles over two wheelbases. The Packard Six (renamed the 48 for 1913) was powered by a T-head engine of 528ci (8652cc) and 74bhp, joined

OPPOSITE and THIS PAGE
Hard hit by the Depression, Packard fought back with an inexpensive Light Eight.

two years later by a smaller 417-ci (6833-cc) L-head version. The fours were dropped that year, leaving Packard with only a six-cylinder range.

This continued until 1915, when it was topped by the Twin Six. This was the world's first 12-cylinder car made in any quantity, and underlined Packard's

determination to leave the single-cylinder far behind. In terms of cubic inches, the new engine was actually smaller than the original six, at 426ci (6981ce) from its 60° V12, but at 88bhp was considerably more powerful. It was also astonishingly flexible, allowing the Twin Six to accelerate smoothly from walking pace to its top

speed of around 70mph (113km/h), all in top gear. The frosting on the cake was that it was also cheaper than the Model 48 six, with prices starting at $2,600.

Who could resist the lure of having more cylinders than anyone else on the road, and at a bargain price? Packard dropped its sixes that same year, and the

OPPOSITE and LEFT
A 1936 Packard straight-eight. Cars like this spearheaded the company's post-Depression recovery. Over 130,000 low-priced 120s were sold in three years.

OPPOSITE and THIS PAGE
A 1937 Packard 115, a six-cylinder version
of the popular eight-cylinder 120.

Twin Six V12 was its sole model for the half-dozen years. When it was dropped in 1923, nearly 31,000 had been sold, making it the most popular American V12 of all.

Single Six

Post-war inflation, however, turned the Twin Six into an expensive car, so a smaller, cheaper Single Six was launched for 1921 to run alongside it. The Single Six started life with a relatively stubby 116-in (2.9-m) wheelbase, but this was stretched to a full-sized 126 or 133 inches the following year. It proved very popular, and over 150,000 were sold in the 1920s. They were joined in 1923 by the Single Eight, with a straight-eight engine of 360ci

(5899cc) offering 85bhp and in the Packard fashion of the time dictating the model designation. Once again, there was a choice of two wheelbases, 136in (3.4m) and 143in (3.6m). In the tradition begun by the Twin Six, they were fine value for money, the shorter-wheelbased Eight starting at $3,650, though rather more could be spent by opting for one of the many coach-built bodies from well-known companies like Judkins and Fleetwood. More power (109bhp) arrived in 1927 from more capacity (387ci/6342cc), while two years later a smaller 321-ci (5260-cc) Standard Eight replaced the Six.

OPPOSITE and THIS PAGE
One of the last. The Packard Clipper for 1957/58 was a rebadged Studebaker President.

The 626 Speedster for 1929 was produced by slotting the big eight into this smaller chassis and clothing the result in curvaceous bodywork. And 'Speedster' it was, with the eight boosted to 130bhp due to high compression and high-lift cams, enough for a top speed of 100mph (160km/h). It was swiftly followed by the

145-bhp 734 Speedster with a longer wheelbase and performance in excess of 100mph. Beautiful as the Speedsters were, they were also expensive, and fewer than 200 were sold.

Packard fought the Depression in 1932 with the much cheaper Light Eight and the existing 321-ci eight in a 128-in (3.2-m)

wheelbase chassis. Although prices started at $1,750, the Light Eight was not a success and was soon dropped, though the idea was revived in1935. The other new Packard of 1932 was an attempt to recreate the glory days of the 1920s Twin Six, and this latest V12 was given the same name. Front-wheel-drive had been

considered for the new flagship, and even a rear-drive straight-twelve, but the new Twin Six was a rear-driven Vl2, a new L-head unit of 447ci (7325cc). Other new features were a three-speed synchromesh gearbox and vacuum-assisted brakes, though the Twin Six also came in two wheelbases and a wide choice of factory- or coach-built bodywork.

Despite all this activity, Packard was hard hit by the Depression, selling 9,000 cars in 1932 and 6,200 or so in '34 compared with 1928, when over 50,000 Packards left the works. But the company persevered with the Twin Six (now renamed the Twelve) though it never equalled the success of its 1920s predecessor. Gradually updated with more power, independent front suspension and hydraulic brakes, fewer than 6,000 Twelves were actually made.

third the year after, when Walter Chrysler must have congratulated himself on the success of the Plymouth strategy.

The new model PA for 1932 brought another boost in capacity to 197ci (3228cc) for 56bhp. But just as significant, and with an eye to the six-cylinder Chevrolets, was the four-cylinder engine's rubber mounting, which suspended the unit along its own centre of gravity. This, said its maker, would make the four as smooth as an eight. The public approved, and a freewheeling transmission with 'Easy Shift' constant-mesh was part of the deal. In April 1932 it was replaced by the PB, now with 65bhp.

The four cylinders may have been rubber-mounted but were no longer enough, and a 191-ci (3130-cc) six was

made standard on the PC for 1933. This produced 70bhp, or 76bhp in high-compression form, though the PC actually had a shorter 107-in (2.7-m) wheelbase than the four which preceded it. But no one could accuse Plymouth of not reacting quickly, and by mid-year it had revealed the PD with five extra inches in the wheelbase and different fenders. But the short-wheel-based car continued as the budget PCXX and was a real bargain, starting at $445 (the same price as a four-cylinder Ford that year); the public response was such that Plymouth maintained its third place in the charts in 1933 and sold almost 200,000 cars.

Plymouths got bigger for 1934, with wheelbases of 108in (PF, PFXX and PG) and 114in (PG), all benefiting from a slightly upsized six increased to 202ci (3310cc). All but the base model PG also came with coil-sprung independent front suspension, which was not a success, and the beam front axle was re-adopted for 1935. That year the PJ series all used the same 113-in (2.9-m) wheelbase, the six now delivering 82bhp. There were few changes in the late 1930s, apart from tweaks to the styling, a hypoid rear axle in 1937 and independent front suspension and a steering-column gear change in 1939.

There was also a restyle that year, bringing recessed headlights and split windshields. Most Plymouths were standard four-door sedans, though the company did offer a long-wheel-based seven-seat version from 1936 and a short-lived four-door convertible. The division's first station wagon had appeared in 1934 in the guise of the Westchester Suburban, and the tough, roomy wagons would become a permanent feature of the Plymouth line-up, though it was many years before they made up more than a tiny minority of sales. Before production was suspended in 1942, the six was enlarged to 216ci (3540cc) for 95bhp.

The public seemed happy with these modest changes and Plymouth sales continued to climb to over 440,000 in 1935, slightly less than that in 1941, though still enough to pass the four million mark since Plymouth began, and this was only U.S. production. By now Plymouths were also being built in Canada and Belgium and were selling all over the world, though not always with Plymouth badges.

OPPOSITE and THIS PAGE
A 1948 Plymouth coupé the year before the marque received all-new styling. The 1948 was a continuation of the '42.

more mild-mannered sedans offered the 132-bhp six or 225-bhp 5.2 litre V8, but from 1958 the Sport Fury hardtop could be had with the 'Golden Commando' V8 of 350ci, twin four-barrelled carburetors and 350bhp: there was even a fuel-injected version with an extra ten horsepower, though this was shortlived.

By 1959, the position of the division was uncertain. Plymouth had regained its third place, with sales that year increasing 11.6 per cent, though overall market share had slipped to 13.2 per cent. Plymouth hoped the compact Valiant, launched in 1960, would turn the tide. With a wheelbase of 106.5in (2.7m), the Valiant was a true compact compared with the full-sized Plymouths – though it was not a true Plymouth, having been built by Dodge. It wasn't such a roaring success as Ford's Falcon, but first-year sales of over 127,000 were good enough. The heavily-styled Valiant had a new ohv slant-six of 172ci (2818cc) giving 101bhp, and a 145-bhp 227-ci (3720-cc) version followed in 1962.

Plymouth's Pony Car
More interesting for enthusiasts was the Barracuda coupé version that followed in 1964, actually beating the Mustang to market by a few weeks. Like Ford's pony car, the Barracuda was a sporty four-seater coupé based on compact-car running gear, though the Barracuda never equalled the Mustang's success. It looked distinctive from the rear, however, due to its huge glass window. With the Valiant slant-six

OPPOSITE and LEFT
The Belvedere hardtop, Plymouth's
intermediate-sized sedan.

beneath the hood, performance was underwhelming, but the Commando 235 V8 was a different matter.

The Barracuda was restyled for 1967, moving it closer to muscle-car territory with new 340- and 383-ci (5572- and 6276-cc) V8 engine options. Other Plymouth performance cars at that time were the Road Runner, hugely popular because of its low price and hot engine options, and the plusher GTX, both of them based on the two-door Belvedere. Many in the market for a Plymouth muscle car would have lusted after the hemi 426-ci (6981-cc)

V8, which was hugely powerful, with over 400bhp in the right state of tune, but was also expensive to buy and insure. This was the second-generation version of Chrysler's legendary deep-breathing V8 of the 1950s. But only a tiny number of Barracudas and Road Runners were ordered with the hemi, and those that were seemed bound for the drag strip. A more sensible choice was the 440-ci (7210-cc) V8, slightly less powerful than the hemi but easier to handle.

The hemi's raison d'être was competition and it certainly delivered, winning many NASCAR races for

Plymouth in the 1960s. To qualify, Plymouth had to make a certain number of road cars with the same modifications as the racers, which led to the outrageous 1969–70 Superbird. With its big front spoiler, droop-snoot and towering rear wing, the Superbird was clearly designed for the big ovals rather than for going to market, but some were bought for the road.

Meanwhile, the Fury had become Plymouth's full-sized sedan, with six-cylinder or V8 options, while the Sport Fury was the full-sized two-door hardtop

or convertible. Full-sized Plymouths later became Gran Furys, while the intermediates were badged plain Furys, still available with the biggest 440-ci V8. Inevitably, all of these were downsized in the late 1970s and and early '80s, and by 1983 the Gran Fury could even be had with a 226-ci (3703-cc) six as well as a 320-ci (5244-cc) V8.

But the 1970s would be the decade of the subcompact, or at least that's what everyone seemed to be thinking when every American manufacturer had its own.

Plymouth's was the Cricket, which was really a U.K.-built Hillman Avenger with different badges. Plymouth's standard compact sedan was still the Valiant, now with a l98-ci (3245-cc) six or the familiar 318-ci (5211-cc) V8, now joined by Scamp hardtop and Duster coupé versions, the latter with a 340-ci (5572-cc) V8 option. The Cricket only lasted a couple of years

and was followed by the Horizon, another European design (the Chrysler Horizon), though this time built in the U.S. It was a roomy five-door hatchback with a 104-ci (1704-cc) four-cylinder engine driving the front wheels. A coupé version, the Turismo, came either with that engine or a 135-ci (2212-cc) four built by Chrysler U.S.

The Valiant gave way to the Volare in

1976, which itself was replaced by the front-wheel-drive Reliant four years later. This was Plymouth's version of Chrysler's K-car, also sold as the Dodge Aries, with a choice of Chrysler (135-ci/2212-cc) or Mitsubishi (157-ci/2573-cc) fours. Chrysler now relied on Mitsubishi for some components for its smaller cars, which extended to complete cars when the

OPPOSITE and ABOVE
A 1968 Plymouth, subtly modified. It was a particular favourite with enthusiasts of hot cars.

351

RIGHT and OPPOSITE
A 1970 Barracuda with a twin four-barrelled hemi. Few were actually ordered with this engine.

Mitsubishi Colt hatchback was sold with Plymouth badges from 1985. The same applied to the Space Wagon (Plymouth Vista), Starion (Conquest Turbo) and Eclipse (Laser).

The 1987 Sundance filled the space between Horizon and Reliant, a two- or four- door sedan using the 135-ci four in standard 97-bhp form or offering 148bhp with fuel injection and turbo.

The 1989 Acclaim, which replaced the Reliant, used a 153-ci (2507-cc) four in 100- or 150-bhp turbo form, plus a less sporty 181-ci (2966-cc) V6 providing 141bhp in the upscale Acclaim LX. That

OPPOSITE and LEFT
The Shaker hood scoop on this 1971
Barracuda is a true period fitting.

same year was the last for the traditional Gran Fury, leaving Plymouth with an all-front-drive and more compact range. The Sundance went the same way in 1994, replaced by the Colt coupé or sedan, once more based on a Mitsubishi though the Neon sedan, announced the year before, was designed and built in the U.S. This came with 123-ci (2016-cc) four-cylinder engines in 133-bhp 8-valve or 152-bhp 16-valve forms, and was exported to Europe under the Chrysler badge. It was joined in 1996 by the slightly larger cab-forward Breeze on Chrysler's J-car platform, again with four-cylinder 123-ci power.

OPPOSITE and ABOVE
A 1972 Plymouth, built before the start of downsizing.

RIGHT
The 2000 Breeze, one of the new generation of front-wheel-drive Plymouths.

BELOW RIGHT
The 2000 Plymouth Voyager SE, a mini people-carrier.

OPPOSITE
ABOVE
2001 Plymouth Neon. This was built alongside Dodge- and Chrysler-badged versions.

BELOW LEFT
Plymouth Pronto Spyder.

BELOW RIGHT
The Plymouth Prowler, a sensational retro-style hot rod.

By U.S. standards these were all rational, sensible and efficient sedans, but the 1997 Prowler threw all of this out of the window. It was an unashamed toy, styled like a 1940s hot rod, with cycle-type front fenders and fat rear tyres. Unlike other Plymouths, it was rear-wheel-drive, and was powered by a 2l6-ci (3540-cc) 24-valve V6 with 214bhp. The Prowler was in limited production, and fewer than 4,000 had been made by September 1999, but it gave a disproportionately large boost to the profile of Chrysler in general and Plymouth in particular. Nevertheless, the Chrysler Corporation decided that Plymouth should play no part in the new Daimler-Chrysler concern, and the division was closed in 2001.

BELOW RIGHT
A 1926 coupé. Early Pontiacs such as this used many Chevrolet components.

BELOW CENTRE RIGHT
1926 Pontiac sedan.

BOTTOM RIGHT
1935 two-door sedan.

FAR RIGHT TOP
Pontiac was one of General Motors middle-class brands, filling the space between Chevrolet and Olds.

FAR RIGHT BELOW
1962 two-door Grand Prix.

OPPOSITE PAGE
The 1953 Chieftain Custom, the start of the million-dollar chrome grin.

PONTIAC (1926–2010)

Pontiac, unlike its cousins Buick, Cadillac and Oldsmobile, had no existence before General Motors, having been created by Alfred P. Sloan as a new marque, purely to fill a gap in the General Motors range.

There is little doubt that without Alfred Sloan, General Motors would never have grown into the giant corporation it is today. Sloan had a natural flair for business, to put it mildly. Aged 20, with a degree in electrical engineering, he joined the Hyatt Roller Bearing Co. as a draftsman and at 24 was managing

OPPOSITE and LEFT
The 1949 Pontiac Silver Streak had the wide, low, post-war look.

BELOW and BELOW RIGHT
A 1953 Chieftain Custom, still without a V8
but selling by the thousand.

OPPOSITE
By 1955 Pontiac finally had an overhead-
valve V8 engine.

director. William C. Durant bought the company in 1916 and with other parts suppliers formed the umbrella group, United Motors, making Sloan president. Two years later. General Motors took control of the group which made Sloan an executive of the company. By the time Durant left, Alfred Sloan had begun to formulate the principles on which General Motors' future success would be based.

Now de facto executive vice-president, the president's job soon to follow, he formed the central committees – Technical, Purchasing, Sales – which would prevent the numerous divisions from acting on their own and allow the giant corporation to take advantage of its huge economies of scale. Pontiac, Chevrolet and the rest were all given clear

price bands to which they should adhere, but with sufficient overlap to allow some in-house competition and keep everyone on their toes. Thus Pontiac competed with Chevrolet at the bottom of its price range, and Oldsmobile at the top. It was a winning formula and one that fulfilled General Motors' slogan of the 1920s: 'A Car for Every Purse'.

It was with that promise in mind that Alfred Sloan recognized the gap between Chevrolet and Oldsmobile and decided to create a new marque to fill it in. At the time, Oakland was still part of General Motors, despite selling poorly, with spare capacity that would enable the new car to be built alongside its own. As for a name, Oakland had its base in Pontiac, Michigan, so Pontiac it was.

Pontiac was to use General Motors parts from the start, in order to cut costs, and the first car borrowed many Chevrolet components, including body panels. It had a new six-cylinder engine of its own, however. This was designed by Henry Crane, who adopted a relatively short stroke and full-pressure lubrication, though the rest of the car was conventional for the time, with two-wheel mechanical brakes. As launched in January 1926, the Pontiac six was offered as a sedan or coupé, both at $825, with a landau sedan and delivery van following in August. It was soon clear that the Pontiac would not only be a success, but that it would also outshine Oakland, with over 76,000 cars sold in the first year, causing the Oakland name to be dropped altogether within a few years. Suitably

A 1955 Pontiac with General Motors' new A-body.

encouraged, the range was widened with two open-top cars – roadster and cabriolet – in 1927, and by 1929 was placed fifth in the manufacturers' league. Even in 1932, one of the worst years of the Depression for the U.S. motor industry, over 46,000

cars were sold. It was a remarkable achievement, given that times were so hard.

Oakland's most significant legacy was a new V8 engine of 252ci (4129cc), which produced 85bhp and a top speed of over 70mph (113km/h). The V8-powered

Oakland became a Pontiac in 1932, slotting in nicely with the company's existing 201-ci (3294-cc) 65-bhp six. The V8, however, proved expensive to make and despite its layout wasn't especially smooth. But Pontiac management was now wedded to

the idea of a broader range, and for 1933 designer Ben Anibal replaced it with a new straight-eight of 225-ci (3687cc). At 77bhp it wasn't quite as powerful as the V8, but was far cheaper to build, using cast-iron pistons among other cost-cutting measures,

its short-stroke design giving it potential for future upgrades. This eight would serve Pontiac well, remaining in production for over 20 years.

To go with the new engine came new styling, with skirted fenders and a V-

shaped radiator, to which the public responded, with sales doubling to over 90,000 in 1933. This is all the more remarkable when one remembers that the six had been dropped.

Leaving the straight-eight Pontiac's

Over 300 horsepower were on offer in this 1957 Chieftain.

OPPOSITE and LEFT
Pontiac entered a new dynamic phase in the late 1950s, helped by more power, new styling and the leadership of Bunkie Knudsen.

only model. A six did return for 1935, first as 209ci (3425cc), though it later grew in power and size. At the same time, Pontiacs benefited from General Motors improvements across the board, such as independent front suspension, all-steel bodies and all-synchromesh transmissions.

There were new body styles, too, such as the station wagon and four-door convertible, both unveiled in 1938. Nineteen-forty saw the launch of the Torpedo Eight which, unlike cheaper Pontiacs, owed nothing to Chevrolet, having been based around the General

Motors 'C'-body instead, also used by Cadillac, Buick and Olds. Selling for around $1,000, it widened Pontiac's appeal, allowing over 30,000 Torpedoes to be sold in 1940.

So successful was the Torpedo that it was followed by the Streamliner Torpedo

for 1941. This time, the basis was the General Motors 'B'-body, shared again with Cadillac, Buick and Olds, which came as a four-door sedan or two-door fastback coupé, with Pontiac's six- or eight-cylinder engines, which had now grown to 240ci (3933cc) and 250ci (4097cc) respectively. But Pontiac was mindful of its bread and butter, and the less stylish but cheaper

Chevrolet-derived cars also continued. This sharing of components was the essence of Alfred Sloan's strategy for General Motors, and made the corporation hugely profitable. Pontiac was able to offer a range of nine different bodyshells and 26 models at a fraction of the cost required by an independent manufacturer. The wide range was reflected in record sales of over

330,000, and even in the truncated 1942 model year, cut short by the war, over 85,000 cars were sold.

From Stodge to Street Racer
Pontiac's immediate post-war scenario was one of transformation, from stodginess to something rather more dynamic. Like most American manufacturers, the division

entered the 1946 model year offering thinly-disguised 1942 cars, in this case the Torpedo and Streamliner, with straight-six or straight-eight engines offering 90 and 103bhp respectively. Sedan, station wagon, coupé and convertible, all saw very few changes for 1946 and '47, with the new option of General Motors' Hydra-Matic transmission from 1948. There was a complete restyle for the following year, Pontiac's first by Harley Earl, which was shared with Oldsmobile and Cadillac, and 1950 saw the announcement of the Catalina coupé.

The end of the Second World War saw an explosion in demand for cars, and the public's insatiable hunger for anything on four wheels gave Pontiac a fifth place in the manufacturers' charts. But as the initial demand for cars was satiated and Detroit began to release genuinely new post-war

models, anyone without an overhead-valve V8 and up-to-the-minute styling was at a distinct disadvantage. True, the Pontiacs styled by Harley Earl did seem innovative, but they still used the side-valve six and straight-eights out of the 1930s.

Consequently, the division acquired a middle-aged image – solid enough, in its own way, but not exactly exciting. However, this didn't appear to have affected sales too badly, if at all. In 1951 and '53 the division sold over 400,000 cars and managed to hold its fifth place right through the early 1950s.

It was clear, however, that if Pontiac was to compete for younger customers, it would have to change its image, and an opportunity arose in 1955 when it was the

last General Motors division to receive a new V8. The 289-ci (4736cc) unit offered 173bhp with synchromesh gearbox or 180bhp with the Hydra-Matic, which 90 per cent of buyers chose. Together with the fresher styling of General Motors' new A-body, it was the first step in Pontiac's transformation from stodge to stallion.

The second came the following year, when Semon E. Knudsen, known as 'Bunkie', became general manager of Pontiac, at 44 the youngest head of a General Motors division. Bunkie was keen on hot cars, and over the next ten years would complete the transformation of Pontiac, helped by Pete Estes and John DeLorean. That same year, the Pontiac V8 was boosted to 318ci (5211cc), while an

optional power pack of twin four-barrelled carburetors and a peakier camshaft took power to 285bhp. The cars were now named Chieftain and Star Chief, in keeping with Pontiac's Native American associations: throughout the late 1950s they were given ever more power and cubic inches: 349ci (5719cc) and up to 317bhp for 1957; 372ci (6096cc) and 330bhp for '58; and 391ci (6407cc) and 345bhp for '59. Even the base V8 for 1959 offered 260bhp. The same year saw the introduction of the low-slung 'Wide Track' Pontiacs, which for the next six years would provide the division with a line in high-performance full-sized cars. Bunkie Knudsen also encouraged racing, and the late 1950s and early '60s saw the development of the

OPPOSITE and THIS PAGE
The 1967 Pontiac Grand Prix, in an age when full-sized meant just that.

infamous 'Super Duty' line – racing parts that were offered over the counter. Pontiac won 69 NASCAR Grand National races between 1957 and '63, which came to an end when General Motors imposed its 'no racing' directive soon afterwards.

But even the performance-led Pontiac could not ignore the growing demand for a compact car, and the Tempest, launched in 1960, was its response. It was an advanced machine, with coil-sprung independent suspension all round and a transaxle gearbox. The standard power unit was a 196-ci (3212-cc) four, offering from 110 to 155bhp. A 185-bhp Buick 216-ci (3540-cc) V8 was an option, but only 2 per cent of buyers chose it. The Tempest, in sedan coupé, station wagon, and later convertible form, was a success, with over 100,000 sold in the first year. Like all Detroit compacts of the era the Tempest gained weight, size and power in the 1960s and by 1964 was closer to being an intermediate, with well over half the buyers opting for the

upgraded 260-bhp V8. The Tempest, and the changes effected by Bunkie, saw Pontiac overtake Buick, Plymouth and Olds, climbing from its customary fifth place to third, which it held until 1969.

At least part of the reason for these sustained high sales was the division's continued strong line in performance cars. Take the Pontiac GTO, for example, seen as the car that started the era of the muscle car. This was simply a Tempest Le Mans with the full-sized 389-ci (6374-cc) V8 shoehorned in. This gave 325bhp in an intermediate-sized car, which pushed it to 60mph (l00km/h) in 7.7 seconds and on to a top speed of 115mph (185km/h). All the

characteristics of a hot car were there as part of the package, such as bucket seats, harder springs and low-profile tyres. So successful was the GTO that, in hardtop or convertible form, it became a model in its own right, with increasing power added throughout the decade. 'The Judge' was a budget GTO variant in 1969, though even this came with up to 370bhp. However, the GTO rapidly faded from view in the early 1970s, returned to the status of an option.

Big Cars, Small Cars
Full-sized Pontiacs were based around the Catalina, Ventura and Bonneville, all of them traditional rear-wheel-drive sedans,

also offered as station wagons, convertibles and two-door hardtops. The Bonneville was the luxury variant, while the Catalina offered plenty of space for the money, especially the nine-seater station wagon. All of these could be had with the biggest 389-ci V8 with up to 363bhp; by 1968. the biggest option was a 428-ci (7014-cc) unit with 390bhp. That year also marked a production milestone for Pontiac, with 940,000 cars rolling off the lines. Meanwhile, as the base engine, the Tempest abandoned its four in favour of an overhead-cam straight-six.

It had taken General Motors the best part of three years to produce a car to

OPPOSITE and ABOVE
The GTO started out as an option but became a legend. This is a model from 1969.

THIS PAGE and OPPOSITE
1969 Pontiac GTO. The Judge variant
offered similar performance at a lower price.

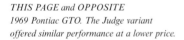

rival Ford's wildly successful Mustang, Pontiac's Firebird appearing in February 1967. It was really a Chevrolet Camaro, which Pontiac engineers had been given as a *fait accompli*, though they could fit their own engines. Despite its hybrid status, the Firebird, a shapely coupé or convertible, was a success for Pontiac, with over 100,000 cars sold in the first full year. At one point the Firebird was even Pontiac's second fastest-selling model of all, outdoing several of the sedans.

Like the Camaro and Mustang, the Firebird came with a wide variety of options to appeal to a wider market, and engine options ranged from the new overhead-cam 231-ci (3785-cc) six of 165bhp to the 400-ci (6555-cc) V8 of 325bhp. The most successful Firebird variant, and by a huge margin, was the Trans Am. It began as a limited option, named after the Trans Am race series, having all the stripes, spoilers, buttoned-down suspension and heavy-duty transmission the aficionado could want, with power from the 335-bhp Ram Air III V8. The Trans Am was so successful that it became a permanent part of the range; in fact, nearly half the Firebirds sold in 1978 were Trans Ams.

As a performance car, it is an interesting fact that the Firebird actually sold better through the 1970s than at the height of the muscle-car boom. As safety and emissions legislation cut performance and power, however, the enthusiast press was bitter in its complaints. But the tact was that Pontiac sold over 180,000 detoxed Firebirds in 1978, more than it ever did of the full-powered originals. The car continued to use the big 400-ci V8 when all around were downsizing, which may have been part of its appeal, a 455-ci (7456-cc) unit also being an option. Not until 1982 would the Firebird be seriously downsized with a new base engine of only 151ci (2474cc) and 90bhp, though it was still possible to have a 175-bhp V8.

Of course, Pontiac had been downsizing long before that. It re-entered the compact market in 1970 with the

Ventura, which was actually a rebadged Chevrolet Nova. In fact, all the smaller Pontiacs, the Fiero sports car apart, would be derivations of other General Motors cars, widening to include most of the range in the 1980s. Pontiac still had a strong sporting image, so the Ventura was soon offered as the Ventura Sprint, with bucket seats and manual gearbox, though few of them were made. The base engine was a 251-ci (4113-cc) six, with a 309-ci (5064-cc) V8 an option. The Ventura was replaced by the Phoenix (still rear-wheel-drive) in 1977, with a four-cylinder base engine, which in turn gave way to the front-drive Phoenix in 1980, it being Pontiac's version of the ubiquitous General Motors X-car.

Pontiac's first venture into the field of subcompacts was the 1973 Astre, though again it was a rebadged Chevrolet, in this case the Vega. Available as hatchback, station wagon or delivery van, the Astre came with a 141-ci (2310-cc) four-cylinder engine and a coupé was added in 1975. It was replaced by the sportier Sunbird in 1977 – sportier because it first came only as a coupé, though a hatchback arrived later with the option of a 232-ci (3802-cc) V6. The Sunbird was very popular, helping Pontiac to sell over 900,000 cars in 1979, and was the division's best-selling model the following year.

Meanwhile, the full-sized Pontiacs were getting smaller, the Bonnevilles, Safaris and Catalinas shrinking in 1976,

while the big 455-ci (7456-cc) V8 was finally dropped. Buyers could still order the 352-ci (5768-cc) V8, though the smaller engines were more popular, while the Olds V8 diesel was another option available from 1980. In 1982, a smaller rear-wheel-drive Bonneville replaced the original, in V6 and V8 guise as a sedan or station wagon. By 1984, this had been joined by the full-sized Parisienne on a 116-in (2.9-m) wheelbase and again with V6 or V8 options.

The big Grand Am had been dropped in 1980, but the name reappeared for 1985 on a smaller two-door notchback coupé, offered with a 151-ci (2474-cc) four or 181-ci (2966-cc) fuel-injected V6, the latter with 125bhp.

OPPOSITE and THIS PAGE
Pontiac continued to offer the Le Mans alongside the GTO. This is the model from 1972.

OPPOSITE and THIS PAGE
The GTO was lightly detoxed and slightly
sanitized for 1973 and would disappear
altogether within a few years.

Phoenix & Fiero

The 1980 Phoenix was the start of a second generation of compacts. It was Pontiac's version of the General Motors X-car, having the same 151-ci (2474-cc) or 174-ci (2851-cc) V6 as its corporate cousins. Offered as sedan, hatchback or station wagon, the new Phoenix sold well at first, but sales soon began to fall. It was joined by the front-drive J2000 the following year (a true subcompact by American standards), sharing parts with the European Opel Ascona and Vauxhall Cavalier. Sold only with a 113-ci (1852-cc) four-cylinder engine, the J2000 was listed until 1983. But it wasn't the smallest Pontiac of the 1980s; this was the rear-drive T1000, another Euro design, this time the Opel Kadett/Vauxhall Astra,

which Chevrolet also sold as the Chevette. This would later be replaced by the Le Mans, based on the later front-wheel-drive Kadett but built for Pontiac by Daewoo of Korea. The Phoenix was supplemented by the A-body 6000 for 1982, which came as coupé or sedan, with the same engine options as the Phoenix but with a 263-ci (4310-cc) V6 diesel added. It would be part of the line-up for ten years. The Grand Prix and Bonneville were Pontiac's mid-sized cars, while the Parisienne and Safari station wagon took care of the full-sized market.

The 1983 Fiero was quite different from any of these, being a mid-engined fiberglass sports car with two seats. It had a striking appearance, rather like an enlarged version of the Fiat X1/9, though

Pontiac aimed to make it fuel-efficient with the General Motors 'Iron Duke' of 15lci and 92bhp. Despite its lack of sports-car performance, the Fiero did well at first, with nearly 100,000 finding buyers in the first year. But the novelty value soon wore off, and sales had halved by 1987; despite the addition of a 181-ci (2966-cc) V6 option and a five-speed manual gearbox, the Fiero was dropped in 1988. By then, the big Safari station wagon was Pontiac's only rear-driven model, and even this disappeared in 1990, replaced by the Trans Sport MPV. For 1992, the line-up consisted of Sunbird (celebrating its tenth anniversary), the Grand Am (redesigned for 1992 and Pontiac's most popular line), the Firebird (due to be replaced the following year, and now with V6 or V8 engines), the Grand Prix (the sporty intermediate, which was also restyled for 1992) and the Bonneville (now with front-wheel-drive and celebrating the 35th anniversary of the badge).

OPPOSITE and THIS PAGE
Trans Am: the most popular Firebird of all.

The fourth-generation Firebird for 1993 initially came only in coupé form, with a choice of 207-ci (3392-cc) 160-bhp V6 or 350-ci (5735-cc) 270-bhp V8, the latter standard on the Formula and Trans Am. Like the Mustang, it had originally been intended to challenge the Firebird and proved to be enduring. For 1995, the Sunbird was replaced by Sunfire, still

occupying the subcompact niche, though it was substantially a new car in sedan, coupé or convertible forms, with a choice of 133-ci (2179-cc) or 138-ci (2261-cc) fours, the latter with dohc and 16 valves offering 150bhp. There was an all-new Grand Prix for 1997, only in V6 form though with 160, 195 or 230bhp and the choice of sedan or coupé bodies, over 94,000 of which were sold.

This range – the Sunfire, Grand Prix, Grand Am, Bonneville, Trans Sport and Firebird – saw Pontiac through to the end of the century, and in 2000 it was joined by the four-wheel-drive Aztek to compete in the growing market for SUVs. As for the 21st century, with Oldsmobile gone and Pontiac's image as a sporty, dynamic badge

OPPOSITE
Early- to mid-1970s Firebirds used twin round headlights.

BELOW LEFT
The 1978 Firebird, with rectangular headlights and the famous flames motif.

PAGE 394
A Trans Am from the 1980s, struggling on through difficult times.

PAGE 395
There was a new shape for the Firebird in the late 1980s. This is a 1989 coupé.

OPPOSITE
*A 2006 Pontiac G6, powered by a 200-bhp
V6 and available as four-door sedan, two-
door coupé and the convertible shown here.*

LEFT
*New for 2006, the Torrent is Pontiac's first
true SUV, based heavily on the Chevrolet
Equinox and powered by the same Chinese-
built V6.*

POPE-HARTFORD (1904–14)

A well-regarded, high-quality car, the Pope-Hartford owed its relatively short life to low production (712 cars in its best year) and a complicated range which its sales could not support. Colonel Albert Augustus Pope was the man behind the cars, his first being a 10-hp single in two-seat runabout or four-seat tonneau forms. It was soon joined by larger cars, including a 20/24-hp four in 1906.

The big 60-hp six was launched in 1910, and Pope-Hartford built it for three years, in the meantime producing a hybrid featuring the company's own engine in a chain-driven Fiat chassis. The company went into receivership in 1913, and although production of four-cylinder engines continued into the following year, it was the end of Pope-Hartford.

QUINCY-LYNN (1975–)

The company never actually built any cars – or even kits – so Quincy-Lynn's status as a manufacturer of automobiles is tenuous to say the least. Instead, Robert Q. Riley and David L. Carey specialized in designing distinctive cars that skilled enthusiasts could build themselves in their spare time. The partners simply sold them the plans, sometimes through *Mechanix Illustrated* magazine, and via the internet later on.

A mere glance at Quincy-Lynn's plans gives some idea of their eclecticism. The Centurion was a front-engined sports car based on a Triumph Spitfire chassis but with a tiny 17-hp Kubota diesel engine providing the power. Then there was an aerodynamic strike called the Trimuter and petrol/electric hybrids such as the Town Car, while the Phoenix was a mini-camper van that could expand to sleep four people. The company was nothing if not versatile, and boats, bicycles and mini-submarines were all part of the Quincy-Lynn repertoire.

RAMBLER (1950–70)

The original Rambler was a two- or four-cylinder car made up to 1913 in Kenosha, Wisconsin. In 1950, however, the name was revived by Nash in its new compact car, though it would be another eight years before the newly-formed American Motors decided to rebadge all its cars Ramblers.

The compact Nash Rambler continued with a 197-ci (3228-cc) six-cylinder engine and its 251-ci (4113-cc) V8 derivative became the Rambler Rebel. Similarly, the 329-ci (5391-cc) V8 Nash Ambassador became the Rambler Ambassador, as a sedan, hardtop or station wagon. AMC also added the Rambler American, another compact using the same six-cylinder engine as the Nash Rambler and with similar styling. Prices, however, started at $1,775. The American range soon expanded to include a convertible and station wagon.

The Ambassador was restyled for 1961 and given a new, far more powerful aluminium ohv six, which delivered 127bhp but no extra cubic inches. The mid-sized Ramblers with the new six were renamed Classics, a fastback version of which, the Marlin, was unveiled in 1965. This had several styling cues taken from pony cars – fast back, bucket seats and so on – but, unlike the Mustang, failed to capture the public's imagination, despite two V8 options alongside the six of 289ci (4736cc) and 329ci (539Icc). Around 10,000 were sold in the first year, with sales slumping thereafter.

The Marlin was replaced in 1968 by the sportier and faster-selling Javelin, though it was badged an AMC rather than a Rambler, the name being possibly too pedestrian in this muscle-car era of the 1960s.

The American retained the Rambler name for 1969, coming as a muscle car in the form of the Hurst SC/Rambler, with a 392-ci (6424-cc) 315-bhp V8 and four-speed transmission. The Rambler name endured until 1970 in America, but only as a model name, and eventually disappeared later that year.

REEVES (1896–1912)

Milton Reeves built cars sporadically between 1896 and 1912. His main aim was to develop a variable-speed belt-pulley transmission, a system now universal in scooters but probably unique in a motor vehicle at the time. He built between six and 12 vehicles in the late-1890s to demonstrate the procedure, from the little two-cylinder Motorcycle, which was a car despite its name, to a 20-seater bus with rear wheels nearly 6ft (1.8m) across.

He also built air-cooled engines, which he supplied to various car-makers, though

Reeves built cars himself, presumably to utilize unsold engine stock when an order fell through. These included a four-cylinder shaft-driven car and a six with chain-drive. But Reeves is best remembered for the Octo-Auto, a massive four-axle, eight-wheelbed conversion of the Overland produced in 1911, none of which was sold.

REO (1904–36)

Reo was formed from the initial letters of Ransom Eli Olds' name, and was his second excursion into the car business after he left Oldsmobile, the firm that also bore his name. He originally intended the second company to be called R.E. Olds, but the new owners of Oldsmobile objected, so Reo it was.

The first Reo was a 16-hp twin, larger than the familiar Curved Dash Oldsmobile but with the same transmission layout of epicyclical gears and chain drive. The engine measured 209ci (3425cc), which wasn't unusual, but utilized one-per-cylinder twin carburetors which was. At $1,250 it was also rather more expensive than the Olds, but a single-cylinder runabout, only $35 more expensive than the Curved Dash, was soon added. Both of these cars entered production in 1905 and were joined by a 24-hp four-cylinder machine in 1906.

By 1907, Reo was outselling Olds – which must have given Ransom considerable satisfaction – capturing third place in the production league behind Ford and Buick. This was quite a feat: Reo was only in its third year in business, while

An 18-hp tourer from 1907, when Reo was second only to Ford and Buick.

Oldsmobile was firmly established, building thousands of cars a year. It would be another decade before it finally overtook Reo.

The company finally bade farewell to the little single-cylinder runabout in 1910, launching a new 35-hp four with shaft-drive and left-hand-drive when most early American cars still had it on the right. It was updated in 1912 with a centrally-mounted gear lever, which Ransom Olds declared was his greatest work and 'The Car That Marks My Limit'. Though less involved in Reo design from this point on, Ransom made a habit of vetoeing any feature he thought too modern. The Reo

the Fifth, as the 1912 car was named, was evidently as far as he thought any car should go.

Whatever Ransom may have thought, Reo had no choice but to keep up with the competition, and he agreed to the launch of a six-cylinder car in 1916. This was the 45-hp Model M, considerably more costly than Reo the Fifth's $875, but with the added sophistication of a closed Sheer-Line body. The M was later dropped, but eventually a six-cylinder successor appeared in the form of the 1920 T-6. It turned out to be one of Reo's most enduring cars, virtually unchanged in production for seven years. It was replaced in 1927 by the Flying Cloud, which was given the significant update of four-wheel hydraulic brakes and an L-head six-cylinder engine of 251ci (4113cc) and 65bhp.

The Flying Cloud was also long-lived, built almost until the end, but Reo evidently felt the need for a cheaper car, announcing the Wolverine only five months later. The Wolverine was certainly cheaper, at $1,195 for the two-door brougham, which was the only body style on offer at first. However, it was not a big-seller: it was thought that Reo's traditional, slightly upmarket clientele did not take to the car, seeing it more as a bitzer than a real Reo. Since the First World War, the company had been busy making trucks as well as cars, and it had no spare capacity to make parts for the Wolverine. So the engine was bought in from Continental, the gearbox from Warner, and so on. Reo also bought in a Continental engine for a smaller version of the Flying Cloud, quaintly naming it the Flying Cloud Mate in 1929.

But lack of capacity was the last thing on Reo's mind as the Depression began to bite. It sold 29,000 cars and trucks in 1928, its best year ever, but sales had fallen to around 6,000 by 1931. Because of its thriving truck and bus business, it is possible that Reo was not as pressurized as other small manufacturers, and was able to carry on marketing luxury cars even when times were hard. The Flying Cloud received a bigger 265-ci (4342-cc) engine in 1930, and 1931 saw the launch of the Royale, a longer-wheelbased straight-eight

with one-shot chassis lubrication. At 361ci (5916cc), its engine was an eight-cylinder version of the Flying Cloud six, and at $2,485 it was moderately well priced.

Nevertheless, the market for such cars was shrinking year on year. Reo found itself unable to weather the Depression of the mid-1930s, with the result that fewer and fewer cars were made. Even a new 85-bhp Flying Cloud was unable to prevent the decline, and Reo car production ceased in September 1936, leaving the truck and bus side to continue.

RICKENBACKER (1922–27)
The name Rickenbacker had plenty of kudos in the aftermath of the First World War. Why? Because Captain Eddie Rickenbacker had been a flying ace during the war, having brought down 26 German aircraft. However, car production proved a trickier matter and Rickenbacker the manufacturer failed after only five years, even though a creditable 27,500 cars had already been produced.

The Rickenbacker ('A Car Worthy of the Name') was launched in January 1922, being a side-valved 214-ci (3507-cc) six of 58bhp, and with the unusual feature of twin flywheels for smooth running, one at each end of the crankshaft. Prices for the tourer, sedan and coupé began at $1,485, making it well-priced for a mid-range car. After it had been in production for a few months, it was given four-wheel-brakes, an advanced feature for the time. So advanced, in fact, that Rickenbacker thought it prudent to warn other drivers of the fact

by placing a notice to the effect on the rear spare wheel.

The six was boosted to 256ci (4195cc) and 60bhp in 1925, and was joined by a 270-ci (4424-cc) straight-eight of 80bhp. The latter came in various styles, including a Super Sports two-door sedan tuned to 107bhp and capable of an alleged 90mph (145km/h). In spite of this, sales were disappointing, and Captain Rickenbacker resigned in September 1926, the company closing four months later.

RIKER (1897–1902)
The name Andrew Lawrence Riker, who built his first car in 1895, appeared on a number of electric vehicles. The following year he built an electric racing car, which later set a new American record, covering a mile in 63 seconds and beating a gasoline car in the Narragansett Races. His Electric Motor Company went on to make everything from three-wheeled runabouts to heavy tracks, all of them battery-powered, though the company merged with Columbia late in 1900.

Despite his success with electrics, Andrew Riker was convinced that the future lay in gasoline and designed a car accordingly. Rejected by the Electric Motor Co., he formed the Riker Motor Vehicle Co. and built an 8-hp twin and 16-hp four, which later formed the basis of the Locomobile.

RUXTON (1929–30)
The story of the engineering of the Ruxton is a short one: much longer was its

struggle to reach production. After the project folded, moreover, it took 30 years or so to resolve the legal wrangles that were left behind.

William Muller worked for the body-builder, Edward G. Budd of Philadelphia. In 1928, in conjunction with designer Joseph Ludwinka, also of Budd, he built a prototype front-wheel-drive car. The car had some interesting features in that its 270-ci (4424-cc) Continental straight-eight was quite conventional, but drove through a split gearbox, while constant-velocity universal joints allowed a relatively tight turning circle of 19ft (6m). The car was remarkably low to the ground, being only 63.25in (1.6m) high but with 10in (25cm) of ground clearance. There were also designs for both roadster and sedan.

The car was named the Ruxton, after financier William Ruxton, who in spite of the honour decided not to invest after all. In fact, the saga of getting the Ruxton built was only just beginning as Budd had no facilities of its own. Budd's director, Archie Andrews, tried to sell the project to Hupp, but to no avail, and attempted deals with Gardner and Marmon, both of which came to nothing. Finally the Moon Motor Car Co. agreed to build the car, and actually completed over 200. But the Moon factory was somewhat antiquated and its directors resisted what they saw as a takeover by Andrews. He defeated them, however, gaining control of the company but was forced to bring in the Kissel Motor Car Company to help build his car. But Kissel soon went into voluntary

receivership, apparently having the same fears as Moon. The whole project collapsed in November 1930, proving that building cars and making a profit is rather more difficult than signing them.

SAXON (1912–22)

Saxon is an excellent example of how quickly early American car-makers appeared and disappeared. Its successful small car placed the company seventh in the manufacturers' league in 1917, when over 28,000 cars left the factory. Yet production slumped by 50 per cent the following year, and within five years the whole enterprise had collapsed.

It is not difficult to see why 7,000 Saxons found buyers in 1912, their first year. With a bargain price of $357, the car had a four-cylinder Ferro engine and two- speed selective transmission, though electric lighting cost extra. This was made standard in 1915 and the original two-seater runabout was joined by a tourer. There was even a six-cylinder Saxon from 1916 and a closed sedan was launched the following year.

But the decline was swift after the 1917 peak. Plummeting sales and production were accompanied by internal problems, to which the company responded by dropping model after model despite a brief hiatus in 1920. Production recovered to 6,000 that year, thanks to a new ohv four named the Duplex. But none of this was enough to overcome Saxon's internal problems and production ceased in 1922.

SCRIPPS-BOOTH (1912–22)

Looking at the early career of James Scripps-Booth it would be easy to dismiss him as a dreamer with some eccentric ideas and a rich uncle. His early experiments appear to confirm this, but when Scripps-Booth cars finally reached production they were relatively conventional. Around 60,000 were built, many under the aegis of General Motors.

James was the son of a Detroit newspaper publisher, but it was his uncle, William Scripps, who funded the majority of his early endeavours. His first car was more of a motorcycle than a car, the two big fore-aft wheels supplemented by two smaller ones to keep the 'Bi-Autogo' upright at low speeds. Power was supplied by a 387-ci (6342-cc) V8, air-cooled using 450ft (137m) of copper pipe instead of a conventional radiator. Only one three-seater Bi-Autogo was built, followed by the Rocket cycle-car which used a Spacke V-twin engine and offered tandem seating. At $385 in 1914 it was actually cheaper than a Model T and 400 were built before America's brief flirtation with cycle-cars came to an end.

Booth's next idea was a more sustainable one, and once again his uncle provided the cash. He decided to build a 'luxury light car', and the Model C, launched in early 1915, seemed set to fit the bill. Offered as a coupé, with a large area of glass, or as a roadster, the Model C came with a Sterling four-cylinder engine of 104ci (1704cc). It was hampered by the difficulty in obtaining parts, and the unreliable

RIGHT
A lightweight English chassis and American
V6 power added up to the Shellby-Cobra.

BELOW
The man himself: Carroll Shelby at the
wheel of a Cobra.

Sterling was replaced by a Chevrolet unit to
produce the Model G, with a V8-engined
Model D coming in between.

By the end of 1917, James, his uncle
and company president, Clarence Booth,
had all departed, leaving Chevrolet to take
command. But Scripps-Booth didn't
immediately disappear into the General
Motors machine. In fact, thousands more
cars were built, though they were based on
bought-in parts, such as Oakland chassis
and Northway engines. But the numbers
were too small for General Motors to be
bothered with and Alfred P. Sloan ordered
production to stop in 1922, turning the
factory over to Buicks. As for James
Scripps-Booth, he moved to California and
became an artist, though his final attempts

at car production – the Da Vinci and the
associated Pup – came to nought.

SHELBY (1962–70, 1998–)
The image and legend of some cars far
outweigh the actual number made – the
Shelby Cobra being one of these. Fewer
than 1.200 of them were made, and yet the
Cobra became one of the world's iconic
marques, the ultimate marriage of
lightweight English sports car with
American V8 muscle.

It wasn't a new idea: Sidney Allard
had been building V8-powered sports cars
since 1946 and even before the war, but it
was the Cobra that would achieve
legendary status as one of the hairiest,
most exciting cars of all time. Carroll
Shelby, from Texas, was a successful

racing driver, but in the late 1950s began
to explore ways of building an American
sports car at reasonable cost. He was
rebuffed by General Motors and several
European companies before hearing that
the AC Ace needed a new engine.
Built by AC at Thames Ditton, near
London, the Ace used a lightweight steel
chassis and had a formidable record in
club racing. Supplies of its Bristol six-
cylinder engine, however, were beginning
to dry up.

Shelby's solution was to shoehorn
Ford's lightweight 261-ci (4277-cc) V8 into
the car and the Cobra was born. It was an
Anglo-American hybrid, as AC still built
the body/chassis before shipping them over
for fitment of the V8 by Shelby, first at
Sante Fe Springs, later in Venice,

California. The cars were sold as Shelby Cobras in America, AC Cobras in Britain.

Ford's later 289-ci (4736-cc) V8 was used after 75 cars had been built and nearly 600 cars utilized this engine. Of course, the little AC was not equipped to take anything so powerful, so Shelby funded a complete redesign, a joint effort between Alan Turner of AC and Phil Remington of Shelby. This enabled them to fit Ford's big-block 427-ci (6997-cc) V8 from 1965, with the addition of all-round coil-sprung suspension for a top speed of 165mph (265km/h). But even Shelby admitted that a Cobra was not for the inexperienced, remarking that 'the 427 will kill you in a second'. But the Cobra lost something of its impetus when Ford became more interested in its own racing programme, and Californian production ended in 1967. However, AC did build a few more 289s until 1969.

By then, Carroll Shelby was making his name with an indigenous performance car. The early Mustang was the stylish personal car that had been envisaged by Ford, but it was no sports car: Shelby decided to turn it into one. The first series of Shelby Mustangs formed the basis of another legend: later versions may have had more cosmetic and performance improvers, but the first GT350 was a wild, hairy machine that was near-ready to race. The 289 was hopped-up to 306bhp, and Shelby stiffened up the suspension all round, taking out the rear seat and even some of the soundproofing. At $4,567, the Shelby GT350 cost nearly $2,000 more than the standard 289 Mustang, but all of them were sold. Many ended up on the race track, winning the SCCA Class B Championship in both 1966 and 1967.

ABOVE
A 1965 Shelby Mustang GT350.

ABOVE RIGHT
A modern-day take on the classic Shelby
and a potential Cobra for the 21 st century.

RIGHT
The 1969 Shelby Mustang GT500.

The Shelby Mustang became more civilized as the years went by but the image was unchanged. Nearly 1,000 cars were famously supplied to Hertz, which rented the special black-and-gold GT350-Hs to weekend street racers. A more mundane Shelby was the big-block GT500 from 1967, offered as both fastback and convertible before Ford launched its own big-block Mustang: if that was too relaxed, the revvier GT350 now came with a 302-ci (4949-cc) V8.

Later Shelby Mustangs were assembled by Ford after the lease on Shelby's California factory had expired, and the series ended in 1969, by which time over 14,000 had been built. Carroll Shelby went on to modify various Dodges, and he was also involved in the development of the Dodge Viper. He returned to sports-car production in 1998 with the Series 1, a modern-day Cobra powered by a 350-bhp 243-ci (4015-cc) Northstar engine, mounted in a lightweight carbon-fibre body. As for the original, fewer cars have been the subject of more fibreglass replicas, built on both sides of the Atlantic, a sure sign that even in the 21st century the Shelby Cobra is regarded as the ultimate sports car.

SIMPLEX (1907–24)

Simplex built large and expensive cars in the Edwardian tradition. Its first was a 600-ci (9832-cc) four of 50hp, with T-head layout and square bore and stroke dimensions, which was unusual at the time. This substantial motor was mounted in an equally substantial chassis with twin chain-drive and a four-speed gearbox (also unusual). About 250 Simplexes were built in New York between 1907 and 1913, the limited production being largely due to their price: even the cheapest roadster was $5,500, though one could spend far more if coach-built bodywork was preferred.

A smaller Model 38, with a 479-ci (7849-cc) engine, though based on the same layout, was offered from 1911 and in 1914 the original big four was replaced by a new car of similar size but with a long-stroke engine, while the chain-drive was retained.

Later that year, the company bought the Crane Motor Car Co. of Bayonne, New Jersey: the renamed Crane Simplex company began to build Crane's six-cylinder shaft-driven car, and continued to offer its big, expensive machines until 1924.

STANLEY (1897–1929)

In the first few years of the 20th century, it seemed as though electric and steam power were as much fuels of the future as gasoline. But by 1910, no one was in any doubt that gasoline was in the ascendant, though the brief flowering of steam left some interesting stories behind. Of these, that of the Stanley brothers must surely be the best-known. They may not have been

the most prolific producers of steam cars, but they were the longest surviving; moreover their cars were practical and fast and managed to acquire several speed records along the way.

Identical twins Francis Edgar and Freelan Oscar Stanley had made their fortune in the photographic industry, perfecting a process for coating dry plates which they later sold to George Eastman of Kodak. They also experimented with steam cars, completing their first prototype in 1897. It was small and lightweight, with a two-cylinder steam engine weighing only 35lb (16kg) driving the rear axle by chain. The boiler was strengthened by winding piano wire around it, thus allowing it to accommodate higher pressure than most of its contemporaries.

The Stanley steamer was shown at an exhibition in Boston in 1898, where

onlookers were impressed by the practical trials, in which a mile was covered in two minutes 32 seconds while scaling a 30 per cent incline. Orders flowed in, and about 200 steamers were built up to 1899. In that same year, John Brisbane Walker, publisher of *Cosmopolitan* magazine, bought the business for the colossal sum of $250,000, on condition that the brothers made no cars for at least a year. By 1901, they had bought it back at a fraction of the price and were building a lightweight steam car that tipped the scales at 700lb (317kg) and cost only $650. The range soon broadened, and several Stanley steamers were coaxed up to very high speeds. The most spectacular was the Stanley Rocket, taken to a new world speed record of 127.659mph (205.44km/h) by Fred Marriott in 1906. Fred tried to improve the record the following year, but was lucky to escape with his life when the car flipped at an estimated 150mph (241km/h).

Thereafter, the Stanley brothers were content to sell steamers like the Model H Gentleman's Speedy Roadster, which with 20hp could top 75mph (121km/h). There were improvements for 1907, including rear-wheel brakes, a fully lubricated engine and a new line in commercial steamers. But with thousands of cheap, simple and quick-starting Model Ts coming onto the roads, it was clear that the days of steam power were numbered. In 1916 Stanley responded with a much updated car. This had a steel chassis, the former having been of wood, with semi-elliptical front springs, left-hand-drive, and a condenser to recycle used steam into water and thus improve the range. The Model 720 tourer now cost $3,400, its origins as a lightweight having been left far behind.

Francis and Freelan resigned from the business, but the Stanley steamer soldiered on into the 1920s, surviving on ever smaller sales. By 1923 the firm was bankrupt and was bought by the Steam Vehicle Corporation of America, which carried on making Stanley steamers in ever-decreasing numbers until it too gave up the struggle in 1929.

STAR (1922–28)

Several American car-makers were known as Star, but by far the most prolific was the company run by William C. Durant. It was Durant's ambition to build an automotive giant to challenge the biggest in the country. By 1921, his mid-priced Durant car was in production, but he also needed a cheaper car to tackle Henry Ford head-on. This was the Star Four, with costs cut to the bone so as to match Ford's rockbottom prices. Durant managed to achieve this, the Star Four roadster and tourer selling for $319 and $348 respectively – exactly the same as their Ford counterparts. Typically, Ford soon slashed his prices by another $50, which Durant couldn't hope to match, but the Stars were still on a par with Chevrolet prices and over 170,000 cars were built in 1923.

The basis of Durant's Ford-beater was a conventional four-cylinder car using a 131-ci (2147-cc) Continental engine, the only unusual feature being the gearbox mounted separately from the engine instead of bolted to it. The Star came as sedan and coupé as well as roadster and tourer, and an open-sided station wagon soon followed, together with a delivery van.

A larger 152-ci (2491-cc) four-cylinder engine was offered for 1926, also a 170-ci (2786-cc) six. Both were from Continental, which remained the supplier of Durant's engines, he being its biggest customer. The Star range was extended again with the Compound Fleetruck, and four-wheel brakes were standardized for 1927. But the glory days of Billy Durant's attempt to out-Ford Ford were long since gone. Sales declined, and he renamed the Stars Durants in April 1928, with the result that sales plummeted even more. Fewer than 21,000 were produced in 1930, the final Durant cars appearing in 1932.

STEARNS (1901–1929)

Although it was in the car-making business for over 30 years, Stearns never built cars in big numbers, concentrating, with one exception, on the top end of the market. Frank Ballou Stearns began early, being only 17 when he built his first car in the basement of his parents' home. By the time he was 19, and with the help of the Owen brothers, he was building cars to sell, this time in a workshop at the back of the house.

There was little radical about these first Stearns cars, apart from the steering wheel, as most small cars of 1901 used the simpler tiller steering. Power came from a relatively massive single-cylinder of 230ci (3769cc), the piston measuring over 6in (152mm) across and working through a stroke of over 7in (178mm). The following year this was joined by a 24-hp twin of 337ci (5522cc) and by 1904, after an injection of capital allowed Stearns to move out of his backyard workshop, by a 36-hp four.

The Stearns increased in size and sophistication over the next few years, adopting mechanically operated side valves and featuring a 45/90-hp car with a 798-ci (13077-cc) six-cylinder engine in 1908. But a new technical era began in 1911 when the company adopted the sleeve-valve engine. Chief engineer, James G. Sterling, had gone to England to study the Knight sleeve-valve engine, of which Daimler was the leading exponent, returning so impressed that the entire Stearns range had been given sleeve valves by 1912.

In 1913, these comprised two engines, a 28-hp 313-ci (5129-cc) four and 43.8-hp 417-ci (6833-cc) six. They came in a choice of five wheelbases, from 115 to 140in (2.9 to 3.5m), and were joined by a smaller Light Four of 22.5hp and around 245ci (4015cc) in 1915. With prices starting at $1,750, the Light Four took Stearns into a new market, boosting sales to over 3,700 by 1917.

This turned out to be the zenith of Stearns production. Frank Stearns retired that year to make his name in diesel research, and James Sterling left the year after, taking several key staff with him. John N. Willys bought the company in 1925, seeing the classy sleeve-valved Stearns as a suitable addition to his existing Willys-Knight. By 1927, the range consisted of two sixes and a 100-bhp straight-eight, the cheapest of which was nearly $4,000. However, only around 1,000 cars a year were sold in the late 1920s, the truth being that Stearns was finding it difficult to compete with established luxury cars such as Packard. Production ended shortly before Christmas 1929.

STEVENS-DURYEA (1901–15, 1919–27)
The Stevens-Duryea had two periods of activity, both of them limited to the production of around 100 luxury cars a year. Its roots lay in the Hampden Automobile & Launch Company, which had been started by J. Frank Duryea after he left his brother Charles and the Duryea Motor Wagon Company. A prototype car soon followed, which was renamed

Stevens-Duryea after the J. Stevens Arms & Tool Company acquired an interest in the company.

By late 1901, the Stevens-Duryea runabout was in production: it was a little 5-hp car, with tiller steering like many of its contemporaries but with a sliding gear transmission instead of the usual epicyclical arrangement. From small beginnings the company progressed swiftly upmarket, launching a four-cylinder car in 1905 and a six the following year. A 20-hp four and smaller 338-ci (5539-cc) Light Six were added soon afterwards. By 1912, only sixes were being made and the company was running out of cash. Production was suspended in 1915.

It resumed four years later, after Ray S. Deering with a group of former employees bought the name. The old six reappeared as the 80-bhp Model E, though it now cost up to $9,500, with production strictly limited as before. Receivership came three years later, but the company re-emerged 14 months after when it was purchased by a syndicate. This time, production of the renamed Model G was strictly to order, and very few were made before Stevens-Duryea finally expired in 1927.

STUDEBAKER (1902–66)
Studebaker was not the first company in America to build cars but it was certainly the longest-lived. The Studebaker brothers, Henry and Clem, had begun business back in 1852, making wagons, and 20 years on were the largest wagon builders in the world, using an early form

of mass-production to complete a vehicle every seven minutes.

This gave them plenty of capital to diversify into cars, with the result that the Studebaker Corporation was one of America's major car producers for many

Detail of the spinning prop on a 1950 Studebaker Starlight.

years, second only to Ford in 1911 and building over 100,000 cars a year by 1923. But the company's later history demonstrates how difficult it was, especially after the Second World War, for an independent manufacturer to compete with Detroit's Big Three, even with the styling talent of Virgil Exner, the early adoption of an ohv V8 and such stunning post-war cars as the Hawk and Avanti and the successful compact Lark.

The first Studebaker cars were electrics, developed from a prototype built as early as 1897, the first production cars arriving five years later. They were designed by none other than Thomas Alva Edison, being simple two-seater machines with single motors. Bigger twin-motored cars arrived the following year with a four-seater and a commercial, while the stately 'china-closet' coupé was added in 1906. Studebaker would carry on making electric

cars up to 1912, though only in small numbers, with fewer than 2,000 built in all.

The reason for this early concentration on electrics was John Mohler Studebaker, younger brother of the two founders, who complained that gasoline cars stank to high heaven. But Frederick Fish, his son-in-law, had a more positive attitude and bought the remains of the General Automobile Company in 1903. Twenty-five complete cars were part of the deal, and

OPPOSITE
1950 Studebaker Starlight.

ABOVE
1953 Studebaker Hawk.

RIGHT and OPPOSITE
Studebaker stole a march on the Big Three
with all-new styling for 1946, then followed
it up with this Hawk coupé six years later.
Ford, General Motors and Chrysler had
nothing that could match it.

these were sold as Model A Studebakers, powered by a 12-hp flat-twin engine mounted beneath the seat.

Fish intended to continue production, but the Studebaker factory had no facilities for gasoline engineering, so he contracted the Garford Co. of Ohio to build chassis, while Studebaker made the bodies. This arrangement would last for several years, and 1904 saw both a more powerful 16-hp Model C and a Model B delivery van. A 20-hp four-cylinder shaft-driven car followed in 1905, when the twins were dropped, the Garford fours being offered in a range of sizes up to 40hp until 1910.

The drawback of the arrangement with Garford was that the cars were expensive (up to $4,000) and Frederick Fish's ambition was to become a major manufacturer. He achieved this by buying the EMF company in 1908–10, maker of the EMF 30 that sold for $1,250. At that time the wastage of pioneer companies was high, and Fish also bought several defunct car factories, dramatically expanding Studebaker's capacity. As a result, nearly

8,000 cars were made in 1909, 15,000 in 1910 and nearly 27,000 the year after, confirming its second place behind Ford.

By 1913, the company was finally building complete cars, no longer having to rely on subcontractors like EMF. There were three cars: the 193-ci (3163-cc) A25, 269-ci (4408-cc) AA35 (both of them fours) and the six-cylinder 290-ci (4752-cc) Model E, the latter claimed to be the cheapest six in America at $1,550. Production boomed to over 65,000 in 1916. By 1920, the fours had gone and a new factory was built at South Bend, Indiana, where the Studebakers had always been based, to make the new 208-ci (3408-cc) Light Six. Studebaker was now well-established as a maker of mid-priced six-cylinder cars, ranging from $975 to $2,750, the Light Six, Special Six and Big Six, the latter two derived from the 1913

OPPOSITE and LEFT
Despite its graceful lines, the Hawk had too limited an appeal to give Studebaker the major sales it needed to survive.

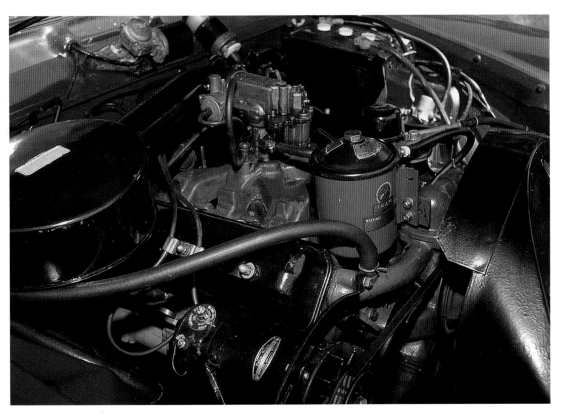

1963 Studebaker Avanti. This was a stylish fibreglass coupé designed to compare with imported sports cars.

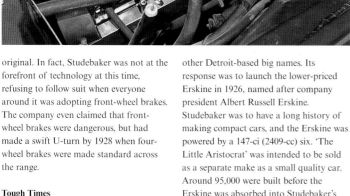

original. In fact, Studebaker was not at the forefront of technology at this time, refusing to follow suit when everyone around it was adopting front-wheel brakes. The company even claimed that front-wheel brakes were dangerous, but had made a swift U-turn by 1928 when four-wheel brakes were made standard across the range.

Tough Times

Sales were booming once again, to over 146,000 in 1923, but Studebaker was now falling well behind Ford, Chevrolet and the other Detroit-based big names. Its response was to launch the lower-priced Erskine in 1926, named after company president Albert Russell Erskine. Studebaker was to have a long history of making compact cars, and the Erskine was powered by a 147-ci (2409-cc) six. 'The Little Aristocrat' was intended to be sold as a separate make as a small quality car. Around 95,000 were built before the Erskine was absorbed into Studebaker's main range.

Albert Erskine took the company upmarket around this time, offering coach-built bodywork on the existing sixes and launching a new straight-eight in 1928. The President Eight was a 100-hp car, its side-valved engine measuring 315ci (5162cc). Prices started at under $2,000 for a five-seater sedan, there being eight body styles from which to choose, which made the stylish President seem like good value when compared with a Lincoln. A bigger 339-ci (5555-cc) version of 115bhp followed, as did longer wheelbases; but the bigger Presidents were dropped as the Depression made itself felt, leaving a 251-ci (4113-cc) derivative to carry on.

ABOVE LEFT and ABOVE
A powerful V8 and sports-car interior gave the Avanti great appeal.

Meanwhile, Studebaker was having a rough time. Albert Erskine had engineered a merger with Pierce-Arrow, but the Depression hit both firms hard. With profits plummeting, Erskine continued to pay out large dividends to its shareholders, with the result that by 1933 the corporation was $15 million in debt. Studebaker went into receivership and a personally bankrupt Erskine committed suicide soon after. But the company not only recovered but also prospered. Harold Vance and Paul Hoffman, respective vice-presidents of sales and engineering, took control of the company, sold off Pierce-Arrow and began to set their house in order.

They concentrated on lower-priced cars, which was the correct thing to do in the mid-1930s. Another attempt at a compact car, the Rockne, was only moderately successful, but the six-cylinder Dictator Model A and Commander and President straight-eights were well-priced quality cars that sold well. Over 49,000 Studebakers were sold in 1935, when all the debts were cleared, with 85,000 the following year. These bigger cars were gradually updated throughout the late 1930s, but Studebaker couldn't resist the promise of compact cars, launching the Champion in 1939. With this, it finally achieved true success, selling over 215,000 before production was suspended on the outset of war. At a starting price of $660, the Champion offered a 78-bhp six-cylinder engine, column gear change and distinctive styling by the Raymond Loewy studio. Consequently, by 1941, although Studebaker was still well behind the Detroit

Big Three, it was now the leading independent make.

In fact, for a brief period after the war, the company from South Bend looked like catching them up. The big manufacturers made do with warmed-over pre-war cars until the 1949 model year, but Studebaker launched its new post-war styling in March 1946. It was a real coup, especially as it featured the distinctive style of Virgil Exner, with curved windshields and rear windows, short hoods and big trunks. The company had considered such radical moves as a rear-mounted flat-six engine to go with the new look, but in the event stuck with the pre-war side-valve sixes of 170ci (2786cc) and 227ci (3720cc) for the Champion and Commander respectively.

Rapid Decline

Compared with a lightly disguised 1941 Ford, these new Studebakers were sensational, and sales leapt to over 228,000 in 1949 and 268,000 the following year. Other independent manufacturers of the time were soon disadvantaged by their lack of an ohv V8, but Studebaker offered a new 232-ci (3802-cc) V8 from 1951. Neither did it allow the 1947 styling to get stale, introducing an all-new look for 1953. Long, low and elegant, it was another product of the Loewy studio (though not Virgil Exner, who had since moved to Chrysler) and the Land Cruiser sedan and Starlight coupé made a particular impact. There were Custom, Deluxe and Regal trim levels, while engine options were limited to the venerable Champion 170-ci (2786-cc) six of

85bhp and the new Commander V8, offering 120bhp from 232ci.

The 1953 Studebakers were stylish and classy and could still offer something different from mainstream Detroit, but the company seemed to be losing its golden touch. Sales dropped to fewer than 190,000 that year and halved in 1954. The company had enlarged the Commander V8 to 26lci (4277-cc) and 210bhp and finally to 29lci (4769cc), but it wasn't enough to compete in the horsepower race that was sweeping Detroit. Post-war Americans wanted power, performance and glamour at an affordable price, and Studebaker began to find itself increasingly sidelined. The Hawk coupé, which continued the 1955 look, was good-looking and fast in later Packard-powered Golden Hawk form, but was still a niche product. Styling, moreover, which had been such a strong point in early post-war Studebakers, lost its way from the mid-1950s, lacking the grace and individuality of the earlier cars.

A merger with Packard in 1954 failed to yield the promised solution to combat the Big Three, though Packard's 275-bhp V8 was a useful addition. Two years later, Studebaker-Packard was bought by aircraft-maker Curtiss-Wright, and for a while looked like a company with a new focus. A new president, Harold Churchill, was part of the Curtiss-Wright package, who determined that the way for Studebaker was to respond with a new compact car.

The 1958 Lark was just that, based on a 108-in (2.7-m) wheelbase with the

Champion six or Commander V8 engines, the latter in 261-ci (4277-cc) guise. There were sedan and coupé versions, both somewhat boxy in appearance. Like the Rambler, it managed to steal a march on Detroit's own compact cars, and did very well in its first year, selling 138,000, which brought total Studebaker production to nearly 154,000. It carried on with minor improvements right to the end, and was the last car to leave the Studebaker line. Meanwhile, the Hawk coupé was now the only other car in the range. It continued up to 1963 with Studebaker's own V8s, the bigger 291-ci (4769-cc) unit offered in 335-bhp supercharged form.

But although Studebaker was struggling, it certainly went out on a high note with the Avanti, a striking fibreglass coupé with European looks, based on a shortened Lark chassis. All Avantis used the 291-ci V8, but in various states of tune, from 240bhp, in supercharged, bored-out form, to 335bhp. Even with the base engine, the Avanti slipped through the air cleanly enough to reach 124mph (199km/h), a specially prepared car reaching 168.24mph (270.75km/h) over a flying kilometre, setting a new American stock-car record in the process. Sadly, production and problems with the quality of the unfamiliar fibreglass delayed the car's delivery, and many buyers lost interest. Less than 4,000 were sold in 1963 and only 809 the following year.

By this time, Studebaker sales had dropped so low that the parent company decided to close the South Bend factory

and move Lark production to Hamilton, Ontario, where Studebaker had long maintained a plant. Straight-six and V8 Larks were made here until March 1966, later with General Motors engines. That was the end of Studebaker, but the Avanti lived on, made in limited numbers by two ex-Studebaker dealers (see Avanti).

STUTZ (1911–34)
In terms of models, marques and makes, the American motor industry has produced relatively few sports cars, despite its prolific output. Of these, even fewer are household names, but alongside the Corvette and Shelby Cobra must come the Stutz Bearcat. Harry Clayton Stutz was a farmer's son from Ausonia, Ohio, who built his first car as early as 1898, yet didn't go into production until 1911. Within a few years, his young company came under the control of financier Alan Ryan, leading Stutz to resign, disillusioned, by the new boss's preference for playing

The 1919 Stutz Bearcat, one of America's few true sports cars

the stock market rather than making exciting cars. This should have been the reason for a decline in Stutz engineering and individuality, and yet the company built some of its finest cars, such as a 32-valve straight-eight, after its founder left.

Stutz made not only sportsters but also a huge variety of cars, though its roots really lay in racing. Harry Stutz's early experimental cars never reached production, however, and he worked for a variety of car firms in Indianapolis up to 1910. When he did go into business on his own account, it was to make a combined gearbox and rear axle of his own design, which he proved by building a racing car around it. This finished the first Indianapolis 500 race in the mid-field, with the result that Stutz went on to build replicas of the race car.

This he did from August 1911, using a Wisconsin 391-ci (6407-cc) engine driving through the patented Stutz transaxle. Although based on the racer layout, the car was offered as a four-seat tonneau and five-seat tourer as well as a two-seater roadster. The famous Bearcat was added in 1912, being little more than the roadster with some of its comforts, such as doors, removed. Capable of over 70mph (113km/h), the first Stutz Bearcat was a spartan machine with little in the way of bodywork apart from two bucket seats, a large external fuel tank and a couple of spare tyres.

A cheaper version of the Bearcat was offered from 1915, powered by a 23-hp four-cylinder engine. With a lower price of

$1,475 it wasn't a success and was dropped after a year, which hardly mattered as the full-sized Stutz was already earning itself a reputation on race tracks and hill climbs. The Bearcat name was used right through to 1925, though by then the model had lost some of its austerity, adopting doors and even a windshield. In fact, it's a myth to see all Stutz cars as uncompromising Bearcats: the early tourers were later joined by closed sedans, and from 1912 the company offered a six-cylinder engine as a more civilized alternative to the Wisconsin.

By 1917, sales had climbed to over 2,000, though there was a fallow period between 1915 and 1925, when Stutz was under the control of financiers rather than people familiar with the industry. Alan Ryan, who was the cause of Harry Stutz leaving the company he had founded, lost control in 1920, but steel magnate Charles M. Schwab proved little more sympathetic, though the company was building its own engines by now. These were a 307-ci (5031-cc) T-head 16-valve four, similar to the Wisconsin, and a 270-ci (4424-cc) six.

But a new manager, Frederick E. Moscovics, was installed in 1924, who realized that Stutz needed a straight-eight to keep up with the competition and swept away the four and six, replacing them with an all-new overhead-cam eight of 290ci (4752cc). Designed by Swiss-born Charles Greuter, this 92-bhp engine powered a chassis with underslung worm drive, allowing a low-slung body. The Stutz Vertical Eight or 'Safety Stutz', the windshield being of safety glass, came in

five body styles, all at $2,995, and was highly successful. Five thousand cars were sold in its first year (1926), more than doubling Stutz's output, though its success was shortlived and sales gradually declined thereafter.

The Vertical Eight was given more power for 1927 (95bhp) and '28 (115bhp), with a longer wheelbase that extended the range of coach-built bodies available. It was fast, too, winning all but one of the 1927 AAA stock-car races, and setting a new U.S. Stock Car speed record the following year at 106.53mph (171.44km/h), while another Stutz was second in the 1928 Le Mans 24 Hours. The most sporting variant on the Vertical Eight were the Black Hawk boat-tailed speedsters, which came as two- or four-seaters and were developed with the help of racing driver Frank Lockhart.

Sadly, however, Stutz was now on the decline. Not everyone liked the way Moscovics ran the business and he resigned in January 1929. That same year Stutz launched the cheaper Blackhawk, which was not a success, being outsold even by the pricier cars in the range. Sales were down to a miserable 720 in 1930, but Stutz persevered, developing the straight-eight into the 113-bhp SV16, with two valves per cylinder, and the 156-bhp DV32 with four. The DV32, in particular, was something of a masterpiece, with its hemispherical combustion chambers, and was available as a $1,000 option over the whole range. This now ran to 32 models on two wheelbases, with prices up to $7,495.

With a nod to the past, the Bearcat name was used on the short-wheelbased roadster, with a Super Bearcat on an ultra-short one of 116in. But still sales continued to fall, with Stutz selling only six cars in 1934. Stutz production ended that year.

The name was revived in 1970 on the Virgil Exner-styled Pontiac-based Blackhawk coupé, various forms of which were built in tiny numbers up to 1986.

TERRAPLANE (1932–38)

Terraplane was a cheaper line of cars launched by Hudson, a manufacturer of mid-priced cars, in 1932, intended to steal a slice of the low-price market from Ford and Chevrolet. In this it succeeded, with prices starting at a competitive $425. The Terraplane's chassis was all-new and of a tapered design, being far lighter than a conventional ladder chassis. Its 106-in (2.7-m) wheelbase was also significantly smaller

than that of the Hudson Essex. With the Essex side-valve six enlarged to 194ci (3179cc) and 70bhp, and weighing 500lb (227kg) less than the equivalent Essex, its performance was more than sprightly.

Using a smaller version of Hudson's own eight, a straight-eight was added in 1933, proving successful in competition and setting new records at Pikes Peak and Daytona. With a wider track and longer wheelbase, it wasn't quite as compact as

the original Terraplane, but proved a worthy competitor for Ford's bargain-priced V8. But the eight lasted only a year, as in 1934 all Hudson cars adopted the Terraplane's lightweight chassis design, which blurred the differences between the two lines. This didn't prevent Hudson from selling over 70,000 Terraplanes the following year, however, making the whole company profitable in the process.

Meanwhile, Terraplanes became ever closer to Hudsons in specification, sharing many of the same features, with Hudson-like bodies from 1937 and even a Hudson badge from '38. The Terraplane name disappeared at the end of that year, but from Hudson's point of view it had done its job.

TUCKER (1946–48)
Preston Thomas Tucker's company was in voluntary liquidation even before full production had been realized, but its story lives on. Tucker was a salesman who had partnered the racing-car designer Harry Miller, and now believed he had the car to captivate post-war America.

That prototype Tucker Torpedo seems radical even today. In 1946, when most American cars made do with side-valve sixes, drum brakes and other pre-war technology, it must have seemed like something from outer space. It was a flat-six with fuel injection; transmission was via a pair of torque converters; there was all-independent suspension and all-round disc brakes: and the massive 592-ci (9701-cc) engine was mounted in the rear. At a

time, moreover, when the industry ignored issues of safety as bad for sales, the Tucker featured seat belts, a padded dashboard and pop-out windshield.

Not surprisingly, many of these things never made it beyond the first prototype. The engine, understressed and low-revving, was designed to run 185,000 miles (297 720km) without overhaul, and to produce 170bhp. But it proved troublesome and impractical to build, and was soon rejected in favour of a 336-ci (5506-cc) Franklin flat six, originally designed for helicopters, which Tucker converted to water-cooling. With 166bhp, it was strong enough to push the big six-seater Torpedo to 121mph (195km/h). The twin torque converter set-up also went, replaced by either a conventional automatic or a pre-selector transmission that was based on Cord components.

Tucker had big plans for his car, raising money by selling franchises to 1,000 dealers and launching a $20 million share offer. A large factory in Chicago was leased, but Tucker was accused of fraud by the Securities and Exchange Commission as production approached. It transpired that the car he was about to sell was different from the one on which he had raised the money. This was true, of course, though it could also be argued that the production-ready Tucker had more potential than the 592-ci original

In the event, Tucker was cleared of all criminal charges, but in the meantime bad publicity and financial strain had proved too much and the company went into

voluntary liquidation after only 51 cars had been built. The avant-garde Torpedo, with its swiveling central headlight and 24-volt electrics was dead on the ground, but it had been way ahead of its time in its dedication to both primary and secondary safety. As for Preston Tucker, he reappeared a few years later with a plan to make a small and sporty rear-engined car in Brazil, but died of lung cancer before it could be accomplished.

WALTHAM (1902–08)
Waltham, of Waltham, Massachusetts, built one of the simplest cars ever made. It was the Orient Buckboard, consisting of a frame of wooden slats and a single-cylinder 4-hp engine geared directly to the rear axle. There was no suspension and no transmission. Later Buckboards did become a little more sophisticated when a four-seater surrey-topped version appeared, with fully-elliptical suspension, a steering wheel and a small fairing to protect the driver's feet. At $375 in 1905, bodywork was non-existent, though the Buckboard was cheap for its time.

Waltham also offered a more conventional car from 1905, with a front-mounted 16-hp four-cylinder engine mated to a friction transmission and chain final drive. Production was stopped in 1908 when C.H. Metz returned to take control of the company he had founded back in 1893.

WELCH (1903–11)
It may not be a household name, but the

Welch Motor Car Company can claim a number of firsts. It is thought to have been the first American car with overhead valves and hemispherical combustion chambers, both coming in 1901, and the first with an overhead camshaft (1906). Brothers A.R. and Fred Welch put their hemi-head 20-hp twin into production in 1903, but production ceased when the money ran out after only 15 had been made.

A.R. found a new source of finance and from then on built larger four-cylinder cars such as a 30/36-hp and a 50-hp from 1906. A 70-hp six was added in 1907, which was hardly cheap at $7,000 for the limousine. A smaller 40-hp four followed two years later, but General Motors took over the company in 1910, and production ended soon after. Some Welch features later surfaced in Buick's companion car, the Marquette.

WHITE (1900–18)

White made only steam cars during its first ten years in production. Rollin White's father had a sewing machine company which diversified into cars when a lightweight two-seater steamer, with the engine mounted horizontally under the seat, was produced. It used a semi-flash boiler, which superheated the steam and made the little White quite a practical machine. Eighteen were built in the first year, 191 in 1901 and nearly 400 in '02. The first steam car was superseded by the more advanced four-seater Model C in 1903, featuring front-mounted engine,

tonneau body and shaft drive. It also had a wheel instead of the original steamer's tiller steering. Over 1,500 of these were built in 1906 when Theodore Roosevelt became the first U.S. president to drive a White steamer.

The company was given another boost that year when it split from its sewing machine parent with $2.5 million of capital and a new factory. Meanwhile, by 1910, the steamer had expanded into a 40-hp limousine or landaulet, with a smaller Model O-O also offered from $2,000. White built 1,208 steamers that year, alongside a similar number of gasoline cars, the 30-hp four-cylinder Models G-A and G-B with four-speed transmission.

These were joined by the 40-hp Model E in 1911 when the steamers were dropped, and by a 60-hp six the following year, while a 16-valve four-cylinder engine featured in 1917.

But for White, passenger cars were becoming increasingly irrelevant to its main business, which was commercial vehicles, and they were dropped in 1918. White trucks and buses, of course, had a far longer life.

WILLYS (1914–63)

How does one summarize the story of a company like Willys? It is a roller-coaster tale in which the highlights were the undercutting of Ford, securing third place

The 1903 White steamer, White soon dropped cars, both steam and gasoline, to concentrate on trucks.

ABOVE
The 1940 Willys Jeep heralded the birth of an automotive legend.

RIGHT
The 1949 Willys station wagon was an attempt to broaden the Jeep's civilian appeal.

the name wasn't used on cars for another five years in the Willys-Knight. This was the result of a trip to Europe where John Willys saw a Daimler with a sleeve-valved engine. He was so impressed that he bought a licence to use the Knight patents covering sleeve valves and sailed home.

The first Willys-Knight was no less than a renamed Edwards-Knight, with a 284-ci (4654-cc) sleeve-valved four-cylinder engine, offered at $2,750 as a roadster engine, offered at $2,750 as a roadster or tourer. This arrangement only lasted from late 1914 to the summer of 1915, when Willys transferred production to the large new factory he had built for Overland at Toledo, Ohio. Soon after the move, Willys launched a much cheaper four-cylinder sleeve-valve, starting at only

in the manufacturers' league and building one of the world's iconic vehicles, the Jeep. Lows included two brushes with bankruptcy before finally succumbing to a takeover by Kaiser. Pivotal to much of this story was John North Willys himself, the self-made super-salesman and entrepreneur, who almost single-handedly saved the Overland company, turned it around and made it a thriving business (see Overland).

Overland, in fact, formed the basis of what became Willys. The company was renamed Willys-Overland in 1909. though

$1,095. This was the key to increasing sales and was followed by a Knight-engined six in 1916, with a V8 the following year, all of them very good value indeed.

Then the roller coaster took off, Willys had a profitable First World War, but no sooner had peacetime production resumed than a strike closed the Toledo factory for much of 1919. By the end of the year, the company was over $30 million in debt, the banks only agreeing to a stay of execution on condition that Walter P. Chrysler came to turn the company round. This he did. halving John Willys' salary in the process; by the end of 1921 he had gone and Willys was back in control. Chrysler thought little of sleeve-valves, but Willys proved him wrong, making a success of the Willys-Knight four and selling over 150,000 of

The 1946 Willys Universal, one of the first civilian Jeeps. Willys hoped that farmers, hunters and others needing four-wheel-drive would keep sales buoyant once the war had ended, which they did.

Willys had to update the Jeep for military use, as in this MB, changes which also found their way onto the civilian line.

them in 1925. It was joined by the six-cylinder Model 66, another well-priced sleeve-valve that started at $1,850. The six measured 256ci (4195cc) and gave 60bhp. It was originally a Sterling-Knight design, which Willys bought: he also purchased the top-class Stearns-Knight and backed the launch of the cheaper Falcon-Knight, which was later absorbed into the Willys-Knight range. John Willys, in short, appeared to be on a one-man crusade to promote the Knight sleeve-valved engine in America! These, of course, were all

produced alongside Overland cars which had conventional poppet valves.

But John Willys still had two ambitions: to produce a smaller car and to undercut Ford, both of which he realized in the Whippet. Introduced in mid 1926, this was a remarkably advanced little car, given its low price. It had four-wheel-brakes and balloon tyres, full-pressure lubrication and pumped water-cooling. The four-cylinder engine was of 133ci (2179cc), smaller than that of the Overland Four but offering the same 30hp. Its

lightness also made the Whippet surprisingly fast, like its namesake, and capable of achieving a top speed of 60mph (100km/h). At first, the car was priced slightly above the Overland Four, reflecting its advanced specification, but by 1928 the four-seat cabriolet cost $545 – $5 less than a Ford Model A.

The four-cylinder Whippet was joined by a six in early 1927, and fitting the Overland Six engine to the lightweight chassis, albeit lengthened by 5in (13cm), produced even more sparkling performance. The six was given more power the following year, as was the four. The Whippets were highly successful, taking Willys to its highest ever peak of 315,000 cars in 1927. enough for a third place in the manufacturers' league. But Willys was to experience a spectacular downturn after the Wall Street crash, when it slipped to sixth place. Maybe that wasn't so bad, but it masked a desperate financial crisis.

In the meantime, just before the crash, John Willys had sold all his Willys-Overland stock and had swapped his industrial career for politics, serving as U.S. Ambassador to Poland. But in 1932, hearing how bad things were, he threw in the job and returned to the States to rescue the company. The four-cylinder Whippet had never been replaced, so he hastened the introduction of the Model 77. a similar car with more modern styling and a base price of only $335. By now Willys-Overland was in receivership, permitted to build cars only in batches as finances allowed, but it still managed to build over 77,000 Model 77s over four years, and by August 1935 had emerged from receivership. Sadly, John North Willys had died of a heart attack only 11 days earlier.

Uppers & Downers
But Willys-Overland could not escape from this fluctuation in its fortunes. Sales boomed to over 76,000 in 1937, then slumped to a little over 16,000 the following year. The Model 77 was updated as the 37 and then the 48, with a longer wheelbase, restyling and hydraulic brakes among other

advances. Sales had recovered to nearly 29,000 by 1941, though Willys was still a minnow in a very large pond. What gave the company a new lease of life, and was probably its salvation, was the Jeep. This was designed by American Bantam, which did not have the resources to build it. With war imminent, the American government needed thousands of Jeeps as soon as possible and gave Willys and Ford the contract to build them: Willys would make over 360,000 of them up to 1945.

The Jeep, of course, was a remarkable

vehicle in its own right, regardless of who built it. It combined four-wheel-drive and adaptability in a nimble yet tough package. It could tow, exceed 65mph (105km/h) and negotiate difficult terrain. Best of all, as far as Willys was concerned, it introduced thousands of servicemen and women to the brand and became strongly identified with the war effort as a result. It wasn't a mere tool – people became attached to their Jeeps. So, as well as keeping Willys going during the war it also became the key to its post-war profitability.

One of the first Wintons from 1899, when it was the most popular car in the U.S.A.

Immediately after the war, Willys began to promote the Jeep as a peacetime working vehicle. At first, only farmers were targeted, but the company's new boss, Charlie Sorensen, thought the Jeep could make it into the family market as well. Consequently, Brooks Stevens designed the Jeep station wagon with four seats and windows all round, of which 33,000 were delivered in 1947. It was followed by the Jeepster, an open four-seater fun car that sold in lower numbers due to its higher price. Both were available with a 149-ci (2442-cc) six as well as the basic Jeep's four. But the early passenger Jeeps would never equal the success achieved in the later civilian market.

Fortunately, Willys had ambitions to return to the car market, which it did in 1952 with the Aero compact car. It was quite up to date, with a unitary-construction body, and predated Detroit's own compact cars. The Aero Lark came with a 163-ci (2671-cc) side-valve six of 75bhp, while the upscaled Aero Wing, Ace and Eagle adopted a 90-bhp version of the same unit, with inlet-over-exhaust valves. At first, the Aero's novelty attracted plenty of attention, and over 31,000 were sold in its first year, with 41,000 in 1953. But as the market became more affluent, sales began to shrink. It was not helped by its relatively high price: even in basic side-valve form, the compact Aero was around $200 more than a full-sized Ford.

With the Aero failing and the Jeep still selling in relatively small numbers, it is not surprising that Willys succumbed to a

virtual takeover by Kaiser in 1953. The renamed Kaiser-Willys now built Kaiser and Henry J cars at Toledo, while the Aero was offered with Kaiser's bigger 227-ci (3720-cc) six. But sales continued to decline and the Aero was dropped in mid-1955. Its tooling was shipped to Brazil, where a subsidiary continued to build it until 1967. As for Willys, the name disappeared in 1963 though the Jeep triumphantly endures.

WINTON (1897–1924)
Alexander Winton, a Scotsman who emigrated to the United States in 1878 aged 18, worked as a ship's engineer and bicycle manufacturer before building cars. Little wonder, then, that when sales of Winton cars dwindled in the early 1920s he had another thriving business in stationary

engines in reserve. Thus he managed to avoid the terror of bankruptcy which haunted so many other motor magnates of the time.

Winton built a prototype car in 1896, the first production vehicles following the year after, with a horizontal single-cylinder engine, two-speed gearbox and two-seater body. Twenty-two of these were built in 1898 and 100 the following year, which made Winton the largest producer of gasoline cars in the country, some of which were commercial vehicles; in fact, the company had been responsible for the first gasoline-engined commercial in America.

The cars evolved with bigger, single-cylinder engines, then a 15-hp twin in 1902 and a 20-hp four the year after. The wheelbase was lengthened to make room for four seats, and tiller steering gave way

The 1903 Winton Bullet racing car.

to a wheel. Alexander Winton entered the cars in a number of races in the early years, all ending in failure, but a four-cylinder Winton was the first car to cross America in 1903, with Dr. H. Nelson Jackson and Sewell H. Crocker taking three months to drive from San Francisco to New York.

The company launched its first six, a 475-ci (7784-cc) unit in 1908, and from then on proceeded upmarket with prices up to $5,750 for the six-cylinder landaulet. The fours were dropped and a larger 583-ci (9554-cc) six of 60hp was added in 1909. Winton did offer a smaller six from 1915, starting at $2,285, selling 2,458 cars in 1916 which was its best year ever. Which goes to show what Alexander Winton was about: he had no ambitions to challenge Henry Ford, and his quality cars were not even particularly advanced.

With the motoring world advancing rapidly around it, Winton sales sunk to below 1,000 in 1921, to 373 in 1923 and only 129 in '24 when the car operation was wound up. But Alexander Winton was not too perturbed, in that his Winton Gas Engine Manufacturing Co. was a successful supplier of stationary and marine diesel engines.

ZIMMER (1980–)

One man's neo-Classicism is another's travesty of good taste. Whatever one might think of Paul Zimmer's flamboyant Golden Spirit, it did fulfill a demand. It was basically a lengthened Ford Mustang, with front and rear bodywork in 1930s style. The front end brought to mind a Mercedes 500K or Duesenberg, with a padded top in fake landaulet style. The Golden Spirit was joined by the Quicksilver in 1987, which took the neat little Pontiac Fiero, lengthened it, added large chrome fenders, and turned it into a 1970s coupé. But wouldn't the world be a dull place if we all thought the same?